Buried deep in the past . . . .
and a monstro. . . . .

Earth faces total domination by an alien force.
The Galactic bronze medallion, the only key to freedom,
has been divided and scattered throughout the ages. Now,
a band of heroes, chosen for their extraordinary gifts, find
unexpected, passionate love while braving dangers far
beyond the present in a desperate race against time....

Follow all four books in this thrilling new series that
continues with *Time Raiders: The Protector*.

P.C. CAST

was born in Illinois and grew up being shuttled back and forth between there and Oklahoma, which is where she fell in love with quarter horses and mythology (at about the same time).

Five days after graduating from high school, she joined the United States Air Force, which is where she began speaking professionally. After her tours with the USAF, Ms. Cast attended college as a literature major with a secondary education minor.

Her first novel, *Goddess by Mistake,* was published by a small press in 2001. Thoroughly shocking the author, it won a Prism, a Holt Medallion and a Laurel Wreath, and was a finalist for the National Readers' Choice Award. Since then Ms. Cast has gone on to win numerous writing awards. Ms. Cast is thrilled that her work with her daughter, Kristin, in young adult fiction has won numerous placements on the *New York Times* and *USA TODAY* bestseller lists.

P.C. Cast lives and teaches in Oklahoma with her fabulous daughter, her spoiled cat and her Scotties—better known as the Scottinators. The daughter attends college. The cat refuses higher education. The Scottinators are as yet undecided about their future.

New York Times and USA TODAY bestselling author

P.C. CAST

THE AVENGER

TIME RAIDERS

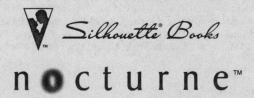

Silhouette® Books

nocturne™

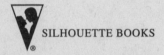 SILHOUETTE BOOKS

Recycling programs
for this product may
not exist in your area.

ISBN-13: 978-0-373-28596-9

TIME RAIDERS: THE AVENGER

This edition published by arrangement with Harlequin Books S.A.

® and TM are trademarks of Harlequin Books S.A., used under license.
Trademarks indicated with ® are registered in the United States Patent and
Trademark Office, the Canadian Trade Marks Office and in other countries.

www.silhouettenocturne.com

Printed in U.S.A.

Dearest Reader,

It was an honor to be asked to write a novel in a series conceived and written by women who have served their country in the armed forces. TIME RAIDERS is a rich world in which to play, and it was fun to bring my prior active-duty USAF alter ego to the sandbox.

I particularly love this period of history. Boudica and her amazing story have intrigued me for years. I love that she was a strong secondary character, and I hope I kept true to her historical spirit in my rendition of her.

And, finally, to be completely honest with you, I have to tell you that it was a pleasant break for me to write a steamy, sexy, paranormal romance again after writing so many young adult books!

I hope you enjoy going back to ancient Briton with Alex. Here's wishing you happy reading and the brightest of blessings.

P.C. Cast

This one is for the enlisted women in the USAF,
with a smile and a semi-insubordinate grin.
Enjoy!

ONE

The dead woman sighed. Her voice sounded wistful and more than a little nostalgic. "It's pretty here, isn't it? There is something restful about all this open space."

"You're dead, Andred. Isn't everything restful to you?" Alex said, lifting a brow at the semitransparent woman who leaned against the low wooden fence beside her.

"Do not be so literal. I am quite certain you are very aware that just because one is dead doesn't mean one is at rest." The spirit paused and gave Alex a knowing, sidelong look. "Your fear of leaving here is irrational."

Alex frowned. The two things that had surprised her most about ghosts when she first started seeing them the year she turned six were they were so damn nosy, which made them ubergossips, and they were so damn free with their advice. As if dying turned them into talk show hosts.

"Look, I'm not afraid of leaving here. I just don't like to.

Even you said how restful this place is, and I love Oklahoma's Tallgrass Prairie. Not to mention my job's here—why should I want to leave?"

"There is quite a difference between loving a place so you choose to stay, and staying in a place because you are too fearful to leave."

"I said I'm *not* afraid to leave! I went to Flagstaff. I was gone for three whole days."

"You hated every moment of it."

"No, I did not. I loved seeing Tessa." *And I'm worried as hell about her.* Alex closed her eyes for an instant and against her dark lids saw smoke and fire and smelled the acrid scent of computers frying in unbelievable heat. Professor Carswell had assured her that Tessa would be fine, but after the terrible accident she'd witnessed, Alex didn't know how that could be true. *But none of that is this damn nosy ghost's business.*

"You have not left the prairie once since you returned. You've even been giving your shopping list to Sam. Alexandra, when you resort to having a hired ranch hand buy tampons for you, I'd say you are turning into a hermit."

"And what about you? Why are you still here? Hello! Aren't you the pot calling the kettle black? How can *you* lecture *me* about being afraid to leave?" Alex glanced pointedly at the woman's archaic looking outfit, which was little more than a brightly colored linen tunic, and leather sandals with straps that wrapped around her calves. "What kind of a name is Andred? How long ago did you die, anyway?"

"Andred is a very old name, as I have been here a very long time."

"And I have a feeling you should have passed on a while ago."

The ghost of the young woman shrugged. "I will. I am in no hurry."

"Well, that's no different than me. I'm in no hurry to leave, either," Alex said smugly.

The spirit turned to face her, her expression sad. "There is a vast difference between us, Alex. As you remind me often, I am not of the living. There is nothing out there for me. But you are alive. The world exists for you, except you're unwilling to live, so you hide in here."

Alex's stomach tightened. "You have no idea what it's like. You ghosts are overwhelming! In Flagstaff, with Tessa, ghosts were everywhere! I couldn't sleep. I couldn't think. Here it isn't so bad."

The spirit shook her head. "It's not where you are, Alex. It's you."

"That's such utter bullshit!"

"You haven't always hidden yourself away out here. You used to be a part of the world. What happened?"

"I am still part of the world! I live and work on the tallgrass prairie. I'm a botanist. I give guided tours. I interact with people all the time. *Living* people. And I'm done talking to ghosts for today." Alex climbed over the fence, and without another word, stomped into the bunkhouse and went directly to the small room she called home, forcing herself not to slam the door behind her.

"Damn know-it-all ghosts! God, they're so incredibly annoying," Alex muttered to herself as she went to the chic wine cooler she kept filled with a stash of her favorite reds and whites. She considered for a second, and then decided to splurge and open a new bottle of her current favorite red, The Prisoner, ignoring the irony of the name on the label. "I live!" she said as she opened the wine. "I just choose to live somewhere that doesn't stress my brains out." While she let the wine breathe Alex pulled off her jeans and sweatshirt, replacing them with comfy silk drawstring pajama bottoms and the matching top. She caught a glimpse of herself in the mirror on the outside of her closet and paused to smooth back her crazy hair. Sometimes it seemed her mood translated to her hair follicles, because nine times out of ten when she was angry her thick mass of strawberry-blond hair frizzed out to look like a lion's mane.

"I should cut this stuff," Alex told her reflection, but she knew they were just words. She would cut her hair when she was really old, and not pushing thirty-five. Hell, she might not even cut it then! It'd be fun to be called "that crazy old woman with the wild hair down to her ass." At least it would give the ghosts something benign to gossip about. "Just pour yourself a glass of wine and stay away from the scissors," she told her reflection.

Alex was curled up in bed with the glass of red wine on her bedside table and a fat copy of Diana Gabaldon's *Outlander*, which she was rereading for the third time in ten years, when her cell phone rang. Annoyed, she glanced at the number, sure it was her mother making her requisite once-a-month call, which Alex would ignore. When she saw the name under the caller ID, she sat straight up and clicked the answer button.

"Tessa! Are you okay?"

"Alex, it's great to hear your voice! You would not believe all the stuff I have to tell you. Man, talk about a wild ride."

"Are you okay?" Alex repeated. "There was that fire just as you disappeared, and—"

"Hey, not over unsecured lines," Tessa said quickly. "And I'm fine. Totally fine." Alex thought she heard a deep male voice in the background, and Tessa giggled. "Well, maybe I'm better than fine." Then her voice sobered and she added, "Oh, you should know that here with us I've also got—"

"Tessa, we need to talk." It was Alex's turn to interrupt. "You scared the living hell out of me. I thought you were dead for sure. And that damn professor wouldn't give me shit for information, not to mention the stick-up-her-ass general. God, I'm so glad I don't have to deal with military mentality anymore." She snorted. "Talk about an oxymoron. Anyway, we gotta talk. I need details."

"Well, Sergeant, we'd be happy to share all the details with you. There's a nonstop flight that leaves tomorrow from Tulsa to Phoenix. I'll have a car waiting at the airport to bring you to Flagstaff."

There was absolute silence on the line as Alex worked on controlling her temper.

"As I was trying to tell you, Alex, I have General Ashton on conference call with us," Tessa said.

"Lovely," Alex said dryly. "Hello, General."

"Sergeant Patton," said the general.

"Look, General, I told you before, I haven't been a sergeant for almost five years, and I have no intention of ever being one again. Just call me Alex."

"As you wish, Alex. Your ticket is wireless. It will be waiting at Tulsa International for you."

"I'm not coming. Not tomorrow. Not the day after. Not ever. I am *not* interested in joining your…" Alex hesitated, wanted to call Project Anasazi a bunch of geeks and freaks. But Tessa was still on the phone, and, in spite of trapping her into this annoying conference call, still Alex's friend—even though she was definitely a psychic freak. After a long breath Alex settled for saying "…your team."

"We need you, Alex." It was Tessa who spoke into the dead air this time. "This is important."

"So is the reason I'm not interested. Actually, so are the *several* reasons I'm not interested, and you know that, Tessa. Look, I'm glad you're all in one piece, and I'm glad you called, even if we do have company on the line. But I am not the girl for this job. I left that life behind me a long time ago, and I'm not ever going back. If you want to come to the prairie and visit, you're invited anytime, *Tessa*." She emphasized her friend's name so there could be no misunderstanding to whom Alex was offering the open invitation. "But I'm not going back to Flagstaff or to the military. Goodbye, Tessa." Alex clicked the end call button.

TWO

The call had pissed Alex off so badly that she couldn't even concentrate on *The Outlander*, which only served to make her even more angry and resentful. Shit! She'd made herself very clear after Tessa had disappeared into the past as the damn lab had gone up in smoke. No, hell no, she wasn't interested in "volunteering" for a time-travel mission—even if it did mean keeping marauding aliens or whatever at bay.

See, the problem was that in Alex's life, what most people would consider alien was her norm. So what if the world had to deal with bizarre crap for a change? Alex's mind flashed back to when she was six years old and her neighbor, Brian Campos, had disappeared. The police had gone door-to-door looking for him. When they'd gotten to her house, she'd told them, in her matter-of-fact little-girl voice, that she knew where he was—then she'd taken the detective's hand and, to the horror of her parents, led him to Brian's body. Everyone had freaked, and then labeled *her* as a freak. At six, how does a kid know not to admit she sees ghosts? At thirtysomething, Alex was a lot smarter.

They'd wanted her talent at Project Anasazi, also known as the Time Raiders. Alex had thought Tessa's insistence on her coming to visit was because her longtime friend was just too damn lonely at her new home in Flagstaff. After all, Tessa was a strong psychic, which meant she was a freak, too. Come to find out, Tessa had wanted to see Alex, but Project Anasazi had *really* wanted her—for a time-travel mission.

Okay, even before she'd witnessed Tessa's messed-up leap back in time, and gotten serious Something's Wrong vibes from the lab fire, Alex had rejected their offer. The reason she'd given— that she was totally not interested in returning to anything re- sembling the military in any form—was true. As was her other reason—the fact that she had a great job as lead botanist, guide and docent for Oklahoma's Tallgrass Prairie National Preserve.

But the truest reason she couldn't handle being a part of Project Anasazi was because she couldn't handle leaving the prairie. It was the only place she could find any measure of peace, any break from the ghosts who haunted her.

It wasn't true that ghosts hung around because they wanted someone to help them with unresolved issues. Well, maybe that was true in some cases. But most of the time ghosts hung around for the same reasons anyone, living or dead, hung around a place. Because they wanted to. Sometimes they were bored. Sometimes they were happy. Sometimes they were sad. Sometimes Alex didn't know what the hell they were, except terrible gossips and seriously noisy. They were just there.

It hadn't been so bad when she was younger. The U.S. Air Force had even helped for a while. At least there she'd been an accepted member of a group, that is until her "knack" for "knowing" what messages needed to get to whom had caused her to be singled out from the herd of airmen who schlepped around the main communications center of Building 500 at Offutt Air Force Base, Nebraska. Her ability, honed from countless hours of listening to gossipy ghosts, had brought her to the attention of the NCOIC in charge of the communications center, CMSgt John Domonick.

One thing had led to another between the two of them, and eventually she'd ended up in his bed and he'd ended up knowing her freakish secret. Oh, she'd also ended up in a special assignment called TA, or Traffic Analysis, which basically meant gathering ghost gossip for John and, eventually, the colonel who was his commander.

It had been early in her comm center debacle that she'd started cramming in botany classes at the local university whenever she could. And when Alex's next reenlistment had come around, instead of re-upping for another four years, she'd said goodbye to John Domonick and the USAF, and hello to a degree in botany—*and* an internship at Oklahoma's beautiful, and mostly untouched, tallgrass prairie—where the ghosts somehow, some way, mostly left her alone. So that's where she planned to stay. Forever if need be.

She was *not* going back into the military—not in any way, shape or form.

Still fuming over the phone call, Alex sucked down the rest of the glass of wine, and only realized when she got up to wash her face—and stumbled into the bed—that the glass had mysteriously been the last in the bottle, which was now empty.

Alex was definitely going to have a headache in the morning. Ugh. And she had to lead a group of wannabe ranch hands out on a sunrise bird-watching tour to Buffalo Ridge, which was a good three miles away.

"Well, crap," she grumbled to herself as she snuggled under the covers. "I'm gonna have to remember to hydrate...."

* * *

It was spectacularly beautiful in Alex's dream. The land around her was lush and so green it almost made her eyes ache. She'd never known there were so many variations of the color green! And the trees! Alex had never imagined trees could be so big and thick and dense. Sure, her dream self had found a path through the incredible woods, but damn! It was like she'd conjured up a version of the *Lord of the Rings* movie set and plopped herself down in the middle of Rivendell. She recognized chestnuts and oaks and even something one of her professors would call a witches' beech. They were all massive and had a look of untamed health—as if a contractor would never even consider cutting them down to build a highway or, worse, a development of suburban double-income-all-basically-the-same houses.

Yeah, she'd definitely dreamed up her version of Rivendell. Now all she needed was to conjure Aragorn and she'd be all set. So while she waited for Aragorn to show up, Alex strolled through the lush woods.

Obviously, it was early morning—just barely dawn. The soft young daylight complimented the deep and varied green of the woods, making everything around Alex magical. She was following a small, winding path. On either side of it the forest floor was spongy, carpeted with thick moss that looked so soft she started to have thoughts about pulling the tardy dream version of Aragorn off the path and having a roll in the moss with him. Or at least she'd do that when he finally showed.

It was then that she heard a voice speaking. At first it was just a faint sound coming from somewhere in front of her. Alex paused, listening hard, and sure enough, the sound came again. This time it was recognizable as a voice, a deep, strong, *male* voice.

She practically skipped down the path in glee. Back in the waking world she might be working on a raging hangover, but here in this gorgeous dreamland she was going to play Arwen to a handsome Aragorn. And in *this* world she was actually going to have sex.

"Come back...."

The words finally became understandable, and they jolted Alex to a halt.

"Come back?" she said aloud, more to herself than to a randy, but invisible Aragorn. "But I haven't found you yet." The voice still came from somewhere in front of her, so she kept walking.

"Come back to me...."

Again the compelling voice pulled her forward.

"I haven't gone anywhere!" Alex shouted, annoyed at her dream self. She got more annoyed as mist started to pour in from the woods, creeping over the moss and washing across the deer path like unsubstantial fingers.

Alex usually liked fog. It had a romantic, mystical quality that appealed to her. Plus, it wasn't like she was scared of any boogey men it might be hiding. She was way too familiar with ghosts to be freaked by them.

But there was something weird about this mist. It moved oddly, swirling around her body, with tendrils of gray licking against her skin. It was almost liquid in its touch.

"Come back to me! I need you!"

He sounded as if he was standing right in front of her, but by this time the fog was so dense she couldn't see through it.

"Where are you?" she called.

"I'm waiting for you! Come back to me...."

"I'm trying to find you! Where the hell—" Alex bumbled off the path and fell, facefirst, into the mossy ground.

"What the hell!" Gasping, Alex tried to sit up, but was totally entangled in her comforter. For an instant she was still in the dream, and she flailed around, thinking that the moss was clinging to her. And where was he? Where was the Aragorn guy with the incredible voice who kept calling for her?

Then a spike pierced her temple and she realized her mouth was dry and disgusting, which meant she had a hangover headache and a cottony mouth.

She wasn't in an amazing, misty dream forest. She was in her room in the bunkhouse on the tallgrass prairie. Alex freed her arms and shoved off the comforter, rubbing her eyes and glancing blearily at her alarm clock. The luminous dial read 5:10 A.M., exactly five minutes before her alarm was set to go off. She sighed and, with a groan that sounded as if she were almost eighty-five rather than almost thirty-five, hobbled into her bathroom, going through her mental to-do list. She'd shower. Hydrate. Take aspirin. Eat breakfast—a light nongreasy one. Lead the city folks to Buffalo Ridge. She would not let her hangover kill her. She would forget about the weird dream.

Later that day Alex would try to convince herself that accomplishing six to-dos out of seven wasn't all that bad.

THREE

Alex figured she should be grateful it wasn't August, one hundred five degrees and perfect tick-swarming weather. *Okay,* she admitted to herself as she resettled her back against the convenient hump in the ground behind her, *today's assignment has been one of the cushy ones.* They'd eaten breakfast in the bunkhouse, and then started the trek to Buffalo Ridge. Alex could have hiked it in less than an hour, but the city folks were chatty and wanted to loiter, so she'd adjusted her pace to theirs, which didn't really bother her since she was decidedly sleep deprived and hungover. After two hours of a leisurely stroll they were on the ridge, which was when her charges broke out their easels, watercolors, sketch pads and mimosas. They'd asked her if it was okay if they just stayed there on the ridge for the rest of the morning, sketching and drinking, instead of finishing the hike.

Alex had said no problemo.

Since she was responsible for them—and no way could they

find their way back to the bunkhouse by themselves sober, let alone after ingesting the half-dozen or so bottles of bubbly they'd brought in their provision packs, Alex settled in to let them sketch the morning away while she caught up on some much needed sleep.

The dream started like the other one. She was in the middle of a dense, gorgeous forest, surrounded by layers of verdant green that could have very easily mesmerized her—had she not already been expecting some weirdness. This time she wasn't a tourist. She was wary and ready for whatever her obviously stressed-out psyche could throw at her.

She walked down the same path as before, only now she wasn't gawking at the nature surrounding her. Alex was paying attention to the fact that there were no damn birds.

Okay, a little detail like that might have escaped most people's radar, especially most dreaming people, but Alex was an experienced hiker and was used to birds chirping away as she hiked. In her dream world, there were no sounds at all, not even the sloughing of wind through the thick green leaves of the ancient trees that formed a living canopy over her head.

"Same place, but it's like someone pressed the mute button," Alex said. "Well, at least in my dream I'm not hungover." She had just decided her previous experience must have been wine-induced craziness when his voice drifted down the path to her.

"Come back to me...."

Had Alex reasoned out what she planned to do on her next visit to this made-up dream world, she would have said that she was going to be logical. She'd demand the man materialize, and if he didn't, then she'd simply ignore him and go on about her dreaming, still hoping her subconscious would come up with a tryst with Aragorn.

But the dream wasn't reasonable. It defied logic. The man's voice had Alex reacting on a visceral level.

"I'm here! I came back! Where the hell are you?"

"Come back to me...I need you!"

"This is just ridiculous!" But even as Alex grumbled, she increased her pace. His voice was coming from down the path in front of her. This time she wasn't going to wake up until she found out what the hell was going on in this dream.

The fog began to slither across the path.

"Damn it, no! This happened last time and I'm not putting up with it again! Hello! Where are you? Hello!" Alex was jogging now, shifting her gaze from the path to the misty space ahead of her, all the while straining to see through the soupy grayness.

The mist enveloped her. This wasn't the romantic, cozy fog she liked to dream about lifting from low spots of the prairie on cool fall mornings. This mist was almost sentient. It was grasping, touching her with frigid fingers that crept into her clothes and down her spine, surrounding her body and soul until, panting, she stumbled to a halt.

"Where are you and what's happening to me?" she whispered as she gasped for air, trying to catch her breath and regain her composure.

"I need your help. You must have the courage to come back to me."

"Well, tell me who you are and where you are, and I will!" Alex blurted, utterly frustrated by this dream version of cat and mouse.

Ahead of her the mist cleared for just an instant and an image materialized. It was a symbol in the shape of an *S,* with both ends of the letter curling in and around to form a thick spiral. Its color was a deep sapphire-blue and she knew that this image held answers for her—somehow the *S* was *his.*

Automatically, Alex reached up, wanting to touch the pattern she glimpsed within the mist, wondering if the thing could be a part of a ghost. She'd never had a spirit get into her dreams before, but after almost three decades of seeing the dead, she figured nothing would surprise her.

Out of the mist someone grabbed her hand! Alex yipped a surprised "Yikes!" and tried to pull away, but the disembodied whatever kept a firm hold on her.

"Just do not say no. You must come back to me."

And then Alex's hand was lifted up into the mist, and she could swear that she felt lips—warm, firm, intimate lips— brush her skin. The touch somehow grounded her, settling her nerves and making her feel calmer, and surer that she was where she was supposed to be. Everything would be okay. This wasn't a ghost—they couldn't touch her. This was a man— a sexy dream man she'd conjured to entertain her sleeping mind. Through his strong grip he telegraphed need.

Alex grinned.

Of course he needed her. Of course he was calling for her. She'd dreamed him up. Now all she needed to do was relax. No doubt the mist would be whisked away—probably to the tune of the theme song from the cool old Lerner and Lowe version of *Camelot*. Oooh! Maybe *that* was who she'd dreamed up—King Arthur! Yep! He was definitely King Arthur. This dream world was a perfect pretend ancient England. No wonder he'd kept disappearing when she'd been imagining him as Aragorn—silly her! She was having a dorky historical fantasy, not a dorky sci fi/fantasy fantasy!

"All righty then," Alex said happily, squeezing the hand that still held hers, "I'm ready. I've come back to you." Still grinning, she braced herself, sure she'd figured out her dream version of the Gordian Knot, and everything would clear right up in an instant.

"It won't be that easy, daughter of man!"

The new voice blasted Alex. Whoever had her hand dropped

it, and, thrown off balance by the force of the voice and by the absence of the comforting presence that had anchored her in the dream world, Alex stumbled backward. And there was nothing behind her. Her arms windmilled, but she couldn't stop herself from falling...falling...falling....

"Hey there, Ms. Patton! You're awake now—everything's okay."

Alex jerked away from the old guy whose big, beefy hand was resting on her shoulder.

"Sorry. Didn't mean to scare you. It's just that you were making some real strange noises and I thought you might be having a doozy of a nightmare."

Alex blinked up at the man—thinning gray hair, silver unibrow, lots of nose hair—and reality rushed back into her frazzled brain.

"Oh, Mr. Thompson, you startled me."

"Were you having a bad dream, dear?" Mrs. Thompson, a plump woman who looked as if she'd be the perfect grandma, peered down at Alex over her husband's shoulder.

"I—I guess I was. I don't really remember." She stood abruptly, brushing nonexistent dirt and grass from her khaki work pants. "I can't believe I fell asleep," she said, trying not to sound as disconcerted as she felt—especially when she realized she was the center the half dozen city folks' attention.

"Sweetheart, you've been out like a light for the better part of two hours!" boomed Mr. Meyers, a retired butcher from Tulsa.

"Oh, Frank, leave the girl alone. I was just thinkin' how tired she looked while we was hiking up here." Mrs. Meyers, who insisted Alex call her Trixi, patted her shoulder. "Don't worry. We all need our beauty sleep."

"Okay, well, are we ready to head back?" Alex said, wishing she could crawl under the nearest rock.

"Yep, sure are! And I'll bet you can set a quicker pace than you did on the way here, after that nap you took!" Mr. Meyers chuckled and slapped Alex on the back.

Thankfully, none of the tourists were staying the night, so Alex's duties were done after she deposited the group in the prairie gift shop. Still feeling out of sorts after the weird repeated dream, she decided to indulge herself in one of her favorite pastimes—watching old BBC Masterpiece Theatre specials on her widescreen iMac. She'd popped some extra-buttery popcorn, poured a huge glass of iced tea—no wine today!—opened her new Netflix envelope and was just getting ready to pop disc one of *The House of Elliott* into her computer when the screen bleeped, telling her she had a new e-mail. Without really thinking about it, Alex clicked on the logo and saw that the new mail was from ACarswell@flagstaff.net.

"Oh, you've got to be kidding," she muttered at the screen. With an annoyed jab, she clicked on the e-mail.

There was one line, which read: If you want to find out more about this, come to Flagstaff. It was signed A. C.

Alex glanced up at the address block and saw that there was an attachment. She almost didn't click into it. What could Carswell possibly send her that she'd want to learn more about? But, grudgingly, Alex had to admit she was curious. She clinked into the attachment.

The symbol that filled the screen had her breath catching in her throat.

It was the sapphire *S* design from her dream.

FOUR

It took her too damn long to dig around in her address book and find the number to the Project Anasazi headquarters Tessa had given her months ago, when she'd first tried to talk her into joining Carswell's team. Alex wasn't at all surprised when the professor answered the phone herself.

"Where did you get that design?" Alex asked without any preamble.

"Alex, it's good of you to call," said the professor smoothly.

"Where did you get that design?" she stubbornly repeated.

"As I explained in the e-mail, if you want to know more about the symbol you'll have to come to Flagstaff."

"That's bullshit!"

"Nevertheless, that is the deal."

Alex drew a deep breath and got a handle on her temper before she spoke again. Then, in short clipped sentences, she said, "I do not know why you're doing this. I will not join the project. My answer there will be the same as my answer here."

"I'm doing this because we need you. The world needs you, Alex."

"That's just more bullshit! The world? I can't save the world. Find someone else—someone who's more like Tessa."

"It's you we need for this particular mission." When Alex didn't respond, Professor Carswell continued softly, "The symbol is important to you. I can tell you that."

"How can you be so sure?"

Alex could hear the smile in her voice. "Because you're not the only freak around."

Alex snorted.

"Come to Flagstaff. It'll change your life," said Professor Carswell.

"I don't want my life changed," Alex insisted.

"Don't you?"

There was a long silence on the line and then Alex heard herself saying, "Is that ticket still at Tulsa International?"

"What's woad?" Alex asked Professor Carswell. She was sitting across from the professor in her office at the Time Raiders headquarters in Flagstaff, staring at a beautiful sketch of the S design the professor had scanned into the computer and sent to her. Only this original had been drawn on the outline of a human face. The face didn't have any detail—it was just a frame for the swirling S pattern that spread from the man's forehead and cheekbones, down to the side of his neck and even onto his torso.

Alex thought she'd never seen anything so exotic, beautiful or compelling.

"Woad is a powerful tattoo that ancient Celtic warriors used to adorn their bodies."

"That's an ancient tattoo?" Alex continued to stare at the design as if she was trying to see the man behind it.

"Well, there is a rather boring academic debate about whether the Celts actually tattooed the images on their bodies, or whether they were painted on. This particular image once adorned the body of a Celt who was a druid and a warrior. He lived about AD 60 in Briton. I'm sure about all of that, but I'm not certain if these designs were painted or tattooed on his body."

"I don't understand. How do you know all of this, and what does it have to do with me?"

"What *does* this have to do with you?" asked General Ashton, who'd chosen that moment to join them in Carswell's office.

"You tell me. I thought that's why I flew down here."

"Why does this particular carrot dangle so enticingly for you that it *did* get you down here?" the general asked.

"Alex, I know this design is connected to you," Professor Carswell said gently.

Ignoring the general, Alex spoke to the professor. "I've seen it in my dreams. I think the man who's wearing this design is calling to me."

"He's asking you to come to him?" Professor Carswell leaned forward, literally on the edge of her seat, waiting for Alex's answer.

"Yes," she admitted reluctantly.

The professor nodded slowly. "Then it is you who must go on this mission. Alex, I've located the next piece of the medallion. I can tell that it is hidden in AD 60 Briton. I can also tell that it is tied to the Celtic warrior queen Boudica. The only other detail I know for sure about the placement of the medallion is that this particular piece in our puzzle is surrounded by death. It's almost as if the dead have paved a path to the hidden piece. They know where it is. I do not."

"So you see, Alex, we need someone on this mission who can speak to the dead," General Ashton finished for her.

"Oh, no!" Alex was shaking her head. "Look, I haven't even been away from the tallgrass prairie for a full day and already I'm sick and tired of seeing ghost after ghost swarming everywhere." It gave her a twisted sense of pleasure that the professor and the general both glanced nervously around in response to her words. "Don't worry about it—you can't see them. Anyway, they don't seem to like this building. There aren't any in here. But here's the deal—I know Tessa told you about my *thing,* and I understand why she did. Tessa's all about being a team player. I'm not. I'm out of the air force. The whole thing..." she paused and gestured vaguely around her "...*this* whole thing is just too much for me. Yeah, I'm curious about the man in my dreams, but you guys are telling me he lived a zillion years ago, so that really doesn't have anything to do with me today. I just want to go back home—to my quiet job—to a world where I can actually get some damn rest and not be driven out of my mind. Besides all that—in case you haven't noticed, I'm not particularly into the military mind-set of do-what-you're-told-and-shut-up anymore. Sorry I've wasted your time and mine." Alex started to stand up.

"Sit down, Sergeant." General Ashton didn't raise her voice, but the tone of command in it had Alex sitting back down before she even registered the fact that she'd complied.

"You're a blunt woman, so I'm going to be equally as blunt with you. This isn't about some dream man. This isn't about you getting your rest. This is about finding the twelve pieces of the medallion, which once reassembled, will stop a race of creatures who have been subjugating women for thousands of years. We are their only challengers, and they will unmake us in order to keep their power. This is about saving your daughters' daughters and all those women who come after them. Suck it up, Sergeant. Stop whining. You can sleep when you're dead."

Alex met the general's sharp gaze. The officer was obviously pissed at her, but that didn't bother Alex at all. Actually, it was like a sweet walk down memory lane—she'd kinda liked pissing off officers. The truth was Alex respected that the general had finally given her the bottom line and stopped dancing around the damn bush. "These creatures, they're really as bad as all that?"

"The Centauri will wipe out human females before they allow us to join the free galactic community."

"I'm not a hero, General. I'm just a woman who hears the dead. And if I'm not buffered by the tallgrass prairie, that usually stresses me out so badly I can barely think."

"How much thinking do you have to be able to do to ask some ancient ghosts to lead you to this?" General Ashton pulled out a drawing of what looked like a piece of a bronze medallion. It was oblong in shape and about the size of two quarters welded together. There was an interesting raised pattern on the piece that looked as if it might be sparkly, and vaguely reminded Alex of constellations.

She shrugged. "Depends on how long I have to go without sleep."

"Alex," Professor Carswell interjected quickly. "Do you know why you find the tallgrass prairie so peaceful?"

"No, except when I'm there the dead don't bother me as much. It's like they're more tied to the earth or something. I've never really questioned it. I've just been glad Tessa and I decided to stop there on a road trip several years ago."

The professor nodded. "Tied to the earth…that's an interesting premise. Did you know the ancient Celts were very closely tied to the earth, too? I can't know for sure, but my guess is you could be a lot less troubled by ghosts in the ancient world than you are in our modern one."

"But whether the professor's guess is correct or not, we need you to go on this mission," said General Ashton.

Alex turned to face her. "I want to talk to Tessa."

Ashton glanced at the professor, who cleared her throat, then said, "Tessa isn't on earth right now, Alex."

"Huh?"

Carswell gave a slight nod. "It's true. She was only here briefly, when she made the call to you. Actually, she was here for a prenatal examination."

"Prenatal!"

The general's smile was self-satisfied. "Had you not hung up on your friend she would have told you herself."

Carswell frowned at the general. "Tessa wouldn't have explained that she's pregnant with an alien's child and is going to raise it to be a star navigator in the father's home world. She would only have said that she was pregnant."

"An alien kid?" Alex felt a little dizzy.

"Half alien, half human," Carswell corrected.

"So her mission was successful," Alex murmured.

"On many levels," agreed the general.

Alex met General Ashton's gaze. "I'm not like Tessa. She's always been one of the good guys. She's always known the right thing to do, and done it. I got sick of doing the right thing when I was six and my parents started to treat me like they were scared of me because I helped lead the cops to a neighbor kid's body. For a long time I've preferred staying on the sidelines."

This time the general's smile looked genuine and softened her face, so that Alex suddenly thought how pretty she was. "So, aren't you tired of getting splinters in your butt from staying on the bench? How about getting into the game for a change?"

"I think you're backing the wrong player," Alex replied.

"I don't think so," Professor Carswell said quickly. "You're linked with the druid who bears that woad design."

"What do you mean by *linked?*"

Instead of answering, the professor cocked her head to the

side, as if she was listening to a whisper in the wind. "You've never been in love."

It wasn't a question, but Alex felt awkwardly compelled to answer. "No. I haven't."

"It's never been right with any man, has it?"

"It's a little hard to concentrate on romance after a guy finds out I can talk to dead people. It's not like on TV. Guys don't so much like it," Alex said sardonically.

"The man who wears that woad design will change that. He is woven into your soul," said the professor.

"And just what the hell does that mean?" Alex blurted.

"Accept this mission, go back to ancient Briton and find out," General Ashton said.

"Ah, hell," Alex groaned.

The professor and the general shared a brief, victorious smile.

FIVE

"Are you sure this bunny's going to act right?" Alex peered into what looked like a cat carrier, at a very ordinary white rabbit.

"The rabbit will do what she's supposed to do. Just unwrap her from the cloak you'll be wearing, speak the lines you've memorized, and then drop her at your feet." Professor Carswell smiled at Alex. "Keep in mind you're the powerful priestess of a mighty goddess, as well as what the Celts recognized as a Soul Speaker—so you need to deliver the lines with some aplomb."

"Aplomb? Seriously?"

"Seriously. You need to be in character."

"I'll do my best. Hope the rabbit does hers."

"Leave that to me. I'm going to be sure you're facing southeast. The rabbit will bolt away from you and directly toward Londinium."

"And that will make Boudica attack London?" Alex said doubtfully.

"History is clear. Boudica was a devout follower of the goddess Andraste. Rabbits were sacred to the goddess, pure white rabbits especially so. Before making the final decision to march her army against *Londinium*…" Carswell paused to be sure Alex caught the correction in calling the city by its ancient name "…she released a rabbit, saying that she would march her army in the direction the goddess commanded. You're posing as a priestess of Andraste, so that moment is the perfect one for you to materialize in the queen's camp."

"Assuming they don't all freak and attack me because I've just beamed down. They have to be superstitious as hell."

"Their specific belief in their goddess, and their more general belief in the magic of the earth, is what is going to ensure our plan works. What we consider science, they considered magic. Also, you don't have to hide your ability to speak to the dead there. You'll be venerated for it."

"I certainly hope so." Alex also hoped Carswell had been right about the ghosts of the past behaving like ghosts did on the tallgrass prairie. Even though the lab, which she hadn't left for days, was insulated against psychic phenomena, Alex could feel the presence of spirits in the city surrounding her, and just that was enough to mess with her sleep and her nerves.

"Use some of that famous attitude of yours that has kept you butting heads with General Ashton these past several days, and no one will have any trouble believing you're the priestess of a war goddess," Carswell was saying.

"Ashton thinks I'm insubordinate."

"War goddesses often are," the professor stated, which made Alex laugh. "Just rely on your instincts. The knowledge that I place within your brain during the transport will be like a very strong gut feeling. Sometimes you'll receive whole strings of information in your subconscious, so be sure you follow your hunches."

Just then Alex's nervous gut felt the urge to empty itself. "I really won't have any trouble communicating?"

"None. The chip implanted in your brain's language center will act as your own internal computer. It'll translate what you say and what you hear. Remember, you aren't Alex anymore. You are Blonwen, priestess of the goddess Andraste. You've escaped the Roman governor Gaius Seutonius Paulinus's slaughter of druids and priestesses on the Island of Mona."

"Who you believe could be a Centaurian."

The professor nodded. "With his historic record of cruelty it's a definite possibility. Plus, we know the medallion is there. No doubt there will also be a Centaurian tracking it and trying to keep it from us."

Carswell handed over a cuff bracelet of beaten gold embedded with a quartz crystal, which Alex slide onto her right wrist. "My get-out-of-jail-free card," she said.

"Don't lose it," General Aston called as she took her seat behind a computer monitor near the glass booth that stood in the middle of the lab. "The Emergency Signal Cuff is the only way we can get you out of there if you're really in trouble."

Really in trouble? Alex mused silently. *Does she mean versus the unreal trouble I'll be in the instant I step into the past?*

"Don't forget that we can correct historical events you accidently impact, but you have to activate the ESC before you're mortally wounded. You aren't a part of history, so you can actually be killed," said General Ashton.

"That is impossible for me to forget," Alex muttered wryly.

"Ready, *Blonwen?*" Carswell asked.

"As I'll ever be," she said.

"All right. Here's Thumper." Carswell pulled the rabbit out of the carrier and handed it to her.

"Thumper?"

The professor smiled. "*Bambi* was a favorite of mine."

Too nervous to smile back, Alex concentrated on not holding the rabbit too tightly.

As the professor put on the crown-shaped headpiece that would allow her to harness sine waves and send Alex back in time, she whispered, "Your druid will be there for you. I know he will. Allow yourself to find him."

Her mouth had dried to a desert, so all Alex could do was nod in response.

Much too soon Professor Carswell was seated comfortably in the plush recliner directly in front of the curved, glass-walled booth Alex had secretly christened the Glass Coffin. Alex stood inside the booth, holding the rabbit and trying to keep her breathing even. She was marveling at how utterly relaxed the professor looked, when the small hairs on her forearms began to tingle and then lift. She'd just tightened her grip on the rabbit when the pain hit. A terrible agony sizzled through her body. Waves of power made the air around her ripple as if she were in a whirlwind. *Don't fight this!* Alex reminded herself. *It's like a wave you're supposed to ride.* But she had never done any surfing. She tried to concentrate on the professor—to focus on the fact that the woman looked calm. Everything must be fine. Carswell knew what she was doing. Everything was going to be okay.

A cloud of light built around Alex, and as she closed her eyes against the incredible brightness and clutched the rabbit to her, she began to feel weightless. She was telling herself not to think about the fact that that lightness meant her molecules were beginning to temporarily disconnect from each other when she felt as if she was being sucked up into the ceiling. As everything went black, Thumper's panicked scream joined her own.

The vertigo was worse than Alex had thought it would be, and she stayed on her knees, bent over and trembling while she sucked in air. Just as Carswell had said, she was wearing a cloak, though how the professor managed to twine sine waves to create clothing was as mind-boggling as time travel itself. Alex still had the rabbit in her arms, and it was definitely alive, because she could feel it shaking.

Then the voices penetrated through the ringing in her ears.

"What is it?"

"A vision!"

"Aye! An apparition!"

"Is she a spirit?"

"Protect Boudica! Shield the queen from the apparition!"

Then a woman's voice lifted above the others. It was filled with confidence and command. "Rise and explain who you are, be you spirit or flesh."

Alex drew a deep breath and prayed silently to whatever god or goddess existed in this time that she could stay on her feet and make her voice work.

She stood up slowly, giving herself a chance to adapt to the dizziness, and kept her arms wrapped around the rabbit, hidden within her cloak. Alex didn't open her eyes until she was fairly sure she wasn't going to fall over.

The first thing she saw was a woman who blazed with power. Boudica—it had to be the queen—stood not twenty feet in front of her. She had more thick red hair than Alex had ever seen on anyone. Her clothes were of supple leather, intricately embroidered with brightly colored thread in complex knots and designs. They wrapped snuggly around her tall, athletic body. The tunic left most of her thighs bare. Flat-heeled leather boots that came to her knees were trimmed in fox fur, as was the cloak she was wearing. She had jeweled bracelets on her wrists and biceps, and around her neck was a thick ring of twisted gold that had stones inlayed on both ends. The words *Torque— ancient symbol of royalty,* whispered through Alex's mind.

Yes! This had to be the queen. Alex lifted her chin and met the woman's cold green eyes.

"Queen Boudica, I am Blonwen, priestess of Andraste. The goddess has sent me here, saving me from the carnage at Mona, so that I might show you her favor." Alex had to pause as the people surrounding them broke into excited shouts.

Boudica raised one hand and easily silenced everyone.

"This is, indeed, a sign from Andraste, as I just evoked the blessing of the goddess on the battle to come."

"I bring news for that battle," Alex said quickly, picking up the thread of the lines she'd memorized back in the lab. "Andraste would have you follow the path she leads, and she has sent her sacred hare to show you the way!" With a flourish that would have made Professor Carswell proud, Alex threw back her cloak, exposing the white rabbit. The people gasped and Alex tossed the bunny to her feet, then held her breath. But as usual, Carswell was spot on. The rabbit leaped forward and ran straight for Boudica. The queen didn't move, but her eyes widened as the hare raced for her. Then, at the last moment, it dodged to the right, coming so close to the queen that it brushed the folds of her cloak, before it darted off into the darkening forest behind them.

No one made a sound for a moment, and then Boudica's face broke into a fierce grin. "The hare makes for Londinium, and so shall we!" She raised her fist in the air as the people shouted in joyful agreement.

Alex was almost positive she was going to be sick.

"Sit, Priestess! You look barely able to stay on your feet." Boudica strode to Alex and put a firm hand under her elbow. "Aedan! Why do you stand and stare like a waterless carp? Aid me with Andraste's servant."

A man who looked as if he could scare croup out of babies just by glancing at them hurried over. He practically lifted Alex off her feet in his haste to get her to an odd looking chair set to the right of an intricately carved piece that was obviously a throne.

"Bring the priestess food and mead!" Boudica barked, and other men scrambled to do her bidding.

Soon a bronze goblet was handed to Alex. Gratefully, she sipped it and then, delighted with the sweet strong taste of mead, gulped thirstily. The cup was quickly refilled and a bronze platter of hot meat and hunks of bread put in front of her, and Alex, feeling as if she hadn't eaten in days, went to work shoving food into her mouth.

Even though she had just materialized from thin air, had let loose a sacred rabbit and was now seated to the right of the queen, talk went on around her without anyone quizzing her about where, when, how or why. So as she ate, Alex surreptitiously studied the ancient Celts.

The professor had told her they were a tall people, but her flat textbook description didn't begin to do them justice. They were savagely beautiful. Tall, yes, but also sleek and athletic. The women were bold looking, with thick ropes of braided hair in all the shades from the blondest of blond to Boudica's striking fire red. The men were muscular giants, dangerous and sharp-eyed. Everyone wore brightly colored clothing—tunics, trousers and cloaks. Many items were as intricately embroidered as Boudica's leathers.

At the sight of a man whose face was decorated with the sapphire woad design, Alex felt a snap of recognition, and her heart thudded almost painfully in her chest. But the design wasn't of graceful S swirls. Instead it was in the shape of a dragon, the tattooed tail wrapping the warrior's neck. But even though it wasn't the image from her dreams, Alex's appetite was gone.

"Better now?" Boudica asked, leaning toward her so that the

two of them could speak intimately, while the men and women around them talked and threw curious glances their way.

"Yes, thank you," Alex said.

Boudica glanced at the half-eaten food on the platter Alex had set aside. "So, you are not a spirit, for though they can take human form and appear corporeal, they can not take in nourishment from this world."

"I promise you I'm not a spirit."

"But you are magical, and you must be greatly beloved of Andraste. It was a most unusual and magical thing, that the goddess made you appear to me this night. I will dedicate to Andraste the first blood my sword drinks from the liver of my first kill in the battle to come."

Not sure what to say, Alex nodded, hoping she looked pleased at the gruesome picture the queen painted.

"Word came to us that the Roman governor Suetonius slaughtered those of the sacred Isle of Mona."

Alex tried to look as confident as possible as she said, "Suetonius did lead the killing on Mona. I was lucky that the goddess saved me."

Boudica had been studying her carefully. Finally she said, "I knew the goddess would not allow this desecration to go unpunished. Andraste saving you and bringing you to me shows me I have been following the right path all along."

As the queen spoke her gaze traveled beyond Alex to a place close to the fire where two young girls sat on thick pallets of furs. Both were beautiful, and Alex noticed one of them had hair the exact shade of Boudica's. The youngest of the two was maybe eleven or twelve. She stared into the campfire, leaving food untouched on the platter in front of her. The older girl, as if sensing Boudica's gaze, turned her head slowly and looked at the queen. Alex was struck by the dark circles under her eyes, and her haunted expression.

With a start of recognition, Alex realized these two girls must be the queen's daughters. She remembered the story Carswell had told her about Boudica's husband dying, and passing the torque of leadership on to his wife. The new queen of the Iceni had been reigning peacefully under a treaty with Rome signed by her husband when, without warning, the Roman tax collector, Catus Decius, attacked her—had her beaten in front of her people, and her young daughters publicly raped. Enraged, Boudica had rallied the Celts against Roman oppression.

Alex had thought the story a gruesome one when Carswell had told it to her, but coming face-to-face with the living people of legend was much different than history being retold in a laboratory. The girls were so young! And so obviously terribly damaged.

"I believe you're doing the right thing," Alex surprised herself by saying.

The queen's smile was sad as she gazed at her daughters. "The goddess is with me and she will truly help us drive the vile Romans from our sacred land."

Alex knew what would happen to this woman—that she would have victory over the Romans, but only a short-lived one. Her fate was to fall with her people, after which the Romans would subjugate the Celts for many years. But at that moment Alex felt herself caught up in Boudica's passion, and she suddenly wished the queen could be victorious.

Boudica's green eyes blazed and her face was framed by her brilliant red hair, which caught the glow of the campfire as if it, too, were made of flame. *She looks like a goddess—like nothing in this world or any other could defeat her.*

One of Boudica's men spoke to her and the queen briefly turned her attention from her daughters. It was then Alex saw the firelight reflect on more than her glimmering hair. The golden torque at her neck flashed, pulling Alex's gaze down—

and she felt her eyes widened. There, in the half circle of braided gold that nestled against Boudica's fair skin, wasn't a large jewel, as she had at first thought. It was the medallion she had been sent to retrieve.

SIX

Alex was staring at her torque when Boudica turned back to her. Without speaking, the queen looked at her for a long moment, and then her hand went up to touch the neck piece of braided gold.

"Sometimes I still believe I feel the warmth of my husband's skin through it," she said softly. "I touch it and remember how like this torque he was—beautiful and strong."

"What is that medallion in the end of it?" Alex blurted. Then she quickly shut her mouth, worried that she'd said something inappropriate, or worse, something she should have already known.

But Boudica appeared unfazed. Her fingers found the medallion, tracing over the raised pattern. "It is an ancient image of the stars. It was thought to be a powerful talisman in my family, and was passed from mother to daughter until it, and its mate, came to me. When I wed Prasutagus I had both pieces set in his torque as a wedding gift." The queen paused, stroking the object as she stared into the fire.

Then Alex's mind caught up with what Boudica had said, and her gaze snapped back to the torque. Her stomach tightened as she saw that, sure enough, the medallion was only half of what Carswell had shown her—as if the original had been broken in two. She looked at the other end of the torque and felt the breath rush out of her as she saw that something was missing.

"It's gone!" Alex gasped.

"Aye, it is indeed, but I shall retrieve it if I have to cut it from that monster's body."

"A monster took it?" Alex was utterly confused.

"Aye, a monster in the form of a Roman tax collector." Boudica's blazing green eyes seemed to pierce Alex. "You know that I was beaten and my daughters raped."

It wasn't a question, but Alex nodded and said solemnly, "I do."

"The monster who ordered it was Catus Decius, a Roman tax collector. When his soldiers were beating me, the medallion came loose. Catus took it, saying it was payment owed to Rome by the Queen of the Iceni. He said my daughters' virginity was payment owed to Rome, too." Boudica curled her lip in a vicious sneer. "I will find him in Londinium and take back my medallion, as well as the payment Rome owes *me* for defiling my children." The queen put her hand on Alex's shoulder, gripping tightly. "And now with a magically given priestess of Andraste by my side, I know I cannot fail to exact vengeance for the wrongs committed against me and my people. You will stay with me, will you not? You must march to Londinium with us."

"I'm here to support you. I'll come to Londinium," she assured her quickly. "I want to be there when you get your medallion back."

How different it was to see the living, breathing Boudica than it had been to be briefed about her, Alex thought. Until moments ago, this mission had been one that had been imposed upon her—one that, other than solving the mystery of the man with the swirling woad, she didn't particularly care about. But meeting the queen and remaining unconnected to her was impossible, especially as Alex knew all too well the tragic end that awaited her.

"Ah, I am glad to hear it." Boudica leaned a little closer and lowered her voice. "Welcome, Blonwen. The goddess must have known that, though I am surrounded by warriors, I have truly felt alone since Prasutagus's death. It will be good to have a priestess as my confidente."

Alex couldn't speak. At that moment Boudica wasn't an ancient queen, long dead and, except for readers of moldy history books, mostly forgotten. She was a woman, younger than Alex at this point in time, and one who needed a friend. As she tried to think of something priestesslike and wise to say, a flicker of movement beside Boudica caught her attention. A man suddenly appeared, not more than two feet away from the queen. He was dressed in a heavily embroidered tunic, and his hair was as brightly blond as Boudica's was red. He was a giant of a man, with thick muscles and an expression so fierce and frightening that Alex automatically recoiled as he shouted at her, "You must help Boudica!"

"What is it, Blonwen? What troubles you? Is it an ill omen?" the queen said, turning to look around her at what might have drawn Alex's attention.

The warriors nearby, standing just far enough away to allow Boudica and the newly arrived priestess privacy to talk, were instantly alerted by their queen's words.

Of course, Alex hadn't needed to see Boudica's nonreaction to the appearance of the man to know he was a ghost—she could tell from her first glimpse of his semitransparent body. *Okay,* Alex told herself sternly, *I'm a priestess. It's normal that I can talk to ghosts.* She cleared her throat and said, "No, it's not a bad omen. It's just a spirit telling me to help you, which is actually a good omen because that is what I intend to do."

There was a hush in the campsite as every eye turned to her.

"I know you are more than what you seem and that you come here for reasons other than to be the queen's confidente, but you must help her," the ghost exclaimed. Though he was speaking to Alex, his eyes never left Boudica.

The queen didn't look nervous or scared, as modern people usually did when they found out Alex was seeing a ghost. Boudica looked calm and more than a little curious. "What else does the spirit say?" she asked.

"Tell her the boy who first kissed her under the hawthorn blossoms on Beltane Eve tells her to stay strong," said the ghost.

Alex swallowed hard and turned to the queen. "He says that the boy who kissed you under the hawthorn blossoms on Beltane Eve wants you to stay strong."

Boudica's eyes widened as the people around her murmured under their breath. Alex thought she could hear the words *Soul Speaker* being whispered through the campsite.

"Where is he?" Boudica asked in a voice that sounded choked.

"There, right beside you."

As the crowd around them watched, talking in hushed tones, their queen turned slowly to where Alex pointed, and said, "Forgive me, my love, for not keeping them safe."

Alex's gaze automatically found Boudica's daughters, who were still sitting, silent and white faced, beside the fire.

"You are not to blame, and you will avenge them," said the ghost.

"He doesn't blame you," Alex told Boudica, though she couldn't make herself repeat his words of vengeance. She knew all too well that Boudica wouldn't avenge her daughters' rapes; rather, the war would end in her death and the subjugation of her people.

"It is with my daughters that you must help her, Soul Speaker," said the apparition, as if he read her mind. "Farewell for now." Before he disappeared completely, Boudica's husband put out a transparent hand to touch her cheek, and then he vanished.

"He's gone now," Alex said to Boudica, who had her own hand pressed against the cheek her husband's ghost had just caressed.

"So you are a Soul Speaker as well as a priestess of Andraste," said the man Boudica had earlier called Aedan.

"Yes, I am," she replied.

"My father died last winter. It was sudden. I did not—" The big Celt's words broke off and he looked down at his hand, which was gripping the hilt of the short sword hanging from a scabbard at his waist. "I did not have time to bid him farewell. If—if you could call him here, to you, so that I might speak with him one last time, I would, indeed, be in your debt."

Alex suppressed a sigh. "I can't do that," she said.

Aedan's nervous look turned dark. "You refuse my request?"

"You don't understand. I'm not refusing to help you, I just can't. I don't call spirits, *they* come to *me*."

The warrior frowned. "What kind of Soul Speaker are you?"

Alex didn't know what else to say but the truth. "I'm a very tired one."

"Enough, Aedan! Have we been so tainted by the Romans that we forget the rules of hospitality?"

"No, my queen," the man said, bowing his head. He sounded contrite, but Alex noticed he kept sending her chilly looks.

"The ways of Andraste are often mysterious—her path difficult and long. She has sent her priestess here to help direct our steps, and not to perform for us like a tamed dog." As she spoke, Boudica's eyes swept the crowd, coming to rest on her daughters. Her stern face softened. "Mirain and Una, show Blonwen to our tent. She is as weary as the two of you look."

The girls got up obediently and walked over to their mother.

"Rest well tonight. The march tomorrow will be long and there will be time for you and me to talk then," Boudica said to Alex.

Alex stood up and then, not sure of correct protocol, followed her instincts and bowed to the queen with what she hoped was at least a little grace. Boudica kissed her daughters, called for more mead, and was staring silently into the fire as Alex followed the girls into the night, which wasn't as dark and impossible to navigate as she would have imagined, thanks to the many campfires dotting the area.

Tents were mostly hides and lines draped from the sides of carts and staked to the ground either with polls or wooden spikes. The camp seemed huge, and was bustling with activity. The sounds of women laughing and men talking carried on the night air with the fragrant scent of roasting meat. All in all it wasn't as crude as Alex had expected. The people, for the most part, weren't dirty barbarians. They were actually attractive and pretty healthy looking. There wasn't opulence and riches scattered about, but everyone seemed well-fed, and the horses and other animals she caught glimpses of appeared fat and happy.

She was still gawking around when she realized the girls had stopped in front of a large tent. This one wasn't draped off the side of a wagon. It was freestanding, with tall poles in the middle and at its five sides. An old woman was tending a cheery campfire burning close enough to the open entrance to cast light within, but not too close to fill the tent with smoke.

The younger of the two girls gestured for Alex to go inside, which she did gratefully. She didn't think she'd ever been so exhausted in her life. *That's something I'm reporting on when I get back—this time travel thing is hard work. The next traveler should be told she's going to be dead on her feet. Unless it's just me…crap, it's probably just me—*

"Priestess, did you not hear me?"

Alex mentally shook herself and focused on the older of the two girls. "I'm sorry. I guess I'm more tired than I thought. What did you say?"

"This is your pallet. If you need anything, Rosin, who keeps the fire, will aid you."

"Thank you. I don't need anything. Except which of you is Mirain and which is Una?"

"I am Mirain," said the older girl. "My sister is Una."

"Mirain and Una, it's nice to meet you. Thank you for showing me here and being so nice to me."

"Our mother believes in the old ways," was all Mirain said. Una didn't speak at all.

After a few awkward moments, Alex turned to her pallet, which was a lovely, thick pile of furs. She pulled off her cloak and tried not to gape at the beautifully embroidered tunic that was revealed under it. Wow! It just seemed so impossible that Carswell could make all of this happen with her mind! Alex curled up on the pallet, using her cloak as a blanket. Just before she closed her eyes, she called across the tent to where Mirain and Una had curled together like puppies. "Good night, girls."

There was a pause and then Mirain said, "Good night, Priestess."

"I don't believe you are from the goddess," said a small voice that Alex knew had to belong to Una.

The girl's words made her stomach tighten, but her reply was purposefully calm. "You don't? Why not?"

"Because I don't believe there is a goddess."

"Shh, Una. Mother wouldn't like it if she heard you say that," Mirain said quickly. "Sleep now. Mornings are always better than nights, remember?"

"I remember too much." Una's whisper carried to Alex.

Alex wanted to say something profound and priestesslike, but she wasn't actually a priestess and she sure didn't know how to talk to a damaged teenager. Hell, it didn't seem that long ago that she'd been a damaged kid herself! Feeling overwhelmed and incompetent, she finally let exhaustion take over, and she slept.

That night, Alex didn't dream at all.

SEVEN

It made her feel foolish, but the first thought she had when she woke up was *he didn't come to me in my dreams.* The second thought was *where the hell am I?* And then all of her mind woke up and Alex remembered—Briton—AD 60 Boudica's camp.

"Wake up, sleepy bugaboo! Time's awastin' and the queen is callin' for ye!"

Alex scrubbed her eyes with her fists and looked up into the face of a true crone. "Rosin?" she asked, remembering the name Mirain had given her before she'd slept.

"Aye! I be Rosin. Boudica wants ye. Ye'd best take this and get movin'." The old woman handed her two slices of bread with a thick piece of fabulously greasy ham stuck between them, and a bronze cup of sweet, strong mead.

"Thank you," Alex muttered. She scrambled to her feet, straightened her clothes, attempted to tame her hair and then hurried out of the tent, bread and meat in hand.

The camp reminded her of a beehive. There was activity everywhere, but the busyness around her wasn't what caught her attention. What she noticed most was the air. Alex drew a deep breath. It was like sucking in the newness of life. Everything around her was green and growing and so free from smog and pollutants and plastic that the world seemed virginal.

"It smells so good!" she exclaimed.

Rosin gave her a sidelong look that said she thought the new priestess might be weak in her head. "Aye. It is the forest, Priestess."

"Well, I like it." She bit into her breakfast sandwich and her eyes almost rolled into the back of her head with pleasure. "Real fat! Real bread! Real meat! I could kiss the cook!" she moaned.

"A simple thank ye will serve very well," said Rosin. "Follow the path that way. Ye will find the heart of the camp and Queen Boudica."

"Thanks!" Alex grinned and, feeling better than she had in days, started down the path. She hadn't taken half a dozen steps when the air to the right side of the path shimmered and an old man materialized. His body was semitransparent, but his frank gaze made it impossible for Alex to ignore him. "What?" she snapped.

We are glad you are here to aid the queen....

Alex paused, looked around her and, not seeing anyone near them, said, "Fine. Okay. Good. But if you want me to help your queen, you're going to have to leave me alone so that I can do my job." She paused when he lifted his brows, and added, "You know what I mean by my job, right? The whole priestess thing."

We know more than you think we do, the spirit said, meeting her gaze squarely before he disappeared.

Great. Just what I need—ghosts that are nosy and cryptic.

She followed the path, and though she kept seeing the

flickery, semitransparent bodies of dead people in her peripheral vision, they didn't approach her. It seemed they were content to simply hover around, which was totally fine with Alex. Left to herself, she enjoyed eating her sandwich and watching the controlled mayhem around her.

The Celts were definitely breaking camp, but this wasn't an army camp like any she'd imagined. There were women and children everywhere. Carswell had told her that the family unit was of the utmost importance to the ancient Celts, and that they even marched to war accompanied by their families: husband, sons, wives and daughters. But seeing it up close and personal was amazing. No, Alex decided. It wasn't amazing. It was intriguing. They were all working together, shouting and laughing and breaking camp. Alex was a product of the twenty-first century. She'd been raised in an antiseptic home where the upper-middle-class mother and father had had one child—her—and provided all the right things—good schools, nice clothes, the house in the suburbs. Yet home had never been warm and comfortable and, well, *family*. The Celts' obvious sense of boisterous togetherness was as alien to Alex as was their ancient world. It was also as compelling.

They survive by depending on one another.

As used to ghosts appearing as Alex was, she was still startled, and then frowned at the see-through woman who had materialized by her side.

"I can figure this out for myself," Alex said under her breath. Several of the people she was passing stopped loading carts and horses to bow respectfully to her and call out "Good day, Priestess!" Alex smiled at them and waved back, hoping this newest spirit would disappear like the old man had.

She didn't.

"I don't mean to be rude," Alex said quietly. "But I'd really appreciate it if you and all your kind would leave me alone for a while."

"I am not here for you, child. I'm here because he will need me."

"He?" Alex didn't have a clue what this woman was talking about.

"Yes, he. You will see."

Alex sighed and kept walking. She glanced at the spirit, who was keeping pace with her. The woman was older and maternal looking. She had a kind, round face with large brown eyes and strong high cheekbones, and when she lifted her right hand to brush back her long silver hair, Alex noticed that tattooed on her palm was a spiraling circle. There was something about it that pricked Alex's interest. The ghost was also wearing an interesting outfit. Even though it was transparent, Alex could see that it had once been beautiful—robin's egg blue with elaborately embroidered roses all over it. For an instant she wanted to ask the ghost about her clothes. Had she decorated them herself? Did the roses mean anything?

Don't seem interested, Alex reminded herself sternly. *Ghosts are worse than stray cats. They stay around forever if you give them attention.* So even though she was curious about the woman, Alex ignored her and kept heading for the middle of camp, trailed by the momlike ghost and too many questions.

"Blonwen! There you are!"

Boudica's voice carried over the noise of the breaking camp. Alex saw the queen waving to her from her place beside a campfire that looked like the same one as the night before. Had the queen even gone to bed? Alex didn't recall anyone joining her and the girls in the tent.

"Good morning, my queen." Alex bowed grandly. She was already starting to like Boudica, and it was easy to catch the spirit of excitement that permeated her camp.

"I'm so pleased to see you. Come close beside me. There is someone I know you will be eager to greet." Boudica's smile was filled with genuine warmth.

Alex's gut immediately began to tighten. Someone she'd be eager to greet? That was impossible. She didn't *know* anyone in this world!

"Look who has just joined our camp! Another survivor of the desecration of Mona. Our goddess is certainly merciful. She has brought him safely here to us, so now I have a priestess and a druid in my camp. Caradoc, my kinsman, this is Blonwen, the priestess I was telling you about. It is she who Andraste brought to me last night, and she who released the sacred white hare that raced toward Londinium. You said her name was unfamiliar, but you must know her now that you see her."

A tall man stepped out from the group of warriors who stood at Boudica's back, and Alex felt dizzy with shock. It was *him!* The left side of the man's face was tattooed with sapphire woad in the swirling *S* of her dreams. She could see that the design went down his neck, spread over his broad shoulder and disappeared under his tunic. She looked from that distinctive pattern into eyes that were an unusual amber color. First she saw shock pass over his face, and then he seemed to draw himself up as he silently studied her with a calculating coldness that chilled her blood.

Before he speaks, tell him you have a message for him from me, and describe what I am wearing. Be certain to mention the spiral circle on my palm. The ghost of the middle-aged woman spoke from her place beside Alex. *Quickly!* she snapped when Alex only stared at her. *Do as I say before he exposes you!*

"I have a message for you from a spirit with a spiral circle on her palm. She is wearing a blue tunic embroidered with roses," Alex said hastily, looking from the ghost to the man Boudica had called Caradoc.

She saw his eyes widen, and he said, "What is the message?"

Alex forced herself not to gasp at the sound of his voice. She'd heard it before! This was the man from her dreams. He had been the one who'd begged her to return to him.

Tell my strong, brave son, these exact words—that his mother would ask him to, once more, wait—think—and consider, or he may once more find himself naked and shoeless and dodging from briar patch to briar patch all the way home.

Alex stared at the woman.

Tell him! she commanded.

Alex turned to Caradoc, who was standing beside Boudica. The queen was watching her with an expression of open curiosity.

"Well…" Alex spoke slowly, making sure she got all the words right. "Your mother asks me to tell you to, once more, wait— think—consider, or you may once more find yourself naked and shoeless and dodging from briar patch to briar path all the way home."

Beside him, Boudica threw back her head and laughed. "I had forgotten all about that! How old were you then, Caradoc? Eleven or twelve?"

He frowned and told his queen, who was still chuckling, "I was twelve." Alex saw his jaw clench and then unclench as he continued to stare at her. Still, he did not speak to her, but said to Boudica, "You did not say she was a Soul Speaker."

Eyes sparkling with amusement, Boudica raised her brows. "Why would I have to tell you that? Her name should have been enough for you to recognize her. Have your wounds affected your mind, Caradoc?"

Alex had been so shocked to see this man whose tattoos and voice were from her dreams that it wasn't until Boudica mentioned it that she noticed Caradoc was injured. There was a gash at his hairline and he had a linen bandage wrapped around his right arm.

"My injuries have done nothing to my memory. The name Blonwen is utterly unfamiliar to me," Caradoc said.

Alex braced herself for him to decry her, and as she did she felt an unexpected wave of disappointment at the thought that she was probably going to have to press the ESC and return to her own time. And that disappointment wasn't just because she hadn't completed her mission. While she waited for Caradoc to expose her as a fraud and call down Boudica's retribution on her for deceiving a queen, she realized that she wasn't ready to return to her old life, and that had nothing to do with Project Anasazi.

"My queen, I do not know her as Blonwen," Caradoc said as his gaze met and locked with Alex's. "I only recognize her as a Soul Speaker."

He wasn't going to expose her? Hesitantly, Alex let out a long, slow breath of relief.

"Ah, well, Soul Speaker, Priestess, Blonwen. Is it not all one in the same? I am simply pleased you both escaped Mona." The queen smiled warmly at her kinsman and Alex, then all traces of amusement faded from her and she continued in a much more sober voice. "Tell me, Caradoc and Blonwen, is the isle utterly destroyed?" Boudica said.

Caradoc gave Alex a long, considering look and then said, "I will defer to the Soul Speaker to answer our queen."

Do not lie! the ghost of Caradoc's mother said quickly. *Negative energy is released with untruths.*

A shiver passed through Alex's body at the spirit's words. She was right; deep in her gut Alex knew that words and oaths, lies and truths, had a different power here than they did in the modern world.

"I can't…" She hesitated, choosing the truth carefully. "I'm sorry, Boudica, but I have to ask you not force me to talk about Mona."

The queen's green eyes were filled with compassion. "Aye,

I understand how difficult it is to speak of great loss to someone who wasn't there and didn't experience it with you. It is too much like reliving the tragedy. Later, perhaps, when the memory isn't so fresh, we will talk." She looked from Alex to Caradoc. "I would imagine the two of you have many things to say to one another. Blonwen, I give you leave to ride beside Caradoc as we march to Londinium. I would ask, though, that before we begin our trek today you offer Andraste libations and evoke her blessing under the rowan." Boudica inclined her head in the direction of a craggy tree that stood apart from the others. It looked unbelievably old. Its bark was gnarled and its many limbs twisted, but it was peppered with delicate white flowers that gave it the appearance of an old woman sprinkled with a jeweled dusting of magic.

Alex had been staring at the tree and smiling at the image of it as an old woman, when she realized what Boudica had just asked of her.

She was supposed to perform some kind of blessing—there, in front of everyone.

"Blonwen, is anything amiss?" Boudica asked her.

Alex felt everyone's eyes drawn to her yet again. She swallowed hard and lifted her chin. She was supposed to be a priestess! There was no way she could balk at asking for her goddess's blessing— that was part of the priestess job description.

"No, nothing's wrong," she stated. "Well, except I don't have any libations." *Libations…libations…what the hell are libations?*

"Oh, of course. Bring the honey and wine," Boudica commanded.

In what seemed like less than a couple frantic beats of her heart, a woman appeared with two jugs and handed them, with a shy smile and curtsy, to Alex.

"We will follow you, Priestess," Boudica said, nodding for Alex to precede her to the old tree.

Numbly, Alex walked toward it. Of all the curious gazes that rested on her, she swore she could feel Caradoc's eyes boring into her back as he waited for her to mess up.

And of course she'd mess up! She didn't have any idea how to give libations to a tree and evoke the blessing of a goddess! She was going to make an utter fool of herself and, worse, expose herself as a fraud. Alex was considering whether she could faint with any believability when the ghost's voice broke through her panicked thoughts.

You can do this. Still your mind and follow your heart.

The ghost of Caradoc's mother was leaning comfortably against the thick bark of the old tree. She smiled at Alex.

Still your mind, she repeated. *Trust yourself, child.*

Having very little choice, Alex listened to the ghost. She walked up to the tree and set the two jugs at her feet. Then she closed her eyes and drew a deep breath, letting it go slowly while she concentrated on relaxing the babble in her mind and the hammering of her heart.

She opened her eyes and stared at the tree. *Rowan—a tree sacred to the ancient Celts. Known for protection. To give libations— sprinkling honey and wine or sometimes milk on the ground in sacred places as offerings to the gods.* The thoughts seemed to pop into her mind. Seeing the tree with new eyes, Alex gazed up at the thick branches and the canopy of lush leaves decorated with brilliant white flowers. The morning light caught the blossoms and, for just an instant, Alex was sure they glistened.

On impulse, she reached out and rested her palms against the tree's bark, gasping as something passed between herself and the rowan. It was as if she could feel the tree breathing, and through the tree she was connected to the world around her. Alex could sense life shifting and growing, and she knew beyond any doubt that there was an energy in this time—in this earth—that she was somehow meant to be a part of.

For the first time in her life, Alex felt completely at home. With a sense of unbelievable joy, she picked up the jugs of honey and of wine, and as she moved in a slow circle around the ancient tree, poured both liquids onto the rowan's roots.

The words of the blessing whispered through her mind like the echo of a pleasant dream. Without any hesitation Alex recited, "We arise today, through the strength of Andraste and her earth—light of sun, radiance of moon, splendor of fire, speed of lightning, swiftness of wind, depth of sea, firmness of rock. As priestess of the goddess I ask blessing and protection for our queen and for her people. Let the justness of Boudica's cause shine pure and visible to all, like the blossoms of this sacred rowan."

Alex poured the last of the libations out as she finished the prayer. Then she bowed to the tree, breathed a deep sigh of contentment and turned to face Boudica.

The queen's smile was as bright as the morning. "With Andraste's blessing, we march on to Londinium!" she cried, and the people surrounding them took up her call, cheering their queen.

Alex sneaked a glance at Caradoc and wasn't too surprised that she caught him staring at her—though she was taken off guard when he slowly, subtly, bowed his head.

EIGHT

Alex was profoundly glad she already knew how to handle a horse. Sometimes horseback was the only efficient way to get to many remote places on the tallgrass prairie. Plus, she'd always preferred the silent ease of riding a horse to the obnoxious motor and jarring shocks of an ATV. Of course, riding a couple hours or so once or twice a week wasn't exactly the same thing as riding with Boudica's army all day long, through what looked like the forest primeval. The one thing Alex didn't have to worry about was that she didn't know how to make a horse start, stop and turn.

The "everything else" she *did* have to worry about was mainly Caradoc. The druid warrior was sticking to her as if someone had joined them at the hip. Under normal circumstances, Alex might not have minded a gorgeous man hanging out with her, but joining Boudica's army and masquerading as a priestess of the queen's goddess definitely did not qualify as normal circumstances.

Caradoc made her nervous. Very nervous.

It wouldn't be so bad if it wasn't just the two of them. The ridiculous part was that it should have been impossible for them to find any privacy in the middle of a marching army, but apparently Boudica had put out the word that the druid and the priestess needed time to speak, time to grieve. *Time,* Alex decided, *for me to start working on one hell of an ulcer.*

So they rode together near the front of the army, within sight of Boudica and her inner circle, but in a little pocket of privacy.

"You did not come from Mona." That was how Caradoc began the conversation once it was obvious they were going to be left alone and uninterrupted.

"No. I didn't," Alex said. His mother's prompting wasn't all that had made her decide to avoid lies. Telling the truth felt right, deep in her gut, and if Alex was sure of nothing else, she was sure that she was going to follow her gut.

Caradoc gave her an incredulous look. "You do not even attempt to deny it?"

"Well, that wouldn't make any sense, would it?"

He stared at her silently.

"I mean, seriously, how long had you lived on Mona before the Roman attack?"

"More than half of my twenty-five years I have lived on the sacred isle of Mona."

Alex was temporarily speechless. The place he'd called home for most of his life had been destroyed. *And he's twenty-five! Ten years younger than me!* Alex shook herself mentally and said, "See, it wouldn't make any sense for me to pretend to you I'd come from your home when you know very well that you've never seen me before."

"I have seen you before," Caradoc said.

"What? How?"

Instead of meeting her curious gaze, the druid warrior stared straight ahead. "In my dreams. The past many nights. I have seen your face and heard your voice."

Shock kept Alex from editing what burst out of her mouth. "You've been in my dreams, too. Only I couldn't see your face. I just heard your voice and I got an image of your woad." She paused, wishing he would look at her so she could read his expression more easily. "But you actually saw me in your dreams?"

Caradoc nodded. "Yes. You were dressed oddly."

Alex glanced down at the druid's linen tunic and leather pants, both of which were embroidered with the same swirling *S* design of his tattoos. Had she actually seen him in her dreams she would have thought he was dressed strangely, too. So it was easy to imagine that her typical outfit of jeans and a T-shirt would have seemed utterly bizarre to this ancient Celt.

"You said you heard my voice. What did I say?" Alex asked, deciding it was best not to mention anything about clothing.

He didn't answer her for so long that Alex didn't think he was going to speak again. Just as she was going to say something banal about the weather, he said, "You told me to wait for you, and promised to come to me." He did turn in the saddle then so that he could look her in the eye, and demanded, "Where did you come from, Soul Speaker, and what is it you want from me?"

While she stalled for time and tried to think of a reasonable answer that wasn't a lie, Alex said, "I really wish you wouldn't call me Soul Speaker."

"Blonwen, then. Where did you come from?" he repeated.

"I can't tell you that," she stated.

"Can you tell me why I shouldn't expose you to Boudica as a fraud?"

"I'm not here to cause Boudica any harm. I respect the queen and think her cause is just."

"Still, that doesn't tell me why I shouldn't expose you."

Alex was trying to formulate a reasonable response to him when the air behind Caradoc shimmered and the ghost of his mother materialized, sitting behind him on his horse's rump. She smiled and motioned for her to go on.

Alex sighed and tried not to let the spirit distract her. "I'm here for a reason that goes beyond Boudica and her war. It has ramifications that will affect the whole world. No, I can't tell you what they are." *You wouldn't believe me anyway,* she added silently to herself. "But I can promise you I want only good things for Boudica."

"Yet you lie to her."

"Only because I have to. I'm telling the truth about everything I can."

"I know you can speak to souls. You could not have described my mother's burial garb had you not seen her, and I know you could not have made up her words. But I do not believe you are a true Soul Speaker. Aedan said he asked for your aid in summoning the spirit of his father, and you denied him."

Totally irritated, Alex snapped, "I told Aedan that I'd help him if I could, but I can't call souls!"

"All Soul Speakers can summon the dead."

"Not this one! This one can only talk to them."

"Is that, perhaps, because your power is based on dark forces?"

"I don't have any idea what you're talking about. I can't call ghosts because I don't know how. Actually, I've never tried. I know as a druid you might find this strange, but not everyone wants to chat with ghosts," she said, unable to keep the sarcasm out of her voice, even though his mother was frowning severely at her. "They tend to be a pain in the ass." She glanced at the stowaway Caradoc didn't know he had, and added, "Plus, they're nosy. Very nosy."

Generalizations are rather impolite, said Caradoc's mother.

"Impolite or not, it's true," Alex said to both mother and son.

He was staring at her with an incredulous expression. "You have had no training in the art of Soul Speaking?"

"No."

He shook his head, still clearly shocked. "Then you could not be a priestess of Andraste. And that deceit is a very grave one."

Alex didn't respond to him. Her gut felt too empty. No, she wasn't a priestess of the goddess Andraste, but for a short time while she'd been performing her blessing ceremony, Alex had felt truly connected to this land, this time, and perhaps even this world's goddess. Caradoc's words had reminded her that she really was nothing more than an interloper here. Her mission was to come, take and leave. It wasn't to belong.

Tell my son it is not his place to judge who is, or isn't, in the service of the great goddess, Caradoc's mother said.

Alex shook her head slightly. There was no point in repeating the words. She *was* an imposter.

Tell him, child, the ghost prompted gently. *It is a mother's prerogative to admonish a child who has become...* She paused, obviously looking for a mom-watered-down-nice-version-of...

"Obnoxious?" Alex suggested aloud.

I was going to say overly judgmental, the ghost said.

"Obnoxious? That is a question?" Caradoc asked.

"Actually, it's an answer. Your mother was trying to describe the kind of guy you've become. I was helping her."

"My mother is with us again?"

"Yes. She's sitting behind you."

Caradoc jerked around, sending his elbow through his mother's semisubstantial form and causing his horse to snort and shy.

Unfazed by his movement, she reached up and placed a hand on his shoulder. *All is well, my selkie,* she murmured.

Touched by the warmth in his mother's voice, Alex said, "She says that all is well."

Caradoc quieted his horse before he spoke again. Still stoking the big bay's neck, he asked, "Does she say anything else?"

His mother raised her brows at Alex. Alex raised her own brows, but said, "When she first materialized she asked me to tell you that it isn't your place to judge who is or who isn't in the service of the goddess."

Caradoc's sharp look snagged Alex's attention. "My mother said that?"

Alex shrugged. "I wasn't going to tell you, but it irritated her that I wouldn't repeat what she said to you. She said it's a mother's prerogative to admonish her child."

Caradoc's bark of quick laughter seemed to surprise him as much as it did Alex. His expression softened, adding a warmth to his chiseled features that was so appealing Alex felt her cheeks warm. When he glanced over at her, Caradoc was still smiling.

"I've missed her. Can you tell her that?"

"I don't have to," Alex said gently. "She's still here. She can hear you just fine." She paused and added, "She's touching your shoulder."

Slowly, Caradoc's hand came up so that it rested on his left shoulder. For a moment it merged with his mother's.

I love you, my golden selkie, she said in a sweet, sad voice as her ghostly body faded and then disappeared completely.

Alex found it hard to speak, but finally managed to clear her throat and say, "She's gone, but before she left she said that she loves you."

Caradoc's hand dropped back to the pommel of his saddle. He nodded and didn't reply.

They rode on in silence. Caradoc was so obviously engrossed in his own thoughts that Alex was able to study him. She didn't have a clue about the selkie part, but she could see why his mom called him golden. His long, thick hair tied back by a leather thong, was the color of spun gold. His tanned skin, flushed with health and stretched smooth over long, lean muscles, had a goldish tint to it. Even his eyes were a deep amber color with flecks of gold in them. As with most of the Celts, Caradoc was tall, at least six feet four, Alex guessed. His face was strong and distinctive. As she continued studying him she had the ridiculous thought that he reminded her of a young, vibrant Marlon Brando, when he was in his prime and exuded confidence and sexuality.

And then Alex felt a jolt as she realized that Caradoc was no longer staring ahead, lost in thought. He was watching her watch him.

"It seems I must ask your pardon," he said.

She blinked in surprise. "What for?"

"For questioning your tie to Andraste."

"Oh, well, I…" Alex stuttered, trying to figure out some way to tell him as much of the truth as she could without totally messing up her mission.

"No, I was wrong to judge your commitment to the goddess. You are not all that you appear, but there is one thing I know—you have been touched by Andraste enough to be considered her priestess."

"How do you know that?"

His smile was sad. "My mother was the goddess's high priestess for the last decade of her life. She wouldn't have admonished me if you did not belong to Andraste. So you see, I must ask your pardon for being hasty in my judgment."

"You're pardoned," Alex said, feeling flushed and short of breath as what he was saying began to sink in.

Caradoc nodded and then continued. "As she followed the goddess's path, my mother did things I found mysterious and oftentimes even strange. She told me over and over that the ways of Andraste could not be understood by men. It seems you may be just another example of my mother being right."

Alex didn't know what to say. His mother had been a high priestess of Andraste! Then why hadn't she been mad at her for pretending to be a priestess of her goddess? Alex remembered the jolt she had felt when she touched the tree, and the serene sense of rightness that had filled her as she'd performed the blessing and evoked the goddess.

A thought, amazing and awe inspiring, drifted through her mind: *Could there really be a goddess who watches over this world, and could she have touched me?*

NINE

The rest of the day the tension between Caradoc and Alex eased, partly because it was impossible for them to be left alone during the entire trek, and partly because Caradoc simply stopped questioning Alex. Then, as the day waned, Boudica ordered the army to leave the rough trail they had been following and cut into the forest. Like everyone else, Alex was busy guiding her horse and dodging limbs. While she fought back foliage there was no way for Caradoc to say much of anything except to call an occasional "Beware the branch!" to her.

By the time the queen ordered camp to be made, Alex wasn't sure she'd ever feel her butt again. After she managed to half fall, half climb down from her horse, it took all her willpower not to hobble over to a fallen tree limb and collapse on it. Everyone else was practically leaping off horses or nimbly climbing down from carts, or even walking briskly up to the campsite. None of them appeared crippled by the day of travel.

No way could Alex curl up in an exhausted ball without calling a lot of attention to herself.

The people worked steadily and seemingly tirelessly to make camp and begin the evening meal, though they were unusually quiet. So she volunteered to help Mirain and Una set up Boudica's tent, one ancient skill she knew she'd be good at, since she often camped out on the tallgrass prairie.

As she worked side by side with the girls, she asked Mirain, "Why is everyone so quiet? It didn't seem like this last night."

"We're close to Londinium. The people will not raise their voices tonight. There will be few campfires. We do not want the Romans to know our army is here and that many of them will enjoy their last night's sleep tonight."

Alex felt a chill at the thought of the coming battle and the deaths that had to happen.

"You glowed today."

Surprised by the younger girl's words, Alex smiled at Una. She didn't have a clue what the child was talking about, but didn't want to discourage her. Boudica's daughters had ridden close to their mother, and Alex had noted that Una rarely spoke. Even when she did her voice tended to be flat and her voice expressionless. Actually, she looked more animated now than she had all day.

"I glowed? When?" Alex asked, still smiling at the girl.

"When you evoked the blessing this morning. You touched the tree and I saw you glow."

Alex was taken utterly off guard by the girl's comments, and while she scrambled to think of something even vaguely intelligent to say, Mirain spoke softly to her sister. "You didn't tell me you saw Blonwen glow."

Una shrugged. "Why should I have told you? You were watching, too. You saw her."

"I was watching, yes, but I only saw Blonwen sprinkle libations and call on the goddess. I did not see her glow. That was something meant for your eyes alone."

Una's eyes, so much like her mother's, widened. Then she pressed her lips together, shook her head twice, crossed her arms in a gesture that was more protective than defiant, and marched out of the tent. Mirain sighed sadly and reached for another fur to arrange on one of the pallets.

"I don't understand," Alex said, frowning at the tent flap through which Una had just disappeared, and wondering if she should go after the girl.

"She saw you glow as the goddess touched you during the blessing." The elder sister said it as if that should clear everything up.

It was Alex's turn to sigh. "That part I understand. What I don't get is why that upset Una so much."

"My sister doesn't want to believe in the goddess anymore, but seeing with her own eyes that Andraste touched you says the goddess does exist and is watching over this camp."

"Why would that upset her?"

Mirain quit arranging furs and faced Alex. "Because if there is a goddess, she allowed the Romans to beat our mother and rape us. It's easier for Una to believe the goddess doesn't exist than to believe she cares so little about us that she didn't intercede."

Alex's stomach felt sick. "I'm so sorry that happened to you two," she said, because she didn't know what else to say.

Mirain gave a short nod and went back to unpacking the bedding.

"And what about you, Mirain?" Alex felt compelled to ask. "Do you still believe in the goddess?"

The teenager looked over her shoulder at Alex. "I believe in my mother's retribution."

★ ★ ★

Dinner at the queen's campfire was a hushed event, but far from somber. As Alex ate her venison stew she thought that the sense of anticipation and excitement in the camp was so strong it was almost a visible entity. Boudica's people were filled with a tension that hummed through camp, albeit silently.

Their queen oversaw everything. As evening melted into night, Boudica moved throughout the camp, speaking softly to men and women, touching children's bright heads. She soothed their nerves with her quiet confidence, and Alex marveled at how the entire army seemed to take on her personality and her sense of calm waiting.

After making her rounds, Boudica returned to her campfire and gratefully accepted a goblet of mead. She drank deeply for a while without speaking to anyone, and then she called for Caradoc and Alex to sit beside her.

"I want to ask a boon from both of you," Boudica said.

"Of course, my queen," Caradoc said.

Alex nodded, agreeing also. How do you say no to a queen's request for a favor?

"It is my wish that the two of you stay with my daughters during the battle tomorrow. Keep my children safe. That is the favor I ask of you."

"I will guard them with my life," Caradoc vowed.

"I'll do everything I can to protect them," Alex said, wishing she'd smuggled an M16 in the folds of her cloak instead of Thumper.

Boudica smiled. "Thank you, my friends. My mind will be at peace knowing that they are being watched over by you." Her hand came up to find the empty circle at the end of her torque where the second medallion piece should be. "Catus will return this to me tomorrow, and my husband's torque will again be whole."

Watching her, Alex saw that there was much more behind Boudica's words than the return of a piece of bronze. She understood that the queen was talking about a wholeness in her soul, and righting the only piece of a terrible wrong that she could control. Boudica couldn't return her children's innocence—she couldn't wipe from their minds the brutality of rape. All she could do was make this one piece of the puzzle fit back into their lives, and then move ahead to deal with the incomplete picture the violence of their past left them with.

At that moment there was a disturbance in the circle of warriors who shadowed Boudica everywhere she went. The group parted, allowing through a young Celt who, breathing hard, ran to the queen and dropped to his knees before her.

"What have you discovered, Heddwyn?" she asked.

"They only have the Ninth Legion for protection!" Heddwyn gasped, struggling to catch his breath between words. "Suetonius hasn't returned from Mona with the rest of the legions. He dallies there, even though he has heard you march against him, my queen. The people of Londinium brag that they have nothing to fear from an army led by a woman."

Boudica's smile was feral. "Then we shall show them how wrong they are to misjudge the Iceni."

He bowed to her. "Yes, my queen!"

Boudica stood. "Rest and prepare. We attack Londinium at dawn from the east, with the rising sun blazing behind us. Tomorrow the Romans will know what it is to harm an Iceni queen and anger her vengeful goddess!"

While the warriors, men and women alike, rallied around Boudica, touching her and asking for her blessing on the morrow, Alex got up and quietly slipped away into the night. Feeling a terrible sense of foreboding, she walked slowly to Boudica's tent.

History reported that Boudica was victorious at Londinium;

it wasn't the queen's possible death the next day that worried Alex. Boudica would win. She would probably even find Catus and get the missing medallion piece.

But then what? Was Alex supposed to rip the torque off the queen's neck and retreat into the future? Just the thought made her sick.

Alex reached the queen's tent, but couldn't make herself go inside. The girls were probably in there. She couldn't face them just then, didn't want to see Mirain's controlled despair or Una's hurt and anger. Wouldn't she just be adding to the trauma the girls had already faced? The torque was their mother's sacred sign of royalty—and all they had left of their father. Alex, who was supposed to be a priestess of their goddess, was going to steal it.

But if she didn't, the world as she knew it might very well be destroyed.

She sighed and walked over to a boulder that sat beside a sweet little tinkling stream not far from the queen's tent. The big rock rested at the base of a thick old oak, making a perfect bench, if Alex ignored the roughness of the bark. She winced as she sat, wishing her butt had stayed numb. She tried to get comfortable, but soon gave up and looked out at the silent forest instead. The moon was almost full, and it gave off a silvery light that glistened on the water's surface, turning it into liquid jewels. The spring night was warm, the air soft. Wearily, Alex took off her shoes, pulled up her tunic and, with a sigh of relief, submerged her tired feet in the cool, clear water. It felt heavenly. She wiggled her toes and was starting to consider whether she could get away with pulling off her tunic completely and taking a quick bath when the ghosts showed up.

They came out of the forest on the other side of the stream. Alex recognized the old man who had spoken to her earlier that day, as well as several others who had hung around during the march here, but who had stayed pretty much on the periphery of things.

There are things we wish to discuss with you, Soul Speaker, said the old man from across the stream.

Yes, we have questions, said a woman who looked way too young and healthy to be dead. But Alex knew the spirits could appear in any form they'd had during their lives. It wasn't as if they were frozen at the time of their death and stuck with appearance, a fact Alex had been thankful for ever since she'd seen her first dead person.

We also have things to tell you, said another man. He was wearing a tunic made of cloth dyed so strong a shade of red that, even semitransparent, it blazed with color.

Alex leaned her head against the tree, closed her eyes and sighed heavily. She'd known that the way the ghosts had backed off earlier was too good to last. Why couldn't they leave her alone for real? She was exhausted. Her job here was already breaking her heart. She just didn't feel up to dealing with whatever it was the dead people wanted, along with everything else.

"I really want you all to go away and leave me in peace," Alex muttered, more to herself than to them.

A sizzle of energy flowed from the ancient tree at her back and shivered through her. Alex's eyes shot open in time to see little wisps of energy—glowing waves of fog—lap from her tree out into the forest. As they reached the ghosts, they engulfed them, carrying the spirits away into the night.

"Holy shit!" Alex said. "How in the hell did I do that?"

"You tapped into the power of this old one, of course." Caradoc stepped out of the shadows. "Where is this place you came from that doesn't teach priestesses about the sacred might of the forest?"

TEN

"Are you spying on me?" Alex asked, neatly sidestepping Caradoc's question.

"Actually, that is a better question to ask of you."

"Me?"

"Aye, you. Do you spy on Boudica for Rome?"

"You've got to be kidding! I'm no more a spy for Rome than you are. And anyway, that makes no sense."

"Why not? We are at war with Rome."

"Yeah, but they don't know that. The Romans believe a few crazy barbarians have been riled up by an even crazier woman. They don't see Boudica's people as an army, so don't see the coming war as anything more than an inconvenience. Heddwyn made that clear from *his* spying on Londinium." Alex knew all that was true from her historical briefing. One of the key reasons Boudica was as successful as she was for so long could be attributed to the fact that the Romans underestimated her, because she was a woman.

"What you say is true, at least in as much as you'll say. Though you still haven't explained where it is you come from."

"How about you and I call a truce and make a pact. I'll promise not to lie to you—ever. But you'll have to understand that, if I *can* only tell you the truth, there will be some things I cannot tell you," Alex said.

Caradoc considered, studying her with his unusual amber eyes. Finally, he gave a brief nod. "Agreed. There will be no lies between us."

"Agreed." Automatically, Alex put out her hand so that they could shake on it. Caradoc hesitated before he touched her, and when he did so his grip wasn't a businesslike handshake. The druid grasped her forearm in the ancient way oaths were sealed, pressing wrists together, pulse point to pulse point, heartbeat to heartbeat, skin to skin.

His touch affected her instantly, but not with a silly Romance Landia zap of instant lust. Caradoc's skin against hers felt familiar—warm, strong, real. He was yet another aspect of this land, this time, that seemed so right.

"I would like it if we could be friends," Alex heard herself saying.

"Mystery doesn't make a good foundation for friendship," he said, yet his words weren't harsh, but almost quizzical, and he didn't release his grip on her arm.

"Truth does make a good foundation, though, and I've promised to always tell you the truth," she countered.

"When you can," he said.

"When I can," she agreed.

Reluctantly, Caradoc let go of her arm. "So can you tell me if it's true that you really have not been trained to tap into the ancient power of the forest?"

Alex smiled. "That's an easy one to answer. No, I have no clue what you mean by the ancient power of the forest, or how to use it."

Caradoc cocked his head to the side and smiled back at her. "You have an odd way of speaking."

Alex felt like the rabbit she'd let loose from her cloak. Carswell had told her the chip in her head would translate for her, both what she said and what she heard. Well, it seemed to be working fine as the words came to her. Sure, the Celts had accents, some more than others, but she definitely understood what they were saying. So she'd assumed that she could just use her normal vocabulary in speaking to them. Apparently not.

Caradoc chuckled. "Do not look so shocked. I meant no offense and I wasn't trying to pry for answers you don't feel you can give me."

He looked nonchalant, but Alex saw in his eyes that there was more behind what he was saying. He *had* been trying to pry, she realized.

"Sorry," she said smoothly. "I'll try to keep my odd ways to a minimum."

He waved his hand. "No need. I find you intriguing."

Alex wasn't sure if he meant intriguing like a good book or intriguing like a car wreck, but decided not to ask. Instead, she barreled on. "So, can you tell me about this ancient power you're talking about, or is it supposed to be a big secret?"

Caradoc sobered instantly. "The spirits in the forest are not to be spoken of lightly, Blonwen. As a priestess of Andraste, you should know that much."

"But I don't," she stated honestly. "I didn't mean to offend you, or the forest." She glanced around nervously before continuing. "And I do want to learn about these things. If you can teach me."

He ran his hand through his thick hair and Alex saw that the leather tie he used to keep the tawny mass back out of his way all day had come loose. She'd never been with a man who had long hair before and was surprised at how sensual it was. She wanted to touch it, to run her fingers through it and use it to pull his face down to hers….

"Blonwen?"

"I'm sorry." Alex jumped. What the hell was wrong with her? Now was not the time to have sexy daydreams about this guy. "My mind was elsewhere," she said quickly. "What were you saying?"

He gave her a look that was much too knowing. *What had her expression been like when she was thinking about kissing him?* But he only said, "I said as a druid I am well versed in the spirits of the forest and the magic they hold, and I have taught young druids often…." Here his words faltered, and he stared off into the dark woods.

Alex realized what he must be thinking—that those young druids he'd taught were now probably all dead, thanks to the barbarism of Suetonius. Slowly, she reached out to him and rested her hand on his arm. "I'm so sorry about your home. It must have been awful."

"They sacrificed themselves for me." Caradoc's voice was strained, his eyes haunted.

"Who?" Alex prompted gently, when it was obvious he wasn't going to say anything more.

"Everyone. The Romans took us utterly by surprise. The elders were sleeping. Some of the young priestesses and druids were finishing a fertility ritual…" His lips twitched at that memory, but his eyes remained sad. "I was restless. I could not sleep, nor could I join in the fertility games. I should have known then that my unease was a warning. Like a fool, I discounted it and went to the cave of springs, where I was soaking, and trying to still my mind." He shook his head and laughed humorlessly in bitter self-mockery.

"That is where my brothers found me. I hadn't heard the attack. It was because of all of them, my brother druids and sister priestesses, that I escaped, to make it to Boudica. They used their bodies as a barrier to keep the Romans from capturing me."

"But Boudica needed to be warned," Alex said.

Caradoc rounded on her. "Do you truly not know who I am and why the others died to assure I remained free?"

"No," Alex said simply. "All I know about you is that your voice called to me in my dreams."

The anger that had flashed in his eyes died, and Caradoc sighed. "Boudica told you I am her kinsman. What she did not also say, because everyone here already knows it, is that I am her *closest* kinsman, the son of her mother's sister. Should Boudica fall in battle, the torque of kingship would pass to me."

Alex's eyes widened. "I had no idea."

"What did I say to you in your dreams?" Caradoc asked abruptly.

"You called to me from somewhere in a forest that was a lot like this one. You asked me to come back to you. You said you needed me and were waiting for me." Alex realized that she was still touching Caradoc's arm, and nervously took her hand away. But as she did he caught her wrist.

"What else did I say to you?" he asked.

"You told me I had to have the courage to come back to you." She looked down at where he was holding her wrist, and remembered the rest of the dream. "I couldn't see you. Well, I got a strange image of your woad, though I couldn't see the rest of you. But you did grab me."

His brows went up. "I grabbed you?"

She nodded, feeling a little breathless. "Yes, like you're doing now."

Caradoc eased his grip on her wrist, and as he stared into

her eyes, his thumb began to caress her skin, tracing a warm circle over where her blood beat close to the surface.

"What else did I do?" he asked.

"Nothing." Her voice was almost a whisper. He was so close to her that Alex could feel the heat of his body. "Fog closed in and you were gone."

"In *my* dream I did not touch you, though I felt drawn to you and was single-minded in believing that you had to be with me," he murmured. "It was a shock to see you today, here in the flesh. I almost thought I was dreaming again." His expression changed, turning sad. "I wished I had been dreaming, so that the last several days would not truly have happened."

Alex reached out and gently brushed the hair back from the gash that marred his forehead. The wound was days old, scabbed over and already healing. "How long did it take you to get here?"

"Four days. I was too dizzy to travel the first day."

"Does it still hurt?"

His lips tilted up. "No, my head is hard."

He looked so young, with his half smile and the healing cut on his head, that Alex impulsively cupped the side of his face with her hand. "I'm glad your head is hard," she said softly.

Caradoc didn't say anything, but slowly, as if he was giving her plenty of time to step away, he bent closer. Sliding his hand from her wrist up her arm, he followed the line of her shoulder and neck until he buried his hand in her hair. Then, gently, he pulled her face forward and pressed his lips to hers.

The kiss began as a question, soft and hesitant and undemanding, and Alex was shocked at her immediate reaction to him. She opened herself to Caradoc, moving forward so that she could step into his arms. Her own arms went around his shoulders, her chest pressed to his, as she explored his mouth. He tasted like the sweet mead they'd had with dinner. The softness of his lips was a wonderful contrast to the hardness of his body. He moaned when she pressed even closer against him, and one of his hands found the roundness of her buttocks so he could keep her there firmly, against his heat, while his kiss went from a question to a deep and intriguing demand for more.

Alex lost herself in the taste and feel of him. It had been so long since she'd felt the heat and hardness of a man! And this man was extraordinary. He was no metrosexual, briefcase-carrying office worker. Nor was he a cowboy wannbe who hadn't ridden a horse in months, but drove a truck big enough to haul around a small herd. Caradoc was an ancient warrior, a man who used his body as a weapon. He was also a druid—and Alex guessed that meant he could also use his mind as a weapon. He was intriguing and sexy and more than a little bit dangerous. And he accepted that she was a Soul Speaker!

Alex wanted him with an intensity that was totally alien to her.

Her tongue teased his, coaxing it into the warmth of her mouth, and she sucked lightly, causing Caradoc to moan again. She felt his shaft pulse against her, and she moved her hips, positioning that hot hardness against the wet center of her. His hand on her buttocks convulsed as she rubbed herself against him. Her body was on fire. Waves of sensation pulsed through her, and all Alex could think was that she wanted this man inside her—deep and long and hard.

A twig snapped behind Caradoc, a sound so sharp that for an instant Alex thought it was a gunshot. He reacted instantly, whirling around and pushing her behind him, blocking her from view with his body. Not two feet from them a doe stepped around some low bushes. Intent on getting to the stream, the deer didn't see Caradoc and Alex until she was almost on top of them, and then she froze, wide-eyed, before leaping over the water and disappearing into the darkness of the forest.

Alex thought her heart would pound out of her chest, and

she dropped her forehead onto Caradoc's back, laughing breathlessly. "Don't say that we scared her more than she scared us, because in my case there is no way that's true."

He turned and looped his arms loosely over her shoulders. "If I say nothing, is there a chance you will believe that small doe didn't almost cause my heart to stop beating?"

She grinned at him and pressed her hand over his heart, which pulsed strong and fast against her palm. "It's still beating."

"Aye," he murmured. "That is an easy truth to tell."

Alex lifted her face, anxious to feel his lips against hers again, then realized he wasn't bending to meet her. She hesitated, feeling both confusion and embarrassment.

"Blonwen, tell me that you mean no harm to Boudica. That being here with me isn't a plan to get close to the queen and then destroy her."

Alex stepped back abruptly, as if he'd just slapped her. Hadn't he felt anything when they'd kissed? While she'd been completely absorbed in him, had he been coolly calculating the chances that she was still a spy?

Her voice shook as she answered, but she held his gaze steadily. "I already told you the truth about that. If you don't believe me—if you can't trust me—there's nothing more I have to say to you. Good night, Caradoc."

Alex turned and, feeling utterly humiliated, walked quickly to Boudica's tent without once glancing back at the silent druid.

ELEVEN

Thanks to the long day on horseback, Alex's exhausted body trumped her restless mind, and she fell asleep more quickly than she would have ever imagined possible. This time she did dream.

She was in a cave. Alex drew a deep breath, recognizing the metallic scent of a mineral spring.

For a second she was disoriented, wondering where her sleeping mind had taken her. And then she understood, and with the understanding came a flush of irritation. This was the cave Caradoc had described—where he'd been when the Romans had attacked the Isle of Mona. He'd somehow brought her here. Setting her shoulders, Alex looked around her, searching for the exit, all the while ordering herself: *Wake up! Wake up! Wake up!*

She took the first passageway from the little candlelit room that she noticed. The arched doorway was wide. It must lead out of the damn place. Alex followed the winding tunnel to her left and noticed almost immediately that the path was leading down and not up toward an exit. She stopped, and was about to turn around and retrace her steps when she heard the sobs. Ahead, somewhere farther into the cave, someone was crying bitterly.

Turn around—get out of here—wake up! Alex's mind screamed at her, but her legs carried her forward. Slowly but steadily she followed the sound of sobbing until she came to a place where another tunnel branched off to the right. She knew from the warm, aromatic fumes that wafted towards her that this chamber held the main mineral spring. It was also, clearly, where the sobs originated.

Quietly, Alex stepped through the stone archway, but stayed in the shadows beside it, gazing around the large inner room. Clearly, the water in the spring was hot, judging by the fog rising in the cool air and condensing on the rough stone walls. The sounds were coming from the side of the pool, and Alex peered through the mist.

Caradoc was sitting on the bench. His elbows rested on his thighs and his face was in his hands. He was sobbing.

He didn't bring me here, Alex realized. *He wouldn't want me to see him like this.* She began to back slowly away, but Caradoc raised his head, looked across the room and met her eyes.

"I keep coming back here." His face was ravaged with grief, his eyes haunted with memories.

"I didn't intrude on purpose," Alex said.

"I know that. What's happening in our dreams is out of our control. I didn't purposely call you, and I don't believe you sought me out."

"But somehow, here we are," she stated. "If this is real."

"Indeed." Caradoc wiped his hand across his eyes and leaned back against the damp wall of the cave. Alex thought he looked young and sad and very vulnerable. When he started to speak, his voice was strained, as if the tears he'd been shedding had seared his throat. "Whether it is real, or mist and dreams, there is something I need to say to you. Before the Romans attacked I was so sure of myself—so certain of my place in the world and of the world itself. Now all I know is confusion and regret and anger. I took some of that out on you today."

Alex felt surprised by his admission, but shrugged nonchalantly. "I'm not a child. I know better than to step into the den of the big bad wolf."

One of his brows went up. "I have never before been compared to a wolf."

"So you don't make a practice of ravaging and then insulting women?"

He looked away from her. "No. I do not." The silence built between them, and Alex was considering retracing her steps and maybe hurling herself off a cliff so that the act of falling might jolt her awake, when his gaze found hers again. "I owe you another apology. This time my mother did not have to prompt it from me. You had already given your word that you would speak only the truth to me, and with that truth you assured me you wished Boudica no harm. It was dishonorable of me to question your veracity. I am sorry."

Alex's history with men hadn't prepared her for Caradoc's honest apology. She'd dated players, geeks, boy-next-door types and your average run-of-the-mill jerks. She'd never dated a man who bared his soul to her.

"What is that about?" she blurted. "You act like I'm your enemy. Then you come on to me. Then you insult me. Now you apologize. Which Caradoc is the real one? Which one do I believe?"

He shook his head sadly. "All of this is me. I am not the man I used to be. The attack on my home, and this war, have changed me. I haven't been able to reground myself and find my center." Caradoc paused and ran his hand through his hair.

"Today, with you in my arms, was the first time in days I have felt anything more than anger and despair, and I ruined that."

Alex stared into his amber eyes. There was only one thing she wanted to say to him, and this was, after all, just a dream. Wasn't it? She could say anything she wanted. Couldn't she?

"You didn't ruin it," she stated.

"Truly?" Hope lightened Caradoc's pain-darkened eyes.

"Truly," she answered.

"Truly! Priestess! You must arise. Our mother is calling for you to bless the army before it attacks. Wake up!"

Alex's eyes opened, and she looked up into Mirain's troubled face.

"Where am I? Wha—" she began, and then knew she wasn't dreaming anymore. She sat up abruptly, brushing her mass of hair back from her face.

"Finally! I have been calling and calling you. When you didn't awaken I thought perhaps you were ill, or your spirit had been carried off to the Otherworld by Andraste," Mirain said.

"I'm fine. I was just…just dreaming, that's all."

"A sacred dream?" Una spoke up from behind her sister.

Alex pulled herself together and smiled at the girl. "I'm not really sure."

Una shot her a wary look. "I thought priestesses were supposed to know whether dreams were sacred or not."

"Priestesses are regular people. We don't know everything. We just do our best to do the right thing." Alex paused, thinking about Caradoc and her dream, and then she let what she was feeling deep inside her answer the girl truthfully. "I think the dream might have been important, maybe even sacred, but only to me. It's private."

"You sound like Mother," Una grumbled.

"Well, that sounds like a compliment," Alex said, climbing out of her pallet and running her fingers through her hair.

"Don't fix it," Mirain said, grabbing Alex's hand. "You look mysterious and a little crazed with all that hair sticking up around you in those big curls. The army will remember you as Andraste's wild priestess who sent them to battle with passion and a great blessing."

Alex grinned at the teenager. Then she bent over at the waist and, upside down, shook her head, letting her long hair get even more tangled and unmanageable. When she snapped upright again, she was rewarded by Mirain's satisfied nod.

"All right. Lead me to your mother."

As they left the tent she heard Una say softly, "Just like everything with priestesses and the goddess—it's all make-believe. None of it's real."

Alex wanted to correct the girl, wanted to explain that her wild hair and passion were harmless theatrics, meant only to buoy the spirits of the people, not to deceive them. But Mirain hurried her forward, so she wasn't able to speak to Una. And then, on second thought, Alex realized she couldn't correct the damaged girl for her comment. "Blonwen" was, after all, playing a part here in the ancient past. She *was* a sham.

Mirain led her quickly to two horses that were saddled and waiting for them. Alex mounted one, and the girls rode double on the other. In the misty predawn light, Alex had to concentrate hard to gallop close behind them, afraid if she fell back she'd be hopelessly lost in the shrouded, silent woods.

And then they were at the forest edge, breaking through the silently waiting army to the little rise on which Boudica waited, at the head of her people. The queen stood in a chariot pulled by two white horses. She was wearing a beaten gold breastplate polished to such a sheen that even in the gray world that waited for the sun to rise, she shone.

Alex saw Caradoc standing with the queen's inner circle of warriors, and then Boudica was speaking to her in a voice tight with excitement. "Bless our army, Priestess of Andraste, and then I will lead them to victory."

There was no time for Alex to panic. No time for her to think—no time for her to plan. At Boudica's command she turned her horse to face the huge army of the Celts, and got her first view of the Iceni poised for battle. Those who were not tattooed, as was Caradoc, had painted woad on their faces and bodies. The sapphire blue of the designs was a stark contrast to the fairness of their skin. Men and women filled the ranks of the army. Many had bared their chests, choosing to cover themselves only in the sacred woad. Their long hair was worn free and decorated with feathers and cloth, and even bells and shells, so that the front lines seemed to ripple with energy, and the wind carry sounds of ancient magic.

They were frightening and awe-inspiring and absolutely breathtaking. At that moment Alex wanted nothing as much as to be a part of their magnificence. She drew a deep breath. In a voice magnified by the energy that lifted in waves from the Celts, Alexandra Patton, a woman from the twenty-first century who had never fit in, never really belonged, spoke ancient words that seemed to rise from her very soul.

"At Londinium today in this fateful hour
I place all of you within Andraste's power.
The sun with its brightness,
The rowan flowers with their brightness,
Fire with all the strength it hath,
And lightning with its rapid wrath,
Winds with their swiftness along the path,
The rocks with their steepness,
And the earth with its deepness,
All these I place
With the goddess's might and grace

Between you and darkness—to protect our home
Against the defiling power of Rome!"

The roar that came from the thousands of warrior throats
lifted the hair on the back of Alex's neck.

Boudica drove her chariot forward and Alex backed her
horse away so that the queen took over the center of the field.
Mirain and Una had joined their mother in the chariot, and
Alex thought Boudica looked like an avenging angel standing
between her lovely young daughters. She rested a hand on each
of the girls' shoulders and addressed her people.

"We do not attack this place because we lust for riches or land
or that which is not ours. We attack this place and these people
because they have wronged us so severely that the goddess
herself has risen and in a loud cry demanded *vengeance!*"

"Vengeance!" The cry was taken up by the army.

Boudica motioned to Alex and Caradoc to join her. Both
hurried to the queen's side.

"Fulfill your promise. Keep my daughters safe," said the queen.

Caradoc lifted the girls from the chariot and, yelling for Alex
to follow them, rushed to where their horses were nervously
waiting. Practically throwing the girls on their horse, he
mounted his own, and then smacked the rump of the children's
animal, driving it from the field that stretched before the army.
As Alex raced after them, she looked back at Boudica, who had
wheeled her chariot around to face Londinium.

"Vengeance!" the queen of the Celts cried again, and this time
when her army responded, it was with a shout so frighteningly
fierce that it chilled Alex's blood with fear.

Then Boudica cracked her whip and her chariot lunged
forward, followed by her army, shrieking for vengeance and
blood and retribution as the sun rose at their backs.

Within moments, Londinium was under attack.

TWELVE

The battle didn't even last through midmorning, though to Alex it seemed those few hours took days to pass. She'd expected the waiting to be terrible. She hadn't expected to be asked to tend the wounded. Not that the Celts thought she was some kind of healer—no, they didn't want her to doctor or even nurse those being pulled from the battle. But they did expect Alex, or rather Blonwen, Priestess of Andraste, to offer the comfort of the goddess to those who were injured—or worse, those who were dying.

When she first learned that she was expected to comfort the wounded, Alex's response was to gape at the message bearer, in this case Caradoc, in disbelief. Luckily, the druid had called for her—said she and Boudica's daughters were to follow him to the hospital tent to tend the wounded, which were already beginning to stream in—and then hurried away, sure that they were following him. He didn't see her mouth drop open as she stared after him, unmoving.

Sadly, girls are more observant than stressed-out druid warriors.

"Why does your face look so white?" Una asked her.

"I—uh—does it?" she stuttered.

"Actually, you look more green than white. You must not like the sight of blood," Una decided, with a preteen certitude so universal that Alex almost smiled.

"Let's go. At least we'll be doing some good there. Plus, anything is better than being stuck here, especially when we should be out there!" Mirain jabbed a finger toward Londinium.

Alex wasn't surprised by the older girl's attitude. She'd watched Mirain become more and more sullen as the morning progressed. Clearly she wanted to be with her mom, exacting retribution from the Romans. And Alex didn't blame her.

"Blonwen? Are you really not coming with us?" Una stood at the tent entrance, holding the flap open and peering back at her, with Mirain waiting impatiently behind her.

"I'm coming." Alex hurried forward, and the three of them followed Caradoc's rapidly disappearing back toward the edge of the camp.

"So, blood makes you sick?" Mirain asked, with a look on her face that said she held anyone so squeamish in obvious disdain.

"It doesn't make me sick, or at least it hasn't so far, but I haven't ever been around a lot of people who have been badly hurt," Alex said honestly.

"It is better to be in the battle," Mirain stated resolutely. "Mother should have let me fight with her!"

"She didn't want you to get hurt," Alex explained.

The girl snorted. "There are a lot worse ways to be hurt than in battle."

Again, a kid left Alex speechless. Who knew that Carswell

should have briefed her in child psychology along with Celtic history before shooting her back in time?

"Blonwen! You are needed here," Caradoc snapped.

Alex didn't seem to have any choice. She hurried over to where the druid was standing in a tent under a huge oak, very near the place Alex had blessed the army. Caradoc was bent over a figure lying on a litter at his feet. Alex steeled herself to see a badly wounded warrior. She could make herself handle blood and such—she had to! She drew a deep, steadying breath, joined Caradoc and peered down at the first casualty of the battle for Londinium.

It was a young woman.

She was splattered with blood and dirt and other stuff Alex didn't want to even begin to name. The bottom half of her body, from her waist down, was completely smashed—flattened as if she were a bizarre cartoon character. Blood seeped everywhere, and Alex knew with a certainty that made her sick that even twenty-first century emergency room doctors couldn't have saved her.

Caradoc straightened, turned to Alex and said softly, "Stay with her. The end is near." He squeezed Alex's shoulder and then he was gone.

Acting on autopilot, Alex moved to take the druid's place, only instead of bending down, she knelt beside the young woman's litter.

"Priestess, you came."

The woman's voice was surprisingly clear and childlike. Her eyes were bright and lucid, and except for the utter lack of color in her face and the shortness of her breath, from her waist up she looked almost normal.

Alex took her hand. "What's your name?"

"Geneth," she said. "Have you seen my betrothed? Have you seen Bran? He will be angry when he finds out how careless I was. I didn't even see the wagon. The horses plunged—it rolled—I was there." She paused, panting and looking around wildly. "Tell him not to be mad at me!"

"Geneth, shh, Bran won't be angry. It was just an accident. It's okay." Alex gripped her hand and smoothed her blond hair back from her wet, clammy forehead.

"Will you find him for me?"

"Yes. Don't worry. I'll take care of everything," Alex soothed.

"Good…good…" Geneth's breath was coming in little pants. "I'm so cold…." she murmured. Her eyes began to roll back and flutter closed. Then, suddenly, she drew a deep breath. Fully alert again, she looked up at Alex. "I'm afraid, Priestess!"

"Don't be," Alex said firmly. "You have nothing to fear."

Geneth's gaze locked with hers. "I'm dying," she said simply.

Alex's stomach clenched so hard she feared she might be ill, but she forced herself to return the girl's gaze calmly. *Speak the truth. There is power in the truth.* The thoughts drifted through her mind, surprising Alex with the peace they brought with them.

"Yes, you are dying," she told her gently.

Geneth nodded. "Would you tell the goddess I'm coming? Ask her to look for me?"

"I will," Alex said. Acting on instinct and gut feeling, she kept holding Geneth's hand, but raised her free hand over her head. This wasn't a time to bow and mutter platitudes. It was a time for truth and the honesty of a soul barred to the universe. "Andraste, your daughter Geneth asks that I tell you she is getting ready to come to you. I ask you to please look for her, to hold your arms out so that when you see her, Geneth will be embraced by you as a beloved child returning to her mother."

Alex added a silent *amen* to the prayer, and then gazed down at the wounded girl. Her lips were tilted up in the beginnings of a smile and her eyes were open and staring at a spot over Alex's shoulder. Geneth was dead.

And then, as Alex crouched there, trying to sort through the horror and sadness this young person's death filled her with, she saw the body begin to glow, quiver, and Geneth's soul lifted from her corpse. The girl stood there for a moment gazing down at what had been her mortal self, and then she grinned at Alex.

Thank you, she whispered, before stepping forward and disappearing into the air beside Alex.

"Priestess! You are needed over here!"

Numbly, Alex looked up from Geneth's body to see someone she didn't recognize calling her over to another litter, which was filled with what looked like pieces of rubble attached to a head.

No! Alex screamed silently. *I can't do this! I'm not who they think I am!*

She dropped the dead girl's hand and took two stumbling steps backward, thinking only that she needed to get out of there. And ran smack into Caradoc. She knew it was him without turning around. She already knew his scent and the feel of his strong hands as they gripped her shoulders.

"They need you," he murmured into her ear. "Boudica told me how you appeared suddenly. Whatever else might be the truth, it is obvious Andraste brought you here for a reason. Let that reason be to ease the suffering of her people." He squeezed her shoulders once, and then let go.

Alex didn't have to look behind her. She could feel his absence as clearly as she felt the sun on her face. *Andraste brought you here for a reason…to ease the suffering of her people.* Clinging to his words, desperately wanting to believe them, Alex walked across the tent to tend to the next mortally wounded Celt.

When it was finally over, twenty-three people were dead, and Alex had eased the passing of nineteen of them. The others had either been unconscious or already dead when they entered the hospital tent.

A rider had thundered up moments after the twenty-third warrior died, proclaiming Boudica's victory over the scanty Ninth Legion that was supposed to be all the protection Londinium needed against an attack led by a "mere woman." Cheers sounded from all around them as the news spread. Alex took a clean linen bandage from a pile near the surgical table, which was awash in blood from limbs that had been severed. She wiped her face and her hands and then, without speaking to anyone, walked out of the tent and into the forest.

She wasn't sure where she was going. Alex just needed to get away. Later, all she remembered from those first moments after the end of the battle was that she had to fight with herself to keep from pressing the crystal in the middle of her ESC bracelet so that she could escape back to the future.

Unerringly, she went straight to the stream that tumbled musically through the forest not far from Boudica's tent.

Cleanse yourself....

Alex automatically obeyed the words that drifted through her mind. Without worrying about modesty, she stripped off her blood spattered tunic and soft underchemise and then pulled off her leather shoes. In a spot where the stream pooled to form an almost bathtub-size basin, Alex sat. Ignoring the cold temperature of the water, she began scrubbing the blood and gore from her hands and face, arms and hair.

She cleaned death from herself, and as her body was washed, Alex's mind settled. Her thoughts became clear again, and she realized that what had shocked her most about the day was the undeniable fact that she had actually helped the dying people. Priestess or no priestess, she'd eased their deaths. And none of the spirits had stayed around after they'd been released from their bodies, not one of them. They'd all thanked her, looked beyond her and joyfully disappeared.

How had that happened? She could rationalize away her

ability to comfort the dying warriors. Maybe all they'd needed was someone's hand to hold—someone to tell them they didn't have anything to fear, and to give them a glimpse, no matter how phony, of a divine power who knew they were coming and was waiting to welcome them to eternity. Alex was obviously good at doing that. Which made sense, because she was definitely experienced with dead folks, and that was really just the next step.

So Alex being there had comforted them. But what about what had happened next? She'd witnessed their spirits joyfully moving on—each and every one of them.

Yes, she'd seen spirits move on before. Lots of times, actually. But not every time one appeared to her. More often than not, the ghost had stuff to say, be it gossip or a comment about her fashion choice. Sometimes they just wanted to talk.

Today had been different. Was it because, here in this ancient place where magic was still firmly attached to the earth, Alex herself was different?

Shivering, she scooted down so that the water lapped around her shoulders. She leaned back against the thick moss that covered the sloping bank of the little pool. It felt like a carpet and, suddenly exhausted beyond words, she turned her head so that her cheek rested against it. Alex drew a deep breath and, as she let it out, whispered the thought that had circled incessantly around the edges of her mind. "Could there really be a goddess in this world? Could I be attached to her?"

Electricity trembled through the soft moss, warming it against Alex's cheek. She froze, then slowly, tentatively, raised her hand from the water and lay it on the moss beside her face. Another rush of warmth shivered through her, rushing into Alex from the cradling earth.

"You're here, aren't you, Andraste? Somehow you're in the earth and you found me."

The warmth that filled Alex intensified, bringing with it a jolt of energy. A sense of belonging washed through her, making her breath catch and tears of happiness pool in her eyes.

"I don't know how, and I don't know why, but thank you. Thank you so much!" Alex said.

"The how is that the goddess is in the earth all around us, and the why is that you are special to her and she has chosen to work through you," Caradoc said.

THIRTEEN

Alex started as if Caradoc's voice had been a gunshot. She sat straight up, and then, realizing she was completely naked, ducked down into the water as far as the shallow pool would allow.

"I brought you clean clothes." Caradoc was looking everywhere but at her.

"Well, leave them on the bank and go away!" she called, crossing her arms over breasts she knew the crystalline water did little to cover.

"Yes, well, of course." Sounding almost as awkward and mortified as she felt, he quickly tossed the clothes beside the pool and turned his back to her.

She waited a heartbeat or two to be sure he was going to stay that way, then hurried out of the water and, teeth chattering, struggled to pull on the clean chemise and tunic over her wet body. When she was decent again she grabbed her old chemise and used the inner, and cleanest part to dry her hair. All this time the tall druid stood silently with his back to her.

"Okay, I'm d-d-dressed," she said, teeth still chattering violently.

Caradoc swung slowly to face her. "You're cold. You should return to Boudica's tent. It is warm in there and—"

"No!" Alex interrupted, not sure for a moment why she had such an adverse reaction to the thought of going to the tent. And then she listened to her heart and her instincts and she knew. "No," she repeated. "I want to be out here for a while more."

Caradoc nodded. "You have found it, haven't you?"

"It?"

"The power of the earth. It's especially strong where the trees are ancient, as they are in this forest."

"Yes, I suppose I have," Alex said.

"Do you want to be alone?"

"Are you going to accuse me of being a spy again?"

"No. I won't be doing that," Caradoc stated.

"Then, no. I don't want to be alone," she told him.

"You could come with me," he said softly.

Alex glanced back toward the camp and the tents that waited there.

Caradoc's lips tilted up. "I mean to my campsite. It is different than those." When she hesitated he added, "I have a fire there, as well as food and mead."

His mention of food reminded Alex that she hadn't eaten anything at all that day, and that she was ravenous.

"Food and mead sounds good." She didn't add that spending time with him sounded good, too.

"This way," the druid said, and he followed the little stream, leading her deeper into the forest.

* * *

He'd been right; his campsite was different than the others. There was no tent, only a large leather hide tacked up by long, thick branches so that it made an awning from a huge oak tree. Under the shelter was a pallet of furs. Caradoc's campfire was banked, but it took hardly any time for him to rekindle it with dried leaves and coax it alive again, which he did after situating Alex on a fallen log near the fire, and handing her a bronze mug filled with mead. He opened the lid of a metal pot that perched on a bed of rocks by the fire, and stirred the contents, releasing the satisfying aroma of stew into the air.

"It'll be warm soon," he told Alex. Then he poured himself a goblet of mead and sat beside her on their makeshift bench. Caradoc cleared his throat. "You did well today."

"It was the hardest thing I've ever done." Alex paused and then added, "And the best thing I've ever done."

He nodded. "The goddess moved through you today."

"I hope so."

"How can you doubt it?"

Alex knew she should keep her mouth shut, but all of this—this world and its goddess—were so new to her that she felt raw and exposed, far more so than when she'd been naked. And Caradoc was a druid—he knew about the power of the earth and the workings of the goddess who was so close to them here. More than anything else, Alex craved answers to the questions milling in her mind.

"I'm not from here. You already know that." She began slowly, but as she spoke, her words came more easily and she felt as if she was unburdening her heart. "I'm sorry I can't explain to you where I'm from, but I can tell you that none of this is there. The power in the earth, even the goddess, is mostly ignored." His look was a mix of horror and disbelief.

"I know. It must seem strange and maybe even impossible to you, but it's true."

"But you are a Soul Speaker! How can you come from a place that doesn't acknowledge the goddess and doesn't feel the power of the earth?"

"I don't know how it happened. I do know I've never felt like I belonged where I'm from. I scared people," Alex admitted.

Caradoc tilted his head and studied her. "You must have lived a lonely life."

He didn't say the words in a pitying tone, but just made a statement, as if it were an undeniable truth.

"Yes, I did," Alex admitted, for the first time in her life.

His amber eyes held hers. "That is over for you now."

If only that were true, Alex thought, but she couldn't say the words aloud.

"You were in my dream again last night," Caradoc said.

She blinked in surprise. "You were in mine, too."

He drew in a sharp breath. "At the water cave?"

She nodded.

Caradoc closed his eyes as if he was in pain.

"I'm guessing today makes us even," Alex said.

He opened his eyes and raised his brows questioningly.

"I saw you naked last night, and today you saw me naked."

His lips twitched as if he considered smiling. "Will you call me 'wolf' again if I say I prefer your type of nakedness?"

Alex felt her cheeks get warm. "Yes, I might."

His smile came then, softening his handsome face and reminding Alex that he was a decade younger than her, which made her cheeks grow even warmer.

Caradoc took her hand in his, holding it carefully, as if he was afraid she might bolt away if he made any sudden moves.

"I would like to begin again with you," he said.

"Why?" She couldn't stop herself from asking. "Because we've seen each other naked?"

"No, Blonwen, because we both know what it is to be homeless and then to perhaps find a new place to belong. I also believe there is much we can learn from one another."

"Such as?" Alex tried not to lose herself in his eyes and his touch, but the warmth of his body was like a drug she craved…

"There is much I could teach you about the spirits within the earth, and how to harness the power of the goddess found there."

"And what do I teach you?" she asked breathlessly.

"You teach me how to find my center again." He lifted her hand and, never taking his gaze from hers, pressed his lips to her palm.

At that instant Alex wanted to forget about the damn medallion pieces and the modern world and Time Raiders. She only wanted to drown in Caradoc—to pull his mouth down to hers and, as he'd said, begin anew with him in this wonderful, magical place.

His lips traveled from her palm to the pulse point at her wrist. Against her skin he said, "And I will admit that I did like your nakedness better than my own." Then he bent and gently pressed his lips to hers. There was passion in the kiss, but it simmered, waiting for Alex to turn up the heat as she became more and more comfortable with him. He was giving her time to trust him, to come to believe that his words and his touch were real, and not something that would turn to anger and accusations again.

Alex kissed him back, slowly and gently, exploring again the already familiar taste and texture of him. She didn't want to be anywhere else but here with Caradoc. She didn't want to think of anything but this magical druid and his world, one she desperately wanted to make her own.

And how do you start a life with him in a new world if you betray your old world?

The thought drifted, unwelcome, through her mind. Alex stiffened and pulled back.

Unshaken by her withdrawal, he smiled at her and touched her cheek. "The first lesson I can teach you is that you must ground and renew yourself after you have been an instrument of the goddess." Caradoc stood and began ladling steaming stew onto a plate for her. "You instinctively renewed yourself already by cleansing in the stream and by drawing power from the earth to you." He handed her the plate and filled one for himself. "Grounding yourself happens when you take in food and drink. It helps to remind your spirit that it still belongs to an earthly, mortal shell."

Instead of there being an awkwardness between them because Alex had ended the kiss, Caradoc's words helped to create the beginnings of an easy camaraderie. He spoke to her as they ate, all the while allowing his thigh to brush against hers and his eyes to linger on her lips. Between bites of stew Alex became even more intrigued with the druid.

"That's how I found you," he explained. "I thought you would be cleansing yourself, and the stream did, indeed, lead me to you."

"I didn't know. I just went there automatically."

Caradoc nodded. "The goddess takes care of her own."

"Caradoc, has she really touched me?" Alex spoke so softly he had to lean closer to her to catch her words. "Am I really a priestess of Andraste?"

"What I saw today assures me that you are. Can you not truly tell that for yourself?"

"I think so. I want to believe it, to understand how…" A flicker of movement from the other side of the campfire stopped her words. Caradoc's mother materialized in her beautiful robin's egg blue tunic.

"What is it?" he asked.

Alex suppressed a sigh. "Your mother."

"Truly?" He looked around the campfire. "Mother, is there something you require of me? I am confused as to why you haven't joined the goddess in her rolling meadows."

Caradoc's mother smiled warmly at her son. *Tell my selkie not to worry for me. I am still about the goddess's business.*

"She says don't worry. She's doing stuff for the goddess."

But there is that which he can do for me, as well as Andraste.

"There is something she needs you to do, though."

Caradoc nodded, clearly eager to do his mother's bidding. Alex suppressed a smile, thinking that it was a good sign when a man doted on his mother, especially if she was a ghost and not a mother-in-law living in the upstairs bedroom.

I need my son to lead you through Londinium so that you might find the Roman tax collector, Catus, and retrieve that which you have been sent to find.

Alex sobered instantly at the spirit's word.

Tell him, and move quickly. Londinium is burning....

The spirit's semisubstantial form wavered, then disappeared.

Alex turned to face Caradoc. "Your mother wants you to take me into Londinium. I have to find the tax collector, Catus."

"The Roman who ordered Boudica beaten and her daughters raped?"

Alex nodded.

"Why would you want to find him?"

Please, oh please, don't turn away from me again. Don't think that I'm acting against Boudica just because I can't tell you everything. "He has the other medallion piece that matches the one in Boudica's torque. I have to return it to her." *And then I have to get both of them back to the future.*

Caradoc gazed steadily at her for a long time before he murmured, "There is more to this than you're telling me."

It wasn't a question, but Alex answered him anyway. "Yes, but I give you my word that what I'm telling you is the truth."

She thought a second and then added, "Your mother called you her selkie."

His eyes widened in surprise. "That was her pet name for me."

"So you believe that she really was here and she really did tell me to pass on to you what she said?"

Caradoc touched Alex's cheek. "I believed you before you said the pet name. I just…" He paused and then began again. "This is difficult for me. I know you are not telling me everything, but I feel compelled to help you." He caressed her neck and rubbed his thumb along her collarbone. "I feel compelled to be with you."

"I need your help, Caradoc," Alex said.

"Someday I hope you will come to me because you need more than my help." He bent and kissed her softly, then stood and held out a hand to her. "I will take you to Londinium to find Catus, so that you can return the medallion to our queen's torque."

Alex took his hand and, feeling like a traitor, went with the druid to find their horses.

FOURTEEN

If there was a hell in this world, Londinium must have been its twin. The city was on fire, a nightmare dreamscape of suffering and disaster juxtaposed with victory and vengeance. The stench of battle nauseated Alex. It was the cloyingly sweet metallic aroma of blood and death, fear and triumph.

She hated everything about it, and it frightened her to her very soul. Celtic warriors cheered and lurched drunkenly down the streets. It was victory, but it wasn't what Alex had imagined victory would look like. It was violent and ugly and base. The good guys had won, but in winning they seemed to have lost what had held them apart from the cruelty of the Romans. They looted and sacked and even raped. And then they set the city on fire.

"We need to leave," Caradoc yelled above the noise of the dying city. "This is too dangerous. Later we'll—"

"No!" Alex grabbed his arm and made him meet her gaze.

"We have to find Catus and the medallion piece. I wouldn't ask this of you if I didn't have to."

The druid still looked as if he was ready to pick her up, throw her back on her horse and ride with her out of there.

"I don't want to be here, either," she told him fervently. "I don't want to see this! But finding the medallion and returning it to where it belongs is more important than what I want. Help me, Caradoc. I don't want to go on without you, but I will if I have no other choice."

That got through to him. Obviously, he wasn't going to leave her alone in the ruined city. He clenched his jaw, nodded shortly, walked up to the next terrified citizen he found hiding in the rubble, and grabbed the man by his tunic.

"Spare me, master!" the man screamed. "I am but a slave! Not even a Roman. I—"

"I only want information," Caradoc interrupted. "Where would I find the tax collector, Catus?"

Even in his terror, the man lifted his lip in a sneer. "When they realized the barbarian queen was going to take the city, Catus and his ilk ran to their god's temple and barricaded themselves within, may they rot in the farthest depths of their accursed Underworld."

"How do I find the temple?"

The slave pointed down a wide road littered with bodies and debris. "There, at the end of that street, is the temple of Jupiter."

Caradoc let go of the man. He and Alex set off resolutely down the main street of Londinium. Alex kept her gaze straight ahead. She tried not to process what she was seeing, tried to convince her mind that her eyes were watching a movie, something that was terrifying and disturbing, but wasn't really part of her. And her denial was almost working until Jupiter's temple came into view.

It was utterly engulfed in flames. Terrified shrieks rose with the cloud of smoke that mushroomed from the temple.

"No!" Alex cried, running forward.

Caradoc ran beside her, keeping a tight hold on her when she got too close to the inferno that had once been a temple. Celtic warriors ringed the burning building, and these men and women weren't taking part in the drunken revelry. They were grim-faced and bloodied, standing armed and dangerous as they watched the temple burn.

There was a scent on the smoke-filled breeze that Alex couldn't quite identify, though it made her stomach feel funny. "No," she repeated more softly. "But maybe he wasn't in there. Maybe he's still in the city somewhere."

Caradoc glanced around until he found a familiar face, then strode over to the warrior, with Alex close behind him.

"Saidear, is Boudica close by?"

He shook his head. "The queen has returned to camp to visit the wounded."

"And she is well and unharmed?"

Saidear's smile was fierce. "She is! Boudica fought like Andraste come to earth."

"I am glad to hear it," Caradoc said. "As the queen is busy elsewhere, perhaps you can aid me."

"Of course, Caradoc." The Celt bowed his head respectfully.

"I am on a mission for the goddess. Her priestess must find the tax collector, Catus. Have you seen the Roman?" Caradoc asked.

"The creature who ordered our queen beaten and her daughters raped? Aye, many of us have seen him. There!" The warrior made a disdainful gesture toward the burning temple. "That is where he and the rest of the Roman cowards ran, hoping our vengeance would be slaked with their slaves and the citizens of Londinium. And there is where Boudica ordered them burned alive, and sent to their Jupiter for judgment."

Sickened by the realization that the disturbing scent wafting on the breeze was human flesh burning, Alex gagged and stumbled away from the temple, not caring that the Celts were watching her with curious expressions on their fire reddened faces.

Caradoc's strong arm went around her. "We're getting out of here," he said grimly.

All she could do was nod. Silently, she allowed him to lead her back to their horses, and then they were galloping for the forest. Alex was unbelievably relieved when the trees closed in a soothing canopy over their heads.

"Do you want to return to Boudica's tent, or to my camp? It is your choice, Blonwen," Caradoc said as she slid down from her horse.

"I want to go with you," she replied with no hesitation. Alex knew she couldn't face Boudica or her daughters just then, as they celebrated their victory over the Romans. The scent of burning human flesh was still in her nose, and the screams of the dead still echoed in her ears.

As she walked beside the silent druid, Alex tried to organize her thoughts and figure out what the hell she was going to do now. But she couldn't seem to make her mind work. It kept circling around and around scenes of the dying Celts, Londinium ablaze and the screams of burning men.

"Drink this and sit close to the fire." Caradoc pressed a goblet of mead into her hands and guided her back to the log near his campfire.

Alex blinked and gazed around her. She hadn't even noticed when they'd reached his camp.

"Do as I say," he told her.

She nodded numbly and drained the goblet, glad for the slow, simmering burn of the sweet, strong mead.

"You have never seen battle before, have you?"

Alex thought about her TDY tours to the communication centers in Turkey and Afghanistan. "Nothing like that," she said.

He nodded. "Warriors want to believe war is glorious and vengeance is sweet. The truth is war is sometimes necessary, but it is always more about death and destruction than it is about fulfilling the vainglorious fantasies of man." Caradoc paused a moment. "I want you to know that what the Romans did to the Isle of Mona and the druids and priestesses and their families was far more terrible than what happened to Londinium today."

"That's hard for me to imagine," she said.

"Don't try to imagine it. Just know that even though war is terrible, Boudica's cause is just. We cannot live as slaves, with the Romans able to discard our lives and our families at whim. We are a free people, and we must remain that way."

"I understand fighting for your freedom," Alex said. "It's just that seeing it makes it…" Her voice trailed off, as if she was unable to put her feelings into words.

"Seeing it makes a magnificent abstract concept real, and reality tends to taint even the most wonderful ideas," he finished for her.

"Yes," she sighed. "I think that's what I mean."

He touched her cheek gently. "Boudica will be calling for me as soon as she finishes with the wounded. I must go to her."

"She'll want me, too," Alex said, and her stomach felt it would turn inside out at the thought of facing the queen and her inner circle of blood-spattered warriors.

"Boudica will understand that your service of Andraste has left you exhausted. Blonwen, you understand that I am saying only truth, don't you? Look deep within yourself. What you witnessed was horrendous, but the despair I see in your eyes is there because the goddess has drained you today. Stay here. Rest. Draw strength and comfort from the forest. I will return as soon as I am able."

With a huge sense of relief, Alex nodded.

Caradoc kissed her softly on her lips and then he was gone.

Alex poured herself another goblet of mead; this one she drank more slowly. as she took the druid's advice and looked within herself. She was exhausted all the way through to her bones. She'd been too busy, too worried to realize just how unimaginably tired she really was. With the understanding that she truly was drained and at the end of her reserves, Alex could acknowledge that some of the horror she was feeling was because her defenses were down. What had happened in Londinium had been terrible, but she was well aware that war wasn't pretty. And she knew from Carswell's briefing, as well as firsthand from the Celts themselves, that the Romans had been brutalizing the Iceni for decades. Alex didn't really want to turn from Boudica just because the queen had exacted retribution from her enemies.

"I do need to recharge and get my perspective back," Alex said aloud. Resolutely, she swallowed the rest of the mead and then got up and, thinking of the cleansing stream, made her way to where it bubbled over smooth stones not far from Caradoc's campsite.

Alex knelt on the mossy bank, cupped the cool, clear water in her hands and splashed it over her face again and again, until she couldn't smell the scent of burning flesh anymore. Then she bent, cupped her hands again and drank deeply of the water. It was so clean it almost tasted sweet. Already feeling better, Alex scooted back until she leaned against the bark of a thick old oak. She ran her damp fingers through her hair, working out snarls and re-forming curls. The act of combing her hands through her hair was soothing, and Alex felt the numbness that had weighed down her spirit begin to lift.

She was still terribly tired, but now it was just a normal weariness, and not the exhaustion that had paralyzed her mind.

Her thoughts didn't circle around the horror of violence and destruction; instead, they were her own again, to put to order and reason through. And reason she did. She had half the medallion, or at least knew where half was. She could see it, and could eventually figure out how to get it from Boudica.

Could Carswell do anything if Alex grabbed the torque and returned with only part of the medallion? Could she make a cast of that and reconstruct from it what the other half of the piece should look like? Maybe. It was a question Alex hadn't posed to the professor. Obviously, no one had, or the answer would have been included in her very thorough briefing.

So, worst-case scenario, Alex could still get a part of the medallion to Flagstaff.

And run away from Caradoc, never to see him again?

Alex mentally shook herself. Now was not the time to get stuck on a man, *literally.* This wasn't her era; she didn't belong in AD 60, no matter what her heart or soul might wish.

"I have to get the mission done. Then I can think about him." She whispered the words as if trying to conjure a spell that would make her heart and soul behave, and quit filling her with thoughts that didn't matter, about a future that couldn't be hers. "Just get the job done," she muttered.

But how was she supposed to do that? Catus was dead and the piece of the puzzle that completed her mission was either burned with him, or hidden by him.

Then Alex's eyes widened. "That's it! Carswell even said the medallion was surrounded by the dead. That's why they needed me for this mission!"

FIFTEEN

Excited, Alex stood and began to pace, still muttering to herself. "So what if Catus is dead? As long as he knew where the medallion was, what difference does that make? I can talk to dead people!" Alex came to an abrupt halt. That was it! That was what she had to do to finish her mission. Caradoc had said Soul Speakers could summon the dead—that they used the power of the forest to do it. She already had some experience with forest power; surely she could figure out how to call one newly dead spirit! She'd ask Catus to tell her where he'd put the medallion, and then she'd retrieve it from his hiding place, even if she had to wait for the temple to turn to cold ashes.

She shivered, not wanting to think about sifting through bodies and rubble to find a little medallion piece. Of course, it might not be in the temple. Actually, it would be logical for it *not* to be. Why would Catus keep his personal things there? It was probably wherever he'd been living.

Feeling more optimistic by the second, Alex continued pacing and thinking, until one thought brought her up short, and she gasped as the final piece of the puzzle fitted into place. She'd been making this mission way too difficult. She didn't have to steal the damn torque from the queen; all she needed to do after she got the medallion piece from Catus was talk Boudica into letting her borrow her torque.

"That should be fairly easy to do. I'll just make up a blessing or cleansing or something that the goddess would want me to do to it."

Once Boudica let her have the torque, Alex would return to the future, give the medallion pieces to Professor Carswell and ask her to make quick copies of them. Alex would fit them into the torque and then return. She didn't have to be the priestess who betrayed the queen and stole the last thing she had from her dead husband, after all!

And what do I do about Caradoc?

"I'll figure that out later," she told herself sternly. "Get one job done at a time, and job one needs to be done now."

Alex looked around her, peering through the dense greenery of the forest for the telltale glimpse of white she needed. She wasn't really surprised to see the snowy flowers of a rowan tree only a few paces beyond the stream.

Alex took off her shoes and, carrying them in one hand, and lifting her tunic with the other, waded across, liking how the cool water and smooth stones felt against her feet. She approached the rowan slowly, taking her time to study it while she slowed her breathing and centered herself.

When her mind was calm and focused, she pressed her palms against the rough bark of the tree.

And realized she didn't know what the hell she was doing. She wasn't really a priestess. She was just a weird girl from a world way off in the future who talked to dead people and really had no damn life at all.

A frustrated tear slipped down Alex's cheek and she brushed her face against her shoulder and sniffled. She was so tired! And she was in way over her head with all of this. Yeah, her plan had seemed doable—if she knew what she was doing!

Have more confidence in yourself, child. The unearthly voice drifted down from above her.

Alex jumped a little and jerked her hands from the rowan's bark as she peered up into the green-and-white boughs, to see Caradoc's mom sitting snuggly where the massive tree formed a *y*. Alex frowned. "You're not the ghost I need to talk to." Then her spirit brightened. "But can you tell me how to call a different ghost here?"

I do not need to tell you something you already know within yourself. You must learn to trust your heart and your soul. Start now. Listen within and act upon what you hear.

"Your son's less cryptic," Alex told her.

My son can instruct you, but his lessons won't do any good if you do not trust yourself, and that is something no one can teach you. You must find a way to believe in yourself on your own.

Alex wanted to scream in frustration. Instead, she clamped down on her temper and looked up at Caradoc's mother again. "Seriously, can't you just tell me what to do? I really don't have the time or energy to waste messing up and starting over a bunch of times."

The ghost's brows lifted, reminding Alex very much of her son. *I didn't take you for the sort of woman who just wished to follow orders given by others.*

Alex felt the shock of the far-reaching truth of the ghost's words. She *didn't* like to take orders. She hadn't left the air force simply because the dead had begun to overwhelm her. She'd left because it didn't rest easy with her to live a life dictated by others,

especially when those others called themselves her "superiors."
Alex liked to make her own choices and her own decisions.

"You're right. I don't like to be told what to do."

Then look within yourself and have the confidence to find your own way, the ghost said, lifting her palm that held the spiral tattoo as if in blessing.

"Okay, I will," Alex said, more to herself than to the spirit.

She raised her hands again and pressed them against the bark of the ancient rowan. Alex closed her eyes and focused her thoughts, and then, with a sense of release, she reached out, searching for the energy she'd tapped into before.

It zapped her just as before, and she gasped. Against her palms, Alex could almost feel the tree breathing, as crazy as that sounded. But there was energy and warmth and…she concentrated harder…there was even a sense of awareness that Alex knew could absolutely not be something she was imagining.

She drew a deep breath and said, "I need your help."

The bark of the tree seemed to quiver under her palms.

"I'm a Soul Speaker, and I need to find a particular soul. I ask that you lend me your power and help me find a spirit that was recently in Londinium. His name was Catus. He was a Roman tax collector—the man who ordered Boudica beaten and her daughters raped." Alex added the description, guessing that trees might not know names and such, but all the Celts seemed to know Catus as the guy who'd caused the queen and her family to be brutalized, so it made sense that the watching forest might know him, too. "So, please, I ask you in the name of the goddess Andraste, who I would be honored to serve, that you show me Catus!"

Her hands heated immensely, so much that she had to grit her teeth and force herself not to pull away. Then there was a shimmering brightness to her right, and Alex watched as what looked like the fabric of reality split, shifted and opened.

Speechless with amazement, she peered through a glittering veil to see Jupiter's temple, only this temple wasn't ablaze. It was in a state of chaos, though. Men wearing togas were rushing in a panicked group into the temple, shouting about barring the doors and keeping out the barbarians. Like a video spotlight, Alex's eye was drawn to the side steps of the temple, where a fat man wearing a richly trimmed toga was talking in a low, urgent voice with a younger, less opulently dressed man. *Catus*...the name came through the bark of the tree and was absorbed into Alex's body. It was the weirdest thing she'd ever experienced, but she knew beyond any doubt that the fat guy was the tax collector.

"I need to see what happens to him!" Alex said quickly.

She watched as Catus sent the man off on an errand. When he was gone, the fat man left the temple steps and ducked into a beautiful marble building situated beside it. Inside, he unlocked an inner room and opened a chest, pulling out several heavy bags that were obviously filled with coins. These he tucked into the huge belt that encircled his midsection, then he rushed out of the building, to pace back and forth.

Minutes later the young man raced up on the back of a horse, leading another.

"Flavius! Here! Come to me!"

Flavius guided the horses to the fat man, pulling them to a skidding halt. Instantly, Catus grabbed the young man's toga and dragged him off his mount's back.

"My lord! What are you doing?" Flavius asked, as Catus literally used his body as a mounting block.

"I am leaving this accursed city," the tax collector said, peering down his long nose at the young man.

Flavius started to move to the second horse, which was saddled and tethered to the other, but Catus guided his mount forward, blocking his path.

"I don't understand," said the young man.

"I am leaving *alone*. I'll need to ride hard and fast to escape, and I'll need the second horse to relieve this one."

"But I've been your assistant for two seasons! I've served you loyally."

Catus shrugged. "And now, Flavius, your time of service is over." The tax collector jerked his fat chin at Jupiter's temple. "Hide there with the rest of the rabble. Perhaps Jupiter will protect you." Then he leaned forward and gouged his heels into the horse, causing his assistant to leap aside to avoid being knocked down. Obviously not knowing what else to do, the young man ran to Jupiter's temple, and to his doom.

The scene shimmered and the veil of reality shifted and closed again.

Breathing hard, Alex leaned wearily against the tree. "Catus isn't dead," she said.

The coward escaped. Sometimes Fate is inexplicably unjust, said Caradoc's mother. She wasn't perched in the tree anymore, but was sitting on the moss-lined bank of the stream.

"Well, at least I was partially successful. I think I know how to call spirits to me. I mean, I needed to see Catus, and the power of the forest let me do so. I suppose the same thing will happen when I call for someone who is actually dead."

But Catus isn't dead.

"No, but he has something I need. Someone who knew him must know where it is—whether it's with him or whether he left it behind."

Do you not think you should try another calling after you have grounded yourself? It isn't wise to traffic in the spirit realm unless you're firmly attached to the mortal world.

"I'm attached." Alex pushed her hair back from her face. God, she was tired!

No, you're exhausted. Your energy is dangerously depleted.

"I'm tougher than I look," she said, straightening up and facing the tree again.

Alexandra, wait for Caradoc to return.

"Who knows how long he could be gone? I just want to get this done and over with." It was not until much later that Alex realized the spirit of the ancient Celt had called her by her real name. Then all she could think of was that she needed to find the other medallion piece, so that she could finally rest and figure out what she was going to do with her own future.

Alex pressed her palms against the rowan tree again. She closed her eyes and focused her tired mind, trying to concentrate.

"Thank you for showing me Catus," she told the tree. "But since he's not dead, I didn't get what I needed from him. So this time I'm calling *only* the spirits of the dead. I need people who knew Catus." Alex paused, and added, "I am especially calling spirits of the dead who knew things about Catus— intimate things, secret things. In Andraste's name, I call those dead to me now!"

Lightning shot through the tree and into her palms, causing her to cry aloud in pain. With a *crack!* the fabric of reality split open. In horror, Alex saw specters of the dead being yanked through the gap. At first their ghostly eyes looked sightlessly around and they seemed disoriented. But then they spotted her and, with an eerie keening cry, rushed toward her.

Alex had never before been afraid of ghosts. As annoying and overwhelming as spirits could be, they'd never been aggressive. These ghosts were utterly different. They exuded anger and hatred and despair. The emotions swirled around them, made tangible in the form of a dark mist that snaked in ominous waves, curling and coiling from the specters, reaching toward Alex.

We who have been wronged by Catus come to claim our vengeance!

"I'm not Catus! Look at me—you know I'm not Catus!" Alex cried at the horde of malevolent spirits that continued to flow through the rip in reality.

Vengeance! They seethed and swarmed, surrounding Alex and her rowan tree.

"What are you doing? Okay, stop! Go back where you came from. This isn't what I wanted."

We shall return to the land of the dead, but we will take you with us!

A tendril of darkness snaked close to her and wrapped around Alex's throat. Ghosts hadn't ever been able to touch her, so she shrieked in shocked surprise when the black, serpent-like tentacle of death closed a frigid noose around her neck.

"No!" she screamed, trying to take her hands from the tree and pull the thing off her. But her hands wouldn't move. It was as if her body was frozen in place, and all that screamed and writhed was her own spirit, skewered by the blind hatred of the conjured ghosts.

As the serpent thing snagged her soul and wrenched it from her body, Alex shrieked in fear. *Andraste! Goddess! Help me!*

A brilliant silver light surrounded Alex, chasing away the darkness that had sought to entrap her. The light soon began to fade, but Alex, drowning in terror, clung to the brightness that had saved her. The might of the goddess was too much for a mortal soul still anchored to its living host to bear, however. Unwilling to return to her body, but unable to fully exist in the presence of the Divine Feminine, Alexandra Patton's spirit shattered.

SIXTEEN

The Celtic army celebrated, surrounding their queen with the loot they'd pillaged from Londinium. Drunk with victory, their thirst for retribution momentarily slaked by the defeat of Londinium and Rome's Ninth Legion, they raised goblets of stolen Roman wine to Boudica and her victorious goddess.

"Next we chase the vermin up the Watling Road, and as we go we will defeat every legion we meet, so by the time we end at the Isle of Mona, the site of the worst of their atrocities, we will have rid our land of the Roman infestation!" Boudica shouted, and the Iceni echoed her words with cheers.

Caradoc raised his goblet along with the rest of Boudica's people, though his thoughts kept circling back to his campsite and the woman who awaited him there.

Blonwen was a mystery. She was no priestess from Mona, though she had been touched by Andraste. She was a Soul Speaker, but she understood little about her gift. She automatically channeled the energy of the forest and used it to comfort the dying and soothe their spirits as they passed on to the Otherworld, yet it seemed she knew nothing about the spirit realms or how to access them.

To add to the paradox that surrounded her, Blonwen had the ability to soothe that which the desecration of Mona had broken within him, and that had shocked the druid to his very soul.

For days he had hated himself because he had escaped the fate of his friends and family on Mona. Caradoc understood why they had given their lives so that he could live and make his way to his kinswoman. The Iceni royal blood must continue and the people must have the security of knowing their line of kings and queens would not be destroyed by Roman brutality. Still, he lived when all the others did not.

And then this woman—this imposter—appeared, claiming to be a priestess from Mona. His first instinct had been to cut her lying throat with his own knife. When his mother's spirit had spoken through her, instructing him not to give her away, Caradoc had been utterly confused. His confusion had only grown stronger as his attraction to her had become obvious. Yes, he recognized her from his dreams, but druids were often gifted with prophetic visions while they slept. His attraction to her had been more shocking than his mother's acceptance of her. He'd thought what he'd witnessed at Mona had killed all the gentleness and passion and ability to love within him. He'd held Blonwen in his arms once and known that, at least with her, that wasn't true.

It had angered him and made him feel racked with guilt, which was why he'd struck out at her, wanting to hurt her and drive her away. But that had been wrong of him, and when he'd looked within himself afterward, he'd been ashamed of what he'd allowed sadness and loss to make him become.

So he'd opened himself to her, and been engulfed by the

desire to learn more—and not because he thought she was dangerous to Boudica. Caradoc wanted to know the truth about Blonwen because he felt *compelled* to know it, and in that feeling he recognized the hand of Andraste. The goddess was at work in the attraction between them. Was Blonwen a soul he'd known before? Was that why he'd dreamed of her and why she had such an instant and intense effect on him? Because she did have a profound effect on him. It was more than her softness, the way she felt against him, the way she tasted and smelled. His need to be with her went beyond the physical, and that truly frightened him. Caradoc was afraid there was something buried within the mystery of her that could take her away from him, and he'd lost too much already. He couldn't bear to lose the woman who had made his soul come alive again.

The longer Caradoc sat there, at his honored place beside his victorious queen, the more restless he became. Thoughts of Blonwen circled obsessively through his mind. He saw the golden red of her hair reflected in the campfire. The deepening shadows of the waning day reminded him of the pools of her eyes. The rich taste of the Roman wine made him think of the sweetness of her mouth.

"Where are you, Caradoc? For surely you are not here beside me." Boudica spoke softly, her words for his ears alone to hear.

"I am sorry, my queen," Caradoc said. "My thoughts are with Andraste's priestess."

Boudica nodded. "Helping the dead pass to the goddess could not have been an easy task." She placed her hand on her kinsman's broad shoulder. "Go to her—I give you leave."

Caradoc had to force himself not to leap up and bolt from Boudica's campsite. Instead he stood and bowed respectfully to her. "Thank you, my queen and my friend."

She smiled at him and then turned back to her celebrating people.

Caradoc waited until he was several paces away before he broke into a run, though his haste made him feel foolish. He was behaving like a callow youth who was unable to spend any time away from the maiden who obsessed him. He almost laughed at himself.

When he reached his empty campsite, the mirth he'd felt at his own expense died. Where was she? A sound from the forest pulled his attention toward the little stream that bubbled not far away, and his feet began to move before his mind consciously told them to.

Then he saw her and his blood went cold. She was lying in a crumpled, motionless heap at the base of a huge rowan tree. Caradoc sprinted to her, pulling her to him with an anguished cry.

"Blonwen! What has—" At that moment he turned her over and saw her open, sightless eyes, and he knew. *By all the gods! Her soul has been shattered!*

Quickly he lifted her in his arms and carried her the short way back to his campsite. He pulled the pallet of furs out from under the protective awning and placed it nearer the fire, then laid her gently atop them. Then he began to ready himself. Moving methodically and with confidence, Caradoc went to the pack he had carried with him all the way from ruined Mona. He took from it a dried smudge stick made of lavender, a candle made of pure, cream colored beeswax, and a stunning amethyst crystal. All the while he concentrated on his breathing and centering himself, and ignored the slight tremor in his hands.

He poured a goblet of mead and set a hunk of bread and cheese on a large rock nearby, then lit the candle and placed it beside the food and mead on the rock. From the lit candle, he set the lavender smudge stick afire, wafting it gently in the air around him until the flame was out and fragrant smoke rolled from the thick braid of dried herb.

Slowly, Caradoc directed the lavender smoke around and over his body as he sat, cross-legged, beside Blonwen. He breathed in and out deeply three times, saturating himself with the smoke and the cleansing and calming effect of the lavender. Then he began smudging Blonwen's motionless body, murmuring whispered words for her to be calm and to absorb the aroma of the lavender smoke, and for her to trust him—he was coming for her.

With his heart and mind still, Caradoc lay down beside Blonwen. They didn't touch, but he could feel how slight she was next to him, and could sense the emptiness of the mortal vessel her spirit had left behind. He cupped the amethyst crystal in his palm and pressed it against his heart. The stone warmed in his hand, and Caradoc thought of the properties of amethyst—a spiritual stone with no negative connotations whatsoever. Its powers enhanced dreaming and healing. It brought with it peace and protection, as well as love and happiness.

Caradoc used the stone as a conduit. Through the brilliant purple crystal the druid found the beat of his heart and followed that ancient, primordial pulse, his lifeline first to the earth on which he lay. And then, as his trance deepened, the two-count beat, with its mesmerizing, timeless pull, led him from his mortal shell.

The druid's spirit lifted and the mists of reality parted around him, opening to reveal three levels of the Otherworld. He hovered there, and sent out a fervent prayer to the goddess.

Andraste, I come after a soul that has shattered. It is your priestess, Blonwen, who I wish to retrieve and make whole. I beg you to help me, Goddess, in my quest to find her.

Caradoc's spirit waited there for a sign from Andraste that would show him which level of the Otherworld he must travel to so that he might find Blonwen.

A girl child appeared before him. She could not have been older than six summers. Her red-gold hair was long and unruly, and her eyes were large and dark. Caradoc breathed a silent sigh of relief. He would recognize this child anywhere as a youthful version of Blonwen.

Hello, little one. Caradoc spoke warmly to the girl. *Can you lead me to your adult self? I have need for her whole and well back in the physical realm.*

The child studied him silently before speaking. *She's scared. Are you here to hurt her?*

No! I would never hurt Blonwen.

The little girl's smooth brow furrowed. *I can tell you are telling me the truth, even though you're calling her the wrong name.*

Caradoc smiled at her. *What is the pet name you would like me to call her, child?*

The girl frowned at him, reminding Caradoc eerily of her adult self. *It's not a pet name we want to be called. We want to be called our name, and that's Alexandra Patton, but I guess if you don't want to say that much you can call us Alex, like everyone else does.*

Caradoc felt a little jolt of surprise. The girl was obviously a spirit version of Blonwen as a child, and spirit versions of children were their purest essence. They did not lie, which mean Blonwen's true name was Alexandra Patton.

Would you take me to Alexandra Patton, child?

Yes. We need you. We're not happy here.

Her words relieved him immeasurably, and he took her hand. *That is because it is not yet your time to join the Otherworld.*

The child shrugged, but led him toward the entrance to all three levels of the Otherworld. Without hesitation, she stepped forward, and a smooth expanse of white marble appeared beneath their feet, stretching up and up.

So she found the Upperworld, Caradoc said, more to himself than the child.

She didn't find it. She just ran up here. She was too scared to find anything.

Caradoc wanted to know what had frightened Blonwen—or Alexandra—so terribly, but he knew asking the child would be pointless. She was a spirit guide. She served only to lead those who were acceptable to her host. She didn't really function separately from her true self.

Time passed oddly in the Otherworld, but it seemed Caradoc had drawn very few breaths before the stairway emptied into a meadow of waving grass, dotted with fragrant wildflowers. The meadow was framed by a dense forest of dark trees, from which Caradoc automatically averted his gaze. He knew there lurked within the depths of that forest things that could delight, as well as destroy the soul—and the druid had time for neither. In the center of the meadow was a beautiful marble fountain, with a silver chalice sitting beside it.

Everything you need is there, the child said, pointing at the well. *I hope you brought payment.*

I did, child.

Good. Bring us back to the world. I don't like it when we're scared. Oh, and you can call me Alex. I hope I see you again soon when we're all together.

Do not worry, Alex. All will be well.

The girl squeezed his hand and then, with the sound of a sigh, disappeared. The child's continued focus on fear worried Caradoc. What would he discover when he found Blonwen? Or would he not find Blonwen at all, but only Alexandra, a terrified stranger whose soul had shattered beyond healing?

He walked into the meadow, keeping his attention on the fountain in the center of it. This was Andraste's realm, and the goddess's fountain. Those who wished to evoke the goddess in the Upperworld must drink of her water and offer her a gift. Caradoc knew all too well that Andraste was Goddess of War, as well as Mother of the Celts, and if his heart was not pure, his intentions clouded with his own greed and need, it wouldn't matter what gift he brought. Andraste's water would turn his faults against him and he would be destroyed by them. To some druids it happened instantly. Others were ousted from Andraste's meadow and allowed to return to the mortal realm, only to see their lives unravel by their own weaknesses.

But the sound of the water soothed Caradoc, as it always did, and without further hesitation he stepped up to the fountain and lowered the chalice into its crystal depths. Though he'd been to Andraste's realm many times before, he hadn't ventured here since the destruction of the Isle of Mona. As he lifted the chalice, Caradoc searched his heart. Yes, he was angry about the loss of his friends and family. Yes, he felt guilty for living, when those closest to him had died protecting him. But had he come here for self-serving means?

He'd come automatically when he understood that Blonwen's soul had somehow been shattered, and she needed his help to find her way back to her body.

Am I being selfish? Caradoc wasn't sure. Blonwen was frightened, so frightened that her spirit had split into pieces. She needed to be healed. But the full truth was that he wanted her back in the mortal realm because *he* needed *her.* Blonwen, Alexandria, Alex—her name made no difference, nor did he care that she wouldn't tell him everything about herself. When he touched her, he felt whole. That was all that truly mattered to him.

So am I being selfish in coming here? Perhaps, he decided, if it was selfish to love and to want to be loved in return, then the goddess's judgment would be harsh. And if that were so, then at least he might have Blonwen returned to him for a little while before his life unraveled....

Caradoc raised the chalice of the goddess and drank until it was drained.

Almost instantly the meadow began to shimmer with a brilliance that defied mortal description, and a woman stepped from the shadows of the forest. As she approached Caradoc, her image kept shifting. One moment she was a maiden, impossibly fresh-faced and utterly innocent in the bloom of youth. The next she was an ancient crone, with long white hair trailing the grass at her feet and skin like the bark of a sacred rowan tree. And then she changed again, taking the form of a woman in the prime of her life, curvy and voluptuous, full of breast and body and quite obviously pregnant.

Caradoc fell to his knees, bowed his head and held out to her the perfect amethyst crystal that still carried the sound of his heartbeat.

Andraste, please accept this gift, from my heart to yours.

The crystal disappeared from his hands.

You may rise, Caradoc, son of Eilwen, one of the most beloved of all of my priestesses.

Caradoc stood. The goddess had chosen to appear to him as if she were a woman of his mother's age. She was beautiful, heartbreakingly so, but this was a form he could more easily look upon than the maiden or the shifting images she so often preferred.

Great Goddess, he began without preamble, knowing Andraste appreciated honestly, especially from those who sought out her meadow. *I follow a soul that has recently been shattered. It belongs to a mortal woman who, I believe, is a servant of yours. I know her as Blonwen, Soul Speaker, confidente of Boudica, but she also carries the name Alexandra Patton.*

She is here, Druid. She is, indeed, a Soul Speaker, though an untrained one. She attempted to call spirits to her, but her body and soul were weary and she did not prepare herself. When the dead turned on her, she was shattered, and automatically fled here in panic.

She is safe and well? Caradoc felt his own soul shiver, imagining the terror of having the dead overwhelm Blonwen.

She is, though she is not herself.

May I call her shattered soul to me, Goddess, and return her, whole, to the mortal realm?

Andraste didn't answer for what felt to Caradoc an eternity. When she finally spoke, her words sent a chill through his spirit.

You are tied to this woman, though it may be easier for you to reject this tie, at least in your current mortal incarnation. For your mother's sake, I give you a choice. Leave Blonwen here. Her mortal body will perish, but I will soothe her soul and she will be at peace. You will live a long, full life, eventually returning here to me, and to her, and the two of you will be reborn in an easier time.

What is my other choice?

Call her to you and accept your love for her, no matter how transient it might be, and you will be her champion. She has a task to complete and she cannot do it alone. But if you help her in completing this task, I see death for you. Will you help her, even if it means losing yourself?

I will do your will, Goddess.

Andraste's eyes blazed and Caradoc had to fight with himself not to bolt from her presence. *That is not my way, as you well know, Caradoc! I have given my people the gift of free will because I do not wish to be served by mindless creatures who act blindly out of fear. Make your choice! Will you aid her in this life, or will you leave here to await more peaceful days and easier times for lovers?*

I choose to aid her in this life. Caradoc let his heart speak for him, and as he did so he felt a great release, as if he'd been carrying around a burden he'd suddenly been freed of.

Even though in choosing to be her champion you will be tested unto the ends of your strength and the depths of your soul? the goddess asked.

Yes.

I see your mother in you, selkie, and I am well pleased. Andraste raised her arms and said, *Call your love, Caradoc. Know that you take my blessing with you. May it lend both of you strength and clarity when you most need it.*

In an explosion of light, the goddess disappeared.

SEVENTEEN

Caradoc was alone in the middle of Andraste's meadow. Her well had disappeared. There was nothing left except grass and the dense woods. This time he didn't avert his gaze from the darkness within the forest depths. Instead he looked straight into it, drew a deep breath and called, *Blonwen, hear me. I am Caradoc, son of Eilwen, beloved of the goddess. In Andraste's name, and with her blessing, I summon you. Come forth, Blonwen, and return to the mortal realm from whence you came!*

With the sound of wind sloughing through leaves, the barrier of trees to his right parted like the drape of a tent opening, and a woman stepped into Andraste's clearing. At first Caradoc didn't recognize her, and then he gasped her name. *Blonwen!*

She cocked her head and her long hair, wild around her shoulders, lifted in a breeze that only she could feel. *I know you,* she said.

As I know you! Caradoc had to remind himself not to go to her. When a soul shattered, the spirit pieces must reunite and return of their own accord. The retrieval could not be forced or cajoled.

But this version of the Blonwen he knew tempted him sorely. She was incredible! It was as if all that was alluring and powerful and utterly feminine had been captured in this version of her spirit, and Caradoc's automatic response to her was as instinctive as his desire to save her.

She smiled at him. *Our souls recognize one another.* Blonwen held her hand out to him. *Join me here, Druid. Let us be lovers in Andraste's verdant meadows and spend a piece of eternity wrapped in each other's arms.*

Ah, that is indeed a tempting offer, as you are fair and fine, and even without touching I feel my blood quicken, just at the sight of you. He returned her smile, but was careful not to take her hand.

Shall we see what happens when we do touch? Her lips curved seductively and her eyes were full of promise.

Don't touch her! We'll never get back if you do! The six-year-old Alex was standing across the glade, to Caradoc's left.

Hello, Alex, he said.

You can't stay here with her! Then we all have to stay!

Don't listen to the child. It's best if we stay here.

No! the child wailed.

Alex, do you trust me? asked Caradoc.

The girl bit her lip and looked worried, but she nodded. Caradoc turned to the alluring Blonwen. *And do you trust me, Blonwen?*

She studied him with that seductive smile still on her lips. *It seems I do, Druid.*

I am glad. Then let us complete this with a triad of souls. Caradoc positioned himself so that he was standing between the two spirit versions of the woman he sought. He looked forward, into the thickest part of the concealing forest that surrounded the meadow, and called once again.

Alexandra Patton, I call you using the other name by which you are known. Come to me, Alexandra, and in answering my call you will see that which you have lost, and be able to fix that which has been broken. Come forth, Alexandra!

The shadows quivered. A woman moved hesitantly from the darkness within the trees. She looked terrified. Her eyes darted back and forth between Blonwen and little Alex. Then she saw Caradoc and she gasped.

Caradoc! It is you! I thought I heard you, but everything is so dark in there—she threw a frightened glance over her shoulder—*that I thought I was making it up.*

It is me. I came for you. He kept his voice steady, but in truth this version of Blonwen shocked him. She was most like the woman he knew, so he realized that in this lifetime her name was, indeed, Alexandra Patton. And this version of his Blonwen was more than frightened. She was overwhelmed. Her eyes were haunted by doubt and indecision. Where was the woman who had stood beside a queen and called forth a goddess's blessing? Where was the woman who had the composure and compassion to gently ease the dying into the Otherworld?

A flicker of movement to his right answered his silent questions.

He came for you, but he wants me, said Blonwen.

The Blonwen version of Alexandra's spirit seemed to be lit from within by confidence and temper and passion. Of course Caradoc was attracted to that part of her, but he also knew that the fiery version of Blonwen would, without the temperance of wariness and restraint, innocence and guilelessness, burn itself out—along with anyone who was unwise enough to bind his life to her.

I came for all of you, Caradoc said, looking from Blonwen to

Alexandra, and finally to young Alex, who was obviously so much more than the spirit guide he'd first taken her for. *I don't want one part of you more than another. I want all of you joined, whole once more, and safe in my arms.*

Safe? said Alexandra.

He nodded.

And out of here, right? 'Cause this isn't where we belong yet, said young Alex.

Yes, we will return to the mortal realm.

Why? Blonwen demanded, tossing back her hair and crossing her arms over her chest. *Why should I leave here? Why should you?*

I must leave because it is not yet my time to enter Andraste's meadow. My body awaits my return in the mortal realm, as does yours.

Druid, you can't tell me it wouldn't be better for us to stay here, she insisted.

It's true. I cannot. But I can tell you… he paused, and his gesture included the other two pieces of her soul …*that you left too early from the mortal realm. There are things you left undone.*

Like what?

He smiled at Blonwen. *Like love me, and you cannot do that here, as I will not be staying.* He turned to young Alex, feeling intensely protective of this childlike version of the woman he loved. *How about you, Alex? Will you return with me?*

I already said I would! You're wasting time.

Caradoc stifled a laugh at her impertinence. He looked from her back to Blonwen. *Isn't love enough to return for?*

The fiery expression faded from her face and Blonwen smiled seductively at him. *Love is all I would return for.*

Then he faced Alexandra. *It is your decision. It has always been your decision. Will you return with me to the mortal realm to live, and perhaps die, by my side?*

Will you protect me? she asked plaintively.

Once you are whole again, I will not need to protect you, only to teach you how to protect yourself. I will love you, though. In that I give you my oath.

Alexandra stood a little straighter. *Okay. Then I'll come back with you.* She started to walk toward him. *For love,* she said.

The child Alex skipped quickly over to the adult, who held out her arm. *For love,* said the little girl as she stepped into Alexandra's embrace and disappeared.

Still approaching Caradoc, Alexandra turned her head to look at Blonwen. The passionate spirit hesitated only for a moment longer, then hurried over to her other self. *For love!* she shouted as she wrapped her arms around Alexandra, and she, too, disappeared.

And then Alexandra was standing before Caradoc. Slowly, the druid opened his arms. *For love,* he said, and the whole Alex stepped into his embrace and lifted her face to him. When he claimed her mouth, the ground dropped open beneath them and, clinging together, they fell.

As they passed through the realms of the Otherworld, the kiss Caradoc and Alex shared became more than a physical sensation. To restore the wholeness of her soul, Caradoc had to literally absorb that which was the essence of Alexandra's spirit. He'd known that, if he succeeded, he would carry her with him from the Otherworld; he just hadn't been prepared for what happened next.

Caradoc couldn't tell where his consciousness ended and hers began. They clung to one another, touching bodies and entwining souls, and in the heartbeats it took to return to the mortal realm, Caradoc looked into Alexandra's mind and saw everything—a vision of her life in a world that was alien to him and a time that was in the unimaginable future.

With a gasp, Caradoc opened his eyes. He was exactly where he'd intended to be, back in his body, lying beside the motionless form of Blonwen. Moving quickly and confidently, he sat up and pulled her into his lap. The druid bent and brought his mouth close to hers. "I carry within me that which must be restored to you." He pressed his lips to hers and blew softly.

Instantly, he felt a rush of warmth leave his body and flow into hers. Her eyelids fluttered, and then she opened them and stared at him.

"Hello, Alex," he said softly.

"You saw everything, didn't you?" she asked, her voice rough, as if she hadn't spoken in days.

"I did."

"Are you sorry you brought me back?"

He touched her face gently. "Did you not see within me, too?"

"I couldn't see things. I could only feel."

"Then what did you feel?" he asked.

"Love," she said.

"And that, Alexandra Patton, will never change, no matter what world or what age you come from."

He kissed her then and he knew some of the passion that burned within him for her was desperation. She wasn't of this time and place, and that meant that no matter how well he loved her, she eventually had to return to her own world.

But not at this moment. Just now she only had to love him. In turn, he would love her, even if their time together was to be measured in days and not years.

As if reading his mind, she pulled back enough to whisper against his lips, "Show me that it's just you and me right now. That for at least a little while we really do have each other." Then she reached up, fisted her hand in his hair and pulled him down to her. Opening her mouth to his, she teased him with her tongue and lips, evoking memories of the seductive Blonwen and how she'd offered herself to him in the goddess's meadow.

Caradoc moaned. His body's reaction was instantaneous and

fierce. Desire speared through him, hot and insistent, like nothing he'd ever experienced before. And he was certainly no inexperienced youth. He'd had his share of lovers and was no stranger to lust, but with Alexandra there was something different between them. It was as if touching her had awakened an instinctual need within him to possess her that his sinews, tendons, blood and nerves remembered, but that his mind had forgotten. He was beyond wanting her—he had to have her.

"Make me yours, Caradoc." Her lips moved against his as their breath mingled. "I want to know that I will always belong to you."

"Yes!" The word was an acknowledgment of everything that had passed between them. *Yes,* he wanted her. *Yes,* he needed her. *Yes,* he would make her his own.

And *yes,* he was scared deep in his soul that no matter what he did or didn't do, he must lose her.

So Caradoc put out of his mind his fears and worries, and simply loved her.

He wanted to go slow, to savor this first time with her. But when his hand skimmed down the side of her body to the edge of her tunic, and then slid under her skirts and up, to find the warm silk of her naked flesh, he couldn't think about savoring anymore. He could only think of satisfying his need to be close to her, heart against heart, skin against skin.

Her chemise and tunic came off easily as she arched her body to allow him to undress her. The firelight licked against her bare skin, and somewhere in the rational part of his mind Caradoc registered that it was so fully dark the sun had to have set hours before. Then he could think no more as Alexandra took his hands and guided them to cup her breasts, and his lips found her again. She arched once more. This time her hips moved restlessly up, pressing the moist heat of her woman's center against his hardness. He had to bury his face in her hair and concentrate on the frantic beating of his heart to stop from spilling his seed as she reached between them and traced his shaft with her soft fingers.

Then she wasn't there against him and he reached out blindly, needing to feel her again. Her hands caught his and he opened his lust-glazed eyes to see her smile.

"I don't like being the only one here who is naked," she said.

Caradoc didn't think he'd ever before shed his clothes so quickly. And then they were in each other's arms again and her body was pressed against the length of him. He thought the heat and softness and scent of her skin would drive him mad.

"Caradoc," she murmured when his lips moved from her mouth to the hollow of her neck. "I have to tell you something."

He looked up from the sweet valley between her breasts. "You may tell me anything, Alexandra."

Her lips lifted in that sassy smile he was coming to love so much. "First, I hate being called Alexandra."

"Blonwen?"

Her brows lifted as she considered. "Yes," she said at last, tracing a finger down his broad shoulder to his back, and allowing her fingernail to dig in ever so slightly.

Caradoc shivered.

She smiled.

"Yes, as long as I'm here I want you to call me Blonwen."

He cupped her breasts and nibbled his way down one soft globe to her blush-colored nipple. When he took it between his teeth, she gasped and her hips automatically moved against him. His hardness slid between her legs and he could feel her wetness on his shaft. He opened his mouth and captured her nipple, alternating between sucking and teasing bites.

"Caradoc!" She gasped his name.

"Yes, my Blonwen. Tell me what is it you want of me." He glanced up at her as he moved his hand down her body to that captivatingly hot place between her legs that was the core of her. Slowly he began to caresses her there, sliding his fingers in and out, back and forth against the satin wetness.

"I want you to know that it has been a very long time since I was with a man," she said breathily.

Caradoc stilled his hand and forced his mind to work. "I would not hurt you," he said. "I will be gentle and we—"

She pressed her fingers against his lips, stilling his words.

"I didn't tell you that because I want you to be gentle. I told you because I want you to know there is no one else for me—that you are the only man in my life. Make love to me, Caradoc, and don't be gentle. I want to feel you inside me, claiming me as yours—hard and fast and now!"

She kissed him with such passion that she made the image of the Blonwen in the goddess's meadow seem a poor shadow of who she really was. She opened her thighs and, grasping him, rubbed the head of his shaft teasingly against her slick opening.

Caradoc could bear it no longer. With a sound that was almost bestial, he impaled her, thrusting inside that center of heat that was so tight and wet he had to stop moving for fear he would explode at that moment.

Blonwen moved against him, pulling him deeper until he was buried within her, and then she moved her hips again, sliding back and forth along the length of him.

"Ah, goddess! I can wait no longer!" Caradoc cried, and then he took over the rhythm…thrusting and thrusting, harder, faster…all the while claiming her mouth and drinking in the taste of her moans. As he felt himself gather for the explosion, Caradoc reached between them, rubbing the sensitive nub he found there. When Blonwen's body began to pulse around his shaft, his voice joined hers in a feral shout that proclaimed to the gods he had, indeed, made her his own.

EIGHTEEN

Afterward, Alex felt well satisfied and more than a little dizzy. Caradoc shifted his weight, obviously worried about crushing her, but she wrapped her arm tightly around his back and held him close.

"No, I don't want you to move. I'm feeling weirdly woozy and I think you're the only thing that's keeping the earth from spinning around underneath me," she whispered, a little surprised that she sounded drunk, her words slurred.

Caradoc's reaction was instantaneous. Speaking a curse that translated in Alex's head as doing something vile to a goat, he pulled easily out of her arms and started rummaging around by the big rock beside the fire. She tried to sit up and ask him what was going on, but as soon as she started to become vertical, the earth really did begin to spin beneath her.

"Here, love, drink this."

Caradoc's strong arms supported her as she drank thirstily from the goblet he handed her.

"And now eat this."

The goblet in her hands was replaced by a hunk of bread and a fragrant piece of cheese. She gave him a questioning look, not liking how worried he appeared, even as he poured a goblet of mead for himself and drained it in one long drink. He wiped his mouth with the back of his hand, and reached for some of the bread and cheese.

"We should have grounded ourselves as soon as we returned from the Otherworld. Our spirits and our bodies needed us to."

Alex chewed the bread slowly and raised her brows. Caradoc's smile was sheepish. "Aye, we were preoccupied. But it is late, as time passes differently in the Otherworld than it does here. I should have grounded us when we first returned, but I…" His words trailed off and he leaned into her, kissing the slope of her neck and sending shivers down her body. Then he leaned back and his smile turned wolfish. "I could not think of anything but getting you naked beside me."

"I'm not complaining," she stated, through a big bite of bread.

"Neither am I, love," he said softly. He got up again and poured them more mead. Then he lifted her, mead, bread and cheese and all, and carried her into the little shelter under the canopy of the oak tree. Snuggled against one anther, they ate and drank in silence, savoring the feeling of being reconnected to the mortal world, almost as much as the new closeness they'd found together.

Finally, after Alex's dizziness had completely passed and she was warmed by the mead, she asked Caradoc the question that had been waiting inside her head since they'd returned to their bodies.

"You know, don't you? I mean, all about where I'm really from and who I really am."

He nodded. "I do."

"Because you read my mind?"

Caradoc's lips tilted up and he touched her cheek in a gentle caress. "No, love. I know the truth because your soul mingled with mine as the shattered parts of it came together and I brought it safely back to your body."

Alex took his hand, threading her fingers with his. "That's absolutely incredible. Almost as incredible as knowing that you came to the Otherworld after me."

"I had to." He stared at their joined hands as he spoke. "I did not want to lose you." He looked up and into her eyes. "I still do not want to lose you."

Alex wanted to tell him that it was okay—that she didn't want to leave him, but the words caught in her throat. He knew the truth. She didn't belong to his world; she didn't belong to him.

"I do not understand everything I learned when our souls merged," he began slowly, as if searching carefully for the right words. "I could tell you are not from this time, but from one far removed and in the future."

"Yes, that's right," she said.

He nodded, considering before he continued. "You are here on a mission. You have come because you must take something back with you to your time."

Alex made her next decision quickly. She was done evading the truth. With him she couldn't pretend to be something she wasn't. Professor Carswell and General Ashton had emphasized not messing with history any more than was utterly necessary. Alex was to slip in, get the medallion and get out. Period. But no one had run a scenario where her spirit had been shattered and an incredible man had traveled to the Otherworld to rescue the pieces of her soul and bring them back. Their souls had merged, and anything less than the truth between them now would be an insult to Caradoc and what they had shared.

"I'm here for the medallion pieces in Boudica's torque, because they're part of a group of medallions that have to be collected, and if all the segments aren't found, the world as we know it will come to an end." She blurted it all in one quick sentence.

Caradoc's eyes widened. "You need the queen's torque?"

"Not actually the torque itself. What I need are the two medallion pieces that were set in the ends. One is there now."

"And the other was stolen by the Roman tax collector," Caradoc finished for her.

She nodded. "I was trying to find Catus when my soul shattered."

"You tried to call his spirit to you." Caradoc took her by the shoulders and gave her a little shake. "But you know nothing about summoning spirits, Blonwen, what you did was incredibly dangerous."

She slid into his arms. "Well, I know that now. I did find out Catus isn't dead. He ran away like the coward he is. I was hoping I could call a ghost to me who might know what he'd done with the medallion piece, but things got out of hand." She shivered and pressed herself more firmly against Caradoc.

He kissed her forehead and held her tightly. "It is over now. You're here, with me, safe."

Alex sighed and reluctantly pulled out of his arms so she could meet his gaze. "But it's not over, Caradoc. I have to get that other medallion piece and transport both of them to my time."

"And if you do somehow find this other illusive medallion, how do you plan on obtaining Boudica's royal torque?" His words were harsh, but his expression was resigned, almost sad, and Alex suddenly understood that he expected her to ask him to help her steal from his queen.

"I'm not going to steal it, Caradoc. I don't have to. I'll take it on the pretext of needing to get Andraste's blessing for it, but I'm not going to keep it forever. I'll transport it to the future, have the medallion pieces copied, fit them into the torque and bring it back to the queen, all in one piece."

"So you will return here?"

"To give the torque back to Boudica, yes."

"How does this time travel happen? What magic do you use?"

Alex hesitated, not having a clue how to explain a future technology to a man from the past, when she didn't actually understand it herself. Finally she told him, "Well, it's a mixture of science and mind magic. I can't use it. Except for this." She held up her wrist, bearing the ESC cuff. "If I press the crystal, I'll be taken to the future."

He was silent for a little while, touching her cuff almost reverently. "When you have returned Boudica's torque to her, you will leave again? Go back to your future world?"

"Yes. When my mission is over I'm supposed to do that," she whispered, staring into the depths of his eyes.

The worry suddenly cleared from his gaze and his grin lit his whiskey-colored eyes so that they sparkled. "Aye, *Alexandra,* and I felt in your soul just how very much you like to do what others tell you you are supposed to do."

Alex blinked in surprise at him. Well, hell! Caradoc was right! She'd be returning to the future because that was what she was expected to do after she completed her mission. But she didn't have to! She wasn't in the damn air force anymore. They couldn't tell her what she could or couldn't do with her life. "After I take the medallion pieces to the future, I'm going to do what I want." As she spoke the words aloud, Alex knew beyond any doubt what it was she wanted to do. She wanted to stay in this time, with this man, more than she'd ever wanted anything.

Caradoc cupped her face in his hands. "Then perhaps I should try to persuade you to consider remaining here, with me, in this time." As his lips met hers he whispered against her mouth, "Though I would never presume to tell you what to do."

She laughed as he kissed her. And then, before he made her dizzy again, this time not because she hadn't been grounded, Alex asked him, "Will you help me, Caradoc? Will you teach me what I need to know so that I can find the missing medallion?"

"Always, love. I will always help you." He paused and then continued, "Will you answer one question for me?"

"I'm through evading the truth with you. I'll answer any question you have," she said.

"Is Boudica victorious? Do we drive the Romans from our land?"

Alex froze. Why hadn't she anticipated this question? What could she say to him? How could she tell him, and yet how could she not?

But as she lay in his arms, unable to speak a lie and unwilling to tell him the harsh truth, Alex saw that she wasn't going to have to answer him.

"Ah," he said, his expression immeasurably sad. "I see. Is there anything you can do to change what happens?" he asked quietly.

Alex shook her head. "I'm sorry. I'm not supposed to change history. We're not even completely sure it can be done."

"I see," he repeated.

"I can tell you that the Celts survive. Your people will live on," Alex said miserably. She wished desperately that she could offer Caradoc more than a vague platitude.

"Then that will have to be enough," he murmured.

"You don't blame me?"

Caradoc pulled her into his arms. "How can I blame you for something fate has decreed? No, love. We will do the best with what fate has allotted us. That is all any of us can do." He slid his hands down her back, pressing her body more firmly against his. "And we will live each moment we are given together to its fullest."

"Yes," Alex murmured as she pulled his lips down to hers. "Yes, we will."

NINETEEN

Alex had never really liked sleeping with a man. She usually stayed awake and worried about whether a ghost was going to show up, and if so, whether she'd slip and somehow let him know a dead person was there—and then the guy would, of course, freak.

Sleeping with Caradoc was nothing like that. It just felt so right to have him next to her. Sleeping in his arms, curled against the side of him, was peaceful. If a ghost had shown up it wouldn't have been a big deal. Caradoc understood her ability to speak to the dead even better than she did herself.

But the dead had left them alone all night, and even this morning no spirit showed up to chatter at her like they would have done back in the modern world. As Alex lay there beside her druid lover, looking up at the pastel colors of the morning sky that peeked between the leaves of the trees surrounding them, she pondered the fact that she really hadn't been deluged by spirits since she'd gone back in time. Yes, sure, she'd seen and spoken with the dead, and she'd helped assuage their fears as they were dying, but they hadn't mobbed her as they had when she'd visited Flagstaff or really anywhere else in the modern world except the tallgrass prairie. Then she remembered how it seemed she had actually pushed the ghosts away from her earlier.

She had to stifle a gasp of surprise and force herself to lie still, versus jumping up and pacing while she thought. *I used the power of the trees to keep the ghosts from overwhelming me, just like I used that same power to see Catus, and finally, to call to me the spirits that frightened me so badly my soul shattered and fled to the Otherworld.*

"What is it, love?"

She shifted in Caradac's arms so that she could look up at him. He was watching her with a sleepy smile. Her first response was to shrug off his question and tell him that "it" was nothing, that she was just woolgathering, as her mother would have said. But then she realized with a little thrill of happiness that she didn't have to shrug off questions; she could actually share this part of her life with him.

"I was just thinking how strange it is that the dead don't overwhelm me here. Well, except for what happened yesterday."

"What happened with the spirits yesterday was because you called the dead to you while you were exhausted, ungrounded and without training." Caradoc's words were stern, but he gently brushed her hair back from her face and then caressed the slope of her neck. His touch soothed as well as reassured her.

"Okay, I understand that. But what I was thinking about was, except for that, the dead have pretty much left me alone. I mean, they do show up once in a while, like your mother, but in my old world I couldn't leave the Tallgrass Prairie without being deluged by them."

"Tallgrass Prairie—what is that?"

She smiled, thinking about the beauty of it. "It's where I work. I'm a botanist and a docent."

He gazed at her questioningly.

"A botanist is someone who knows a lot about plants, and a docent is a guide."

He nodded and looked pleased. "It sounds like a good job for a druid. And you say the spirits of the dead do not overwhelm you there? What is different about this place than the rest of your world?"

"Well, there aren't really many people living there. It's a huge area dedicated to preserving the past and keeping the land as it was naturally meant to be, rather than having a city built on it."

"So it is, in essence, an ancient place among a world of modern marvels."

She nodded in turn. "I suppose you could describe it that way."

"The souls there respect the ancient ways. Blonwen, in this world a Soul Speaker is not at the mercy of the dead. Here you can tap into the power of the spirits of the land to keep the dead at bay, or to call forth those with whom you wish to speak. The dead on your ancient land know that and are following the old ways of the Soul Speaker."

Alex thought about that for a while, soothed by Caradoc's touch and the warmth of his body. She remembered how effortless it had been to push back the spirits with the power of the tree. She could have done that again yesterday, but had been too exhausted to think clearly, and then panic had mingled with her lack of grounding and she'd completely lost control. The more Alex thought about it, the more she knew what she had to do.

"I have to call the spirits of the dead to me again," she told Caradoc. "Or rather *a* spirit of *one* dead. See, that was part of my problem before—I put out this general call for ghosts who

knew Catus, and got many who were filled with hate and bitterness. Not that that's a big surprise, since Catus is a really
awful guy. But I don't need a bunch of spirits. I just need one
who knew him well. Caradoc…" She sat up, reaching for her
chemise and tunic. "I need to call Catus's assistant to me."

"Are you sure he is dead?"

"I had a vision of Catus leaving him behind, and of him
going into Jupiter's temple right before our army got there."

"Then he *is* dead," Caradoc said grimly as he, too, got dressed.

"Will you still help me?"

"I pledged last night to help you," he said solemnly. "And I
will never betray that pledge." His expression lightened and he
kissed her. "First, let us break our fast and ground ourselves,
and then we must go to Boudica and get her permission to lag
behind the army so that you can call the soul of this man who
knew Catus to you."

"She's marching the army out of here already?" Alex asked
in surprise.

"She is. She is following Suetonius."

"That's right! That runner she sent into the city before attacking it said Suetonius had been here."

"He escaped the death that should have been his yesterday,
and Boudica is determined he will not continue to escape it."
Caradoc's voice was filled with a terrible sadness as he went on.
"She is going to take her army after him, and after the legions
toward which he races."

"His legions? You mean the ones that—" Alex broke off.
The pain in Caradoc's eyes didn't allow her to continue.

But he finished for her. "Yes, his legions fresh from the
slaughter on Mona."

"Caradoc, there's something you should know about Suetonius. The team that sent me here believes he is a Centaurian—one of the people who are trying to stop us from finding

all the pieces of the medallion. If they're right, that means he'll stop at nothing to keep me from succeeding."

Caradoc's jaw clenched and unclenched. "Does he know you are here?"

"I'm not certain. I don't think so but..." She hesitated, suddenly remembering the other presence in those long-ago dreams of Caradoc—the presence that kept her from the druid and was definitely malevolent.

"But?" he prompted.

"But I just don't know for sure. The Centaurians have many powers, some we know about, some we can only imagine."

Caradoc pulled her into his arms, surrounding her with his strength and his warmth. "He will have to kill me to get to you."

Alex's stomach tightened in fear. She pulled back and stared into his face. "No! Stay away from him. He's not even human, Caradoc."

Instead of taking her words as a warning, Caradoc seemed to find them amusing. "Well, then he and I are well matched. There are those who do not believe druids are completely human—and many who harbor those beliefs, and fears, are Romans."

"Promise me you'll be careful."

"I am a warrior as well as a druid, love. So I shall promise you that I will be strong."

Alex sighed and thought that men were men, no matter what century it was.

"Let us eat, then find our queen," Caradoc said.

"And what are we going to tell her when we find her?"

"As much of the truth as we are able."

Alex shot him a sharp glance. "Will you tell her that she's not going to win this battle?"

Caradoc looked shocked and shook his head, saying vehemently, "I will not! Boudica's quest is not simply about vengeance for wrongs committed against her. It is a fight for freedom, and it has fired the Iceni and the rest of the Celts with hope. I would not take that hope away from them."

"Some of them live," Alex said, even though the words sounded lame to her own ears.

"And my people will eventually be free?"

Alex nodded, thinking of modern day England and Scotland and Wales, which were definitely not colonies of Italy. "Yes, they will be free."

"Then I choose to let them hold on to hope. I will not lie, but I will not speak of the outcome of Boudica's war. Remember, Blonwen, lies here have a dark power all their own."

Alex sighed and, not saying anything, went to help Caradoc stoke the fire and start breakfast. Sometimes, no matter how much she wished otherwise, she felt like she was one big walking lie.

"And you are quite certain my stolen medallion piece is that important?" Boudica asked Alex.

She nodded soberly, staying with the story of truths and evasions that she and Caradoc had concocted over breakfast.

"It holds the power of matriarchs," Alex explained. And of course, indirectly, it did. Of the human race, only women were intuitive enough to threaten the Centaurians and serve as pilots if they could piece the medallion back together in time to join the galactic federation.

"It being missing from your torque makes the power incomplete." Caradoc took up the thread of the story. "Blonwen's mission is to retrieve the piece and return it to you, with the aid of Andraste."

"I have to cleanse it and get the goddess's blessing on the reunited piece, too, before you wear it again," Alex added.

Then both she and Caradoc waited for Boudica's ruling. As

the druid had predicted, it didn't take the queen long to make up her mind and grant their request.

"Yes, I will allow the two of you to stay behind so that Blonwen might use her gift as a Soul Speaker to locate the other medallion piece." Boudica fingered the empty place in her torque as she spoke. "But do not tarry long. I need those close to the goddess by my side, and we will be riding fast and hard."

The two bowed respectfully and hurried back to Caradoc's campsite. They'd already set out a skin filled with mead and the lavender smudge stick he'd used the night before. In addition, there was a large, noisy chicken sitting beside the campfire in a woven reed cage.

Alex picked up the mead and, following directions Caradoc had explained to her earlier, lit the thick lavender wand and then wafted it around until it was smoking nicely. Then she gave the squawking chicken a leery sidelong glance. "Okay, we might as well get this over with."

Caradoc picked up the chicken in the cage and walked beside her into the forest, the sweet scent of lavender smoke trailing in their wake. "Do not sound as if you are preparing to take on a terrible chore." He smiled at her while they made their way to the stream and the rowan that rested beside it. "You have a great gift in your ability to speak with the dead. It will be an even greater gift when you are able to control it."

"But I'm thirty-five and I haven't been able to control it yet."

Caradoc's eyes widened in shock. "You have lived through thirty-five seasons?"

Alex rolled her eyes. "Yes, almost." She'd forgotten that he was a decade her junior. Okay, she hadn't forgotten it the night before, when they were making love and his amazing body was rock hard and definitely twentysomething versus thirtysome-thing. But other than that he seemed so much older than what she would have normally labeled "a guy way too young."

"But you do not look like—"

Alex put up her hand, stopping him from saying what she was sure would sound like a compliment, but would make her feel like an old hag. "Look, in my world older women have younger lovers. Often," she said firmly. Okay, *she'd* never had a younger lover, but still.

His lips quirked up. "Interesting…"

Alex could feel her cheeks getting warm, and was actually almost glad when she caught sight of the delicate white flowers of the rowan tree. She and Caradoc crossed the stream and stood before the tree. He put down the cage, and took the full mead skin from Alex, setting it on a nearby rock. Then he nodded at her. "Now smudge me, and then yourself, just as we talked of before."

Trying to quell her nerves, Alex began to wave the smoking lavender around Caradoc's body, beginning at his feet, going up the front of his body, and continuing down his back.

"Now smudge yourself," he told her. "Remember to breathe carefully—deep in breaths and deep out breaths. Pull the smoke into your body, and along with it the purifying and protective qualities of the herb."

Alex followed his directions, enjoying the smell of the lavender and the quiet of the forest. When she was finished she ground out the smoking stick and placed it on the rock beside the mead.

"Stand close to the rowan, press your back to it. Think of the tree as your protection and your strength. It is your lifeline to the living earth, in which everything is ensouled."

Alex moved over to the tree and leaned against it. The roughness of the bark felt good, reminding her of its age and strength. It seemed nothing could knock it over, nor break its power.

"You will use the goddess's name to summon the spirit— *one* spirit," Caradoc reiterated carefully. "Proclaim your position as Andraste's priestess when you call the spirit forth. Concentrate your thoughts and the power of the tree on the spirit you summon. This time there will be no mistaking your intent." The druid opened the cage and pulled out the squawking bird, pulling his knife from the sheath strapped to his waist. "This time there will also be a sacrifice as payment for the information you seek."

Alex tried not to look at the chicken. "So none of them will think they can pull my spirit back to the Otherworld with them?"

"Exactly, love. That will never happen again. Are you ready?"

"Yes," she said, more to convince herself than to reply to him.

"Then call forth the spirit you seek, Soul Speaker."

TWENTY

Alex blocked out her nervousness and fears and second thoughts. She lifted her chin and pressed her back, as well as her palms, against the ancient tree that stood like a silent sentential behind her.

"I am a Soul Speaker, and I need your help, ancient one." As Caradoc had instructed her, and as her instincts had led her last time she'd attempted a soul calling, Alex looked to the rowan for the power to fuel her request.

The warmth began slowly, but built to a steady, thrumming tingle that reminded Alex of a heartbeat.

"With the might of this ancient tree, and in the name of the goddess, Andraste, I wish to call the spirit of one recently dead. The one I seek was the assistant to a cruel man. He was young and hardworking, and his name…" Alex paused, thinking back to the vision she'd witnessed. "His name was Flavius. Come to me, Flavius! In Andraste's name I summon you!"

In front of her the air began to quiver, like heat rising from a blacktop road at midday. Then the mirage parted, as would a transparent curtain over a mystical stage, and the veil of reality opened, allowing one lost-looking young man to step through.

"Flavius?" Alex asked. But before he could respond, diaphanous figures of a crowd of spirits, some of whom Alex recognized as malevolent forces from the day before, began to shove through the opening behind him.

"Focus on Flavius and command the other spirits to depart," Caradoc said in a low, intense voice.

Alex swallowed hard and, looking only at Flavius, said in a clear, loud voice, "No! I summoned only Flavius. I command the rest of you depart!" *Oh, please help me,* she silently asked the rowan.

Heat surged through her body and, following her instincts, with her back still pressed to the tree, she lifted her hands and thought about throwing the power that had been building within her out at the spirits. A wave of light the exact color of rowan flowers hit them, tumbling them backward and causing the curtain to the Otherworld to shimmer briefly and then close.

"Did they leave? Did the door to the Otherworld close?" Caradoc asked under his breath.

She nodded.

"Well done, love," he murmured. "Now speak to Flavius and I will ready the sacrifice."

"Flavius, I am Blonwen, Soul Speaker of Andraste," Alex said.

The young man looked at her curiously and then shrugged. "What is it you want with me, Soul Speaker?"

"Were you assistant to the Roman tax collector, Catus?"

The ghost's expression changed instantly. "Catus is an evil man. There are many in the Otherworld who will be very glad to see him join them there."

Although the spirit looked like a harmless guy, little older than a teenager, there was something in his ghostly eyes that made Alex shiver.

"Yes, I know about him. Actually, my question for you has to do with one of the terrible things he's done. Do you remember the medallion piece he took from the Iceni queen, Boudica, when he ordered her beaten?"

Flavius nodded. "I do."

"I need to get that medallion. Can you tell me where it is?"

"I cannot tell you where it is, but I can tell you who has it," said Flavius.

"I would be grateful to know anything about it," she told him.

"You will find it with the monster Suetonius."

Alex's blood chilled. "Suetonius? The Roman who led the attack on Mona?"

The spirit nodded. "He came to Londinium alone, without the might of his legions, because he thought to gloat over the destruction of Boudica by the small Ninth Legion. But when he realized the barbarians were too mighty and that Londinium would be destroyed, he escaped down the Watling Road, running to reunite with the army he'd allowed to stay behind and enjoy the spoils of Mona."

Alex could feel Caradoc's outrage at the spirit's words, but she remained concentrated on Flavius. "How do you know he has the medallion piece?"

"He took it from Catus. I saw him. He and the tax collector spoke in passing as Suetonius was having his horse readied. When he noticed the medallion hanging around Catus's fat neck, the governor flew into a rage." Flavius smiled grimly in remembrance. "It was wonderful to witness. He slapped Catus with the back of his hand so hard that he fell to the floor. Then Suetonius took the medallion from him and hung it around his own neck, saying that he will decorate his himself with Boudica's gold, just as he will decorate the grass of Briton with her blood."

Alex breathed a long sigh of relief. It was bad that Seuton-ius had the medallion, but he must know that he, too, only had part of the prize—which meant he wouldn't be going anywhere until he got his hands on the other piece.

"Thank you, Flavius. You have given me the information I needed," she said, smiling at the young man.

Caradoc stepped forward, obviously following her gaze he walked close to where the spirit was standing. With one quick movement, he twisted the neck of the chicken and then slashed its throat, holding the twitching bird out so that its fresh, warm blood pooled in the moss at his feet.

"Take this blood as a show of the priestess's appreciation for answering her call. When you return to the Otherworld, tell the spirits there that Andraste's Soul Speaker wields the power of the earth. If any would come against her again, she will destroy them. But she does reward those loyal to her call." Caradoc backed away from the pool of blood and whispered to Alex, "When he's finished drinking, command him to return to the Otherworld with Andraste's blessing."

Alex nodded, and then watched in fascinated horror as the ghost fell to his knees and greedily drank the chicken's blood. When he was done he lifted his face, staring around with scarlet-tinged eyes, as if he wanted more and more.

"Return to the Otherworld now!" Alex commanded. "And take with you my thanks and the blessing of Andraste."

The reality veil opened behind him. Flavius reluctantly turned and, wiping his bloody mouth with the back of his hand, walked from one world to another.

Alex turned and pressed her cheek against the rowan. "Thank you so much," she murmured to the ancient tree, and was rewarded with a surge of tingling warmth.

"You must drink the mead and reground yourself quickly, Blonwen." Caradoc was there at her back, supporting her with a strong arm around her waist as he guided her over to the rock where they'd left the mead. She sat beside it, and he opened the skin and handed it to her. "Drink deeply," he said.

She did, and instantly the light-headedness she had been feeling dissipated.

"You did well, love," Caradoc said, taking a long drink from the skin when she was done. "Did I understand correctly? Suetonius has Boudica's medallion piece?"

"He does. He made a big show of taking it from Catus. Flavius says he wears it around his neck for everyone to see."

Caradoc's amber eyes darkened with anger. "Someday soon I will thank him for making it so easy to find that which we seek."

"Caradoc, you have to stay away from him. Suetonius is more dangerous than you can imagine."

"I can imagine very well. I saw his work at Mona. Do you know he impaled priestesses while they were still living?"

Alex shuddered. "No."

"It is something I will never forget, no matter how many lives I live."

"Caradoc, please don't go after him. We'll figure out a way to get the medallion—a way that doesn't involve you taking him on," Alex said.

He surprised her by smiling.

"Love, you are not from this world, so I will not be offended that you have such little faith in my prowess as a warrior. But I assure you, I am skilled and able to protect myself."

"I don't doubt your abilities!" Alex almost shouted. How frustrating that he would take it as an affront to his manhood that she didn't want him to fight the damn alien! "You say that I'm from a different world than this, so I don't understand all I should about you and your awesome warrior abilities. But the same goes for what I've been telling you about Suetonius. He's a creature from another world, Caradoc! At least I'm just from the future." She dropped her head in her hands, feeling completely overwhelmed. "This is all my fault. It's because of me and the stupid medallion pieces that all of this is happening."

Alex felt Caradoc tug at her hands, and reluctantly let him pull them from her face. He was on his knees in front of her.

"Do not ever say that. Do not ever think that. You are not responsible for the evil deeds Suetonius has committed. Yes, he might be here because of the medallion pieces. Did you put them here, Blonwen? And what about the Isle of Mona, and the druids and priestesses there that he slaughtered—did they have the pieces of the medallion?"

"No," she said softly.

"Of course they did not. Suetonius chooses his path, and then Fate guides his feet. It is the same for all of us. Consider this—if the medallion pieces were not here, would Suetonius be in his home world, peacefully living his life?"

Alex considered for a moment and then said, "I don't think so. From what the people who sent me here told me, Suetonius and those like him are at their hearts destructive, violent beings. I don't think it's possible for most of them to find peace."

"Then were he not here, he would be attacking another people in another time."

"Yes, probably."

"What would happen if he fails here? If he doesn't retrieve the medallion pieces?" he asked her.

Alex shrugged. "I'm not sure. His people aren't exactly forgiving, so I would guess he'd be in trouble with them."

Caradoc smiled. "Then if you cause him to be defeated here, are you not responsible for saving a group of people?"

She stared at him.

His smile widened. "You haven't thought of that, have you?"

"No," she said honestly. "I haven't."

"So we defeat him, and by doing so you save the Iceni from

future ravages by him, as well as other nameless peoples *and* the future of your world and mine."

"Well, all the medallion pieces have to be found to actually save the future of the world," she admitted.

"Do your part, love, and the rest will fall into place. I know it in my soul," he said.

"Is it really that simple?"

"That simple and that complex."

Alex laughed. "And to think I told your mom that you were less cryptic than she was."

His smile turned sad. "Is my mother here with us now?"

Alex glanced quickly around and then said, "No, I haven't seen her since I tried to summon Flavius without you. She warned me that I should wait for your help, but she wouldn't give me specifics on how to call a spirit to me."

"She wouldn't know how to summon spirits. My mother was a priestess of Andraste, not a Soul Speaker."

"You're not a Soul Speaker, so how do you know?"

"Were you from this time, Alexandra, you would already understand the answer to that question."

"And that answer is?" she prompted.

"Druids know everything," he said with a cocky grin.

"*Really?* Oh my *word!* I had no idea! I simply must thank you for being here to think for my poor little female self!" Alex batted her eyes and put on her best Scarlett O'Hara accent.

Caradoc lifted a brow. "In your world is that what is called sarcasm?"

"No, in my world that is what is called great acting." Then she giggled as she remembered how often she had attempted a Scottish accent, in honor of Gabaldon's Jamie Fraser, and failed as miserably as she had with a Southern accent. And now, irony of all ironies, she'd been speaking in a perfectly authentic Celtic burr, thanks to Professor Carswell. But she probably wouldn't retain any of it.

"Really?" Caradoc mimicked. "So you're a bard back in your world?"

"Not exactly," she said through giggles.

"Too bad. I've always wanted to seduce a bard."

Alex sobered instantly. "I was mistaken. Back in my old world, I'm definitely a bard."

"Definitely?" he said, eyes shining.

"Absolutely definitely," she stated.

As she started giggling again, Caradoc pulled her off the rock and into his arms, and kissed her until she honestly didn't care whether she'd been a bard, a biologist or a bartender. She simply wrapped her arms around his broad shoulders and kissed him back.

Soon her giggles changed to soft moans and she was pressing her body to his, loving the feel of his hard muscles under her hands.

"Blonwen, would you grant me a boon?" He spoke against her skin as his lips traveled down her neck to the tops of her breasts, barely peeking over the bodice of her tunic and chemise.

"Anything you want," she said breathily, arching back so that he could kiss more of her skin.

"Give me this day and night. Let it be us here, together, without the threat of war or Suetonius, or a future that says we cannot be together."

Alex leaned back and met his gaze. "But we have to follow Suetonius. I have to get that medallion piece."

"And you will, love. *We* will. But we cannot catch him today, even if we left at this moment and rode our horses to exhaustion. We cannot prevent him from reaching his legions. Our confrontation with him will come when Boudica engages him, and not before. That will not happen today, or even tomorrow. So the boon I ask is that you allow us this time together, a day and night we can fill with enough peace and love to last through a lifetime of war and separation."

"I don't want to be separated from you," Alex said softly.

"If the goddess is merciful, you won't be. But can we not gift ourselves with one day to hold dear through all the hard days we know will come?"

"Yes," Alex said firmly. "Yes, we can."

Caradoc's smile was brilliant. He stood and held his hand out to her. "Then come with me and let me show you the magic of my world."

TWENTY-ONE

Caradoc's world was magical—Alex had to give him that.

They'd gone back to his campsite and loaded everything they needed on their horses, and then, without a word to anyone, she had followed him deeper into the forest. He told her they would head in roughly the same direction as the army—northwest—but would detour through one of Briton's densest forests.

"What if we get lost?" she'd asked him.

He'd laughed so hard that he'd had to hold his sides. "Blonwen, love, a druid cannot get lost in a forest."

She frowned at him and tried to pretend she was annoyed that he'd laughed at her, but it was impossible. He was too happy to be angry with. The forest worked on Caradoc like a drug. The stiffness with which he had carried himself disappeared, as did the shadows under his eyes. He smiled. Actually, he smiled a lot.

This was how he must have been before his home was destroyed, she thought as he pointed out to her a different type of rowan, which had red berries instead of white flowers.

Alex adored this Caradoc. Sure, she loved the other parts of him, too: the powerful warrior, the protective lover, the talented druid. But this man—this relaxed, joyful, easygoing man—she adored.

She began to wonder if he would he be like this all the time if he were living in a different time, one where he didn't have to worry about whether he was going to be hunted down and killed or enslaved. A time like the modern United States.

The thought jolted her.

Could he return to her time? As she watched him reach out and caress the leaves on a low hanging oak tree, she could almost see him at the Tallgrass Prairie. He'd love it there, on that land undeveloped by man. Herds of wild bison still ranged there, and by the end of summer the grasses grew so tall they towered overhead like fans of the gods.

What if she went back and had Carswell research Caradoc's life? She'd have to find evidence of his death, and she'd have to retrieve him right before then—but couldn't Alex take him with her if removing him from his time didn't impact history? He *would* find peace on the Tallgrass Prairie. Alex was almost sure of it.

"What are you thinking, love?"

"I was just thinking that you would like my home. There's no sea there, but the land is beautiful."

"If you love the place, then it must be special," he said.

"It is. The Tallgrass Prairie means freedom to me. I think you'd understand that if you could see it."

"I would like to see it," he said. Alex's heart raced, and she was trying to formulate the words to ask him if he would give up his life, his world, and come to hers, when he continued, "I wish I could show you Mona. The way it used to be."

"Tell me about it." *No, now was not the time. She'd ask him later, when she was closer to completing her mission.*

"My isle, 'tis beautiful," he said wistfully. "It was the greenest place on this good earth. The shoreline is rocky where the crystal sea kisses it, but inland is verdant. Streams bubble up from the earth, so pure and clear it sometimes hurt my teeth to drink of them. Sacred groves grew thick and perfumed the air with magic."

He paused and Alex held her breath, waiting for him to continue, aware that he kept shifting tense when he spoke of the home that no longer waited peacefully for him. When he seemed unable to say more, she asked, "What does magic smell like?"

"Magic smells of grass and the sea and moonlit breeze."

"When you say it like that, you make me believe it's true," she said.

He grinned at her. "Follow me, and I'll prove to you it's true." Then he kneed his horse into a rolling canter, and Alex followed him, dodging trees and fallen logs as they went deeper and deeper into the woods.

"Where are we going?" she called to his back.

"To find a stream and a meadow and magic," he yelled over his shoulder, and then with a laugh, urged his horse to a gallop, and there was no more opportunity for talking.

Caradoc found the stream quickly. It babbled through a rocky bed, lined with moss the color of spring grass. Willows wept along it, trailing their sad, delicate branches in the clear water. The spot Caradoc chose to dismount edged a little clearing that was filled with wildflowers so blue it looked as if the sky had sprinkled part of itself over the grasses.

Alex dismounted and waded into the middle of them. "Cornflowers!" she cried with delight. "They're some of my favorite wildflowers, but you don't see them in Oklahoma—it's too hot there for them." She grinned at Caradoc, who was unloading their horses and setting up camp beside the stream. "Is this the magic you were going to show me?"

He grinned back at her. "Aye, 'tis some of it."

"It's plenty!" Among the aquamarine-blue cornflowers, tucked in tufts of dark, emerald green, were bunches of clover complete with puffy reddish flowers. "There's even clover here. In my world finding a clover with four instead of three leaves is thought to be good luck." Alex dropped to her knees and started searching through the patches, breathing deeply and loving the sweet scent of the flowers.

Caradoc's shadow fell over her, and then he was sprawled on the ground beside her, lying back so that he could comfortably watch her sift through the plants. He plucked a clover blossom and, holding her gaze with his own, tucked it behind her ear. "In my world red clover flowers can summon a lover," he said, and handed her the wineskin he'd carried with him.

"Do you feel the need to summon a lover?" She took the skin and drank from it while she watched him watch her.

His smile was long and lazy. "I thought I already had." He pointed at the flower he'd tucked in her hair. "Clover summoning takes time. A tea must be made of the blossoms. For nine days the supplicant must bathe in this tea before dawn, saving the bathwater and pouring it over her head, always rubbing downward and never upward, paying particular attention to her breasts…" He paused, his gaze moving down and lingering on Alex's breasts "…her woman's core and the softness of her inner thighs." As he spoke, his gaze followed his words. Alex's breathing quickened and her cheeks flushed. She could almost feel his gaze as a caress. "On the ninth morning the maiden must carry the washbasin to a crossroads, call the name of the one she desires, throw the clover water toward the rising sun—and very soon, her lover will come."

"Does it always work?" Alex asked, not surprised that her voice sounded a little breathless.

He looked up into her eyes. "As with all magic in my world, if the intention is pure and the priestess is strong enough, it will work."

"What if it's a man and not a woman doing the summoning?"

"It is a woman's spell. Men have other ways of summoning a lover."

"What ways?"

He reached across the space that separated them and traced his thumb over her lip while he stared hungrily at her mouth. "Will you come to me, lover?"

"I can't think of anything I want more," she said.

Alex did go to him. Pressing Caradoc down against the carpet of cornflowers and clover, she straddled him. She took his mouth, kissing him greedily. She tried not to think that this might be the last time they would be truly alone—that the next day they had to catch up with Boudica and the army, and then figure out a way to get the medallion piece from Suetonius so she could return it, and herself, to the modern world, never to see Caradoc again. Alex tried not to think of all that. Instead she concentrated on feelings—on touch and taste and the pleasure she could give Caradoc in the time they had been allotted.

Alex was the aggressor. She couldn't get enough of him. She wanted him with a need that bordered on despair, and that despair coupled with desire and love, lighting a fire within her blood for him. She pulled his tunic off, loving the Celtic tradition of wearing no underclothing. Alex kept straddling him, and when he grabbed her wrists and moved to change positions with her, she pulled back and shook her head, smiling seductively.

"Not this time. This time it's my turn to make love to you."

He pulled her wrist to his lips and nipped her skin playfully, then said, eyes crinkling with humor, "I am indeed a strong druid to have summoned such a demanding lover. I am yours to do with as you will, Priestess." He loosed her wrists and lay back, stretching under her.

In a slow, sensuous movement, Alex began to pull off her tunic. She noticed that almost instantly the teasing went out of his eyes and they began to darken with desire. Sitting astride him in only her sheer chemise, she let her hands play down her body. She shook back her hair, cupped her breasts and arched her back as she tweaked and teased her nipples. His shaft pulsed against her core, hard and hot. Watching his eyes, Alex began to move against him, not taking him within her, but letting her wetness stroke the length of him.

"Ah, gods! You will drive my mind from me!" he growled.

She laughed huskily and leaned forward, trapping his wrists together over his head. "I'll do the touching this time. Will you let me ravish you?" she teased.

"Aye, do as you will with me, you sorceress," he said between clenched teeth.

"It's only right. You called me, remember?" When he opened his mouth to answer her, she brought her breasts to his mouth so that through her chemise he could nip the veiled buds and draw them, and the sheer fabric, between his lips.

Alex moaned. The sensation of his lips and teeth caressing her aroused flesh through the damp material was unbelievably erotic.

"Let me bury myself within you, love," he said roughly against her. "Let me slide my hardness within your soft depths."

"Soon," she whispered. Then she moved down his body until she took him in her hand and stroked him slowly and thoroughly. "You're such a beautiful man," she murmured. "I don't think I told you that yesterday, but I was thinking it. I love your body, Druid. It's strong and tall and perfectly made. And I agree with your mother—you are golden."

His hands were gripping the clover-covered earth in an effort to keep them off her, but there was laughter in his eyes again. "Please assure me my mother is not here, or that shaft you hold will lose its strength."

Alex grinned at him. "We're alone. I promise." Then she took him in her mouth and he gasped, hips straining up. Alex swallowed him, loving the smooth hardness that pulsed in response to her lips and teeth and tongue. She brought him to the edge, and then moved up his body, pulling off her chemise and pressing against him—hot, naked flesh to hot, naked flesh.

When she knew she couldn't bear not to have him for another second, she sat up and guided his hands to her waist. Then, bracing herself with her hands on his shoulders, she took him within her in one long, hard stroke. Both of them cried out at the pleasure of their joining, and then Alex began to move, sliding up and down. Pumping, she drove him into her over and over until she crested a peak of pleasure so intense it was almost painful. And as wave after wave of sensation pulsated through her body, radiating from her core outward, Caradoc cried her name and released his seed into her.

And in that moment, Alex didn't need the druid to tell her she'd made the earth move for him.

TWENTY-TWO

"What are you doing?" Alex asked sleepily as Caradoc stood up and, in one powerful movement, picked her up and started to carry her back toward the camp he'd made by the stream.

"I'm going to show you how a druid worships his lover," he said.

"Okay. I may sleep through it, though." Alex snuggled against his chest and wrapped her arms around his shoulders.

"That I doubt, love."

She yawned. "Is this more of that strong druid stuff?"

"Would you like there to be more of it?" He kissed the top of her head.

"Definitely. I'd especially like it if I could take a nap first."

"No napping yet. There is something I would have you do first," he said.

She gave him a sleepy smile. "Didn't I already do it?"

"Vixen!" he said appreciatively.

"Indeed I am." She snuggled against him again. Truth be told, she didn't feel very vixenlike. At the moment she was too happy to feel anything but a wash of contentment.

She was so amazingly glad she'd found him! And to think she almost hadn't gone to Flagstaff and accepted the stupid mission. She'd almost missed him completely—

Her happy thoughts broke off as reality rushed back in, drowning her contentment.

"Love? What is it?"

"Reality," she said gloomily.

"No reality today. It will keep until the morrow."

She sighed, but didn't say anything else. Hell, she didn't want to consider reality!

He carried her over to the bank of the stream and sat her gently on a moss-covered rock at its edge. Then, naked, he stepped into the crystal water. Alex's toes brushed the surface and she pulled them up quickly.

"Brrr! This is colder than the stream by your old campsite." She raised her brows as he splashed water over himself. "You're going to freeze." Alex hugged herself and considered putting at least some of her clothes back on, and when he started wading toward her she scrambled back. "Oh, no! I'll do the sponge bath version of what you've just done."

He grinned. "I said I would show you some of the magic of my world, did I not?"

"You did," she said guardedly. "Magic does not mean dunking me in cold water, though. There's really nothing magical about that. Right?"

"No, love, there isn't." Caradoc knelt in the stream at her feet and began stirring his hands through the clear, cold water. "As a Soul Speaker and a priestess of Andraste, you are tied to the earth. You understand that, do you not?"

"Yes, well, I understand it enough to know that even in my

old world the land made me feel safe and relaxed—that's why I became a biologist and worked at the tallgrass prairie. It's easier here, though. It's like the land expects me and is already listening."

"That is an excellent way to describe it. The land is listening for you. Well, the way the land listens to you is the same way the waters listen to me."

She blinked at him. "You're going to have to explain that. I thought druids were all earth people."

"It is true that we are all tied to the elements—air, fire, water and earth. Some of us are more closely attached to one element than the others, though we feel the ensouled value of each."

"Selkie…that's a seal."

"Aye." He smiled wryly. "Apparently I reminded my mother of a seal. She used to say I could swim before I could walk properly."

"So what does that mean?"

"It means I can, to some extent, borrow power from the spirit of water, much like you channeled energy from the rowan to open the veil to the Otherworld."

"This I want to see."

"Your wish, love, is as a command to me." Caradoc bowed his head and spread his arms wide, palms down on the water. "Condatis, great god of the waters—father and familiar friend, in your name I ask to share a fraction of this stream's inevitable strength. Not even rock can stand forever against its might. In the name of Condatis, I call upon you!"

The water under Caradoc's hands began to roil. Unbelievably, Alex could see the stream lifting to lap around the druid's forearms, and Caradoc's sun-golden skin literally began to glow. He swirled his arms in the stream, cupped the agitated water and poured it on her toes.

"It's warm!" she gasped.

"It is the magic of my world," he said, holding out one hand in invitation to her.

Alex took his hand and slid off the rock to stand before him in the stream, which was now warm and bubbling around her knees.

"This, my priestess from a distant world, is how a druid worships his lover."

Caradoc bathed her—gently, intimately, erotically. The magic-warmed water was warm oil against her skin. His knowing hands were first gentle, then demanding, and then gentle again. He cleansed her, made sweet, slow love to her there in the water, and as they climaxed together again Alex felt the thrill of power and magic and love all pulse together and join where their bodies joined.

Afterward, they washed each other, and then, wrapped in the cloaks Caradoc carried with them, but still gloriously naked beneath, they sat beside each other, thighs brushing intimately, while they ate a meal of slices of smoked pork, cheese, hard bread and Roman wine.

They talked ceaselessly. Alex loved to hear his stories of the forest, and how each tree and rock, bird and brook, was filled with a unique spirit.

"I'll bet the spirits still exist in my world," Alex said. "I mean, it's obvious on the tallgrass prairie, but I wonder if I came here, to what we call England, if I'd be able to touch a rowan and feel the stirring of its spirit."

Caradoc stared into the campfire without speaking. Then he slowly said, "I think the soul of a land can die from neglect, just as surely as the soul of a man can."

"That makes me really sad," Alex said. She gazed around them at the verdant beauty of the living forest. "It's so hard to believe this isn't all the same, no matter what year it is, or how much time has passed." She met his eyes. "There are still people who believe in the land. I'm sure there are. Maybe all they need is a good teacher to help them bring it alive again."

"What do you propose, love?"

"Come back with me. When this is all over. When I have both medallion pieces and I've returned them to my time—come back with me."

Caradoc closed his eyes as if her words caused him physical pain. When he opened them she saw sadness and loss there. "I already know Boudica does not drive the Romans from our country. Tell me—does the queen survive the war? Does Boudica live?"

Alex wanted to lie to him, but she couldn't. He'd know it, and the lie would ruin the honesty and trust they'd begun to build between them. "No. Boudica doesn't live long after the last battle."

"Is the war a long one?"

"No," she said, remembering Professor Carswell's thorough briefing.

"Then I cannot return to your world with you. The queen's daughters are too young to carry the torque, and even were they older, they may have been too damaged by the Romans' brutality to ever truly be whole enough to lead. The torque will pass to me, and I must wear it for my people, even if they are a people in bondage."

"What if you don't live?" Alex said the words quickly, barely able to stand thinking them. "What if I go back to my time and find out you're killed days or even months after the battle? If you're going to die, couldn't you leave then?"

"You could know this?"

"If your death is recorded in history, and it very well could be. There's a lot we know about Boudica, and you are her heir. There have to be records of what happened to you."

"I do not know. I will have to think on it." He paused and

took her hand before he continued. "You could remain here with me. You're already tied to this world and its goddess. You could have a place here as Andraste's priestess, and as my wife."

"Your wife?"

He lifted her hand to his lips. "Wife, soul mate, companion—you would be all those things."

"Wife?" she repeated, feeling slightly faint.

He chuckled. "Love, would it be easier to simply ask you for a handfast?"

"Handfast?" Her face felt numb and she wondered if she might be having a heart attack.

"A handfast is a marriage vow that is observed for one year. At the end of that year, or even any time during the year, the couple can decide whether they want to continue with a true marriage, or go their separate ways, with no enmity between them."

"A handfast sounds less scary." She'd never really believed she would get married. Ever. And that had been okay, *before* Caradoc. Now it wasn't okay to be without him, but marriage wasn't any less scary.

"Then a handfast it will be!"

Alex's heart was hammering fast in her chest as Caradoc almost leaped up from their place beside the fire and strode over to the packs, pulling from one of them a short sword in a sheath, ornately decorated with Celtic knots that joined to create waves. She stood up nervously, not sure what she was supposed to do. When he rejoined her he began speaking in a deep voice so filled with passion and joy that his words seemed to shimmer around them.

"I do truly desire to handfast with thee. To show my intent I present you with my blade of power." Caradoc dropped to his knee, pulled the sword from its sheath and offered it to her, saying, "Gracious and lovely one—my heart, my love—accept my promise to thee. I pledge this sword, as

I pledge my soul, ever to be in your service. Like this blade, you shall see my love be strong. Like this steel, you shall see my love be enduring. Accept it, love, for that which is mine shall also be yours."

Alex stared at the sword, then into Caradoc's amber eyes. *Listen to your heart....* The words swirled through her mind. Was it really that easy? She knew without a doubt what her heart was telling her. Time and distance and war and turmoil didn't matter between them. She belonged with this man, and she belonged in this world. She'd never belonged anywhere else, and now she knew why. All hesitation and fear gone, Alex accepted his sword and spoke the words that flowed from her wildly beating heart through her soul and out to him.

"I accept your pledge of love, just as I accept the pledge of your blade. You know what is in my heart, and I know what is in yours. I ask in Andraste's name and by the magic of this ensouled place that I will be yours. And, Caradoc, I will stay with you here, in this world. I know beyond any doubt that this is where I belong."

With a glad cry, Caradoc stood. Taking Alex in his arms, he kissed her, blocking out war and time and impossibilities.

As they watched the sun set over the trees in a fiery orange and pink blaze, Alex asked Caradoc the question that had been niggling at the back of her mind ever since she'd automatically evoked Andraste's name during their handfast.

"Isn't there something I should do to formally pledge myself to Andraste—something like our handfast?"

Caradoc spoke hesitantly, as if the words were difficult for him to say. "There is, indeed, an initiation ceremony that a priestess takes part in when she is chosen by a goddess, to show that she, in turn, accepts the path her goddess would have her follow. She is guided in it by a fellow priestess, or sometimes a druid. It should be performed in one of the sacred groves on Mona." His amber eyes were shadowed with grief. "The Romans burned all the sacred groves to the ground. I saw the island turn to fire as I escaped. Mona is no more. The sacred groves are no more."

Alex twined her fingers through his. She lifted his hand, turned it over and kissed his palm and the pulse point at his wrist. Then she leaned forward and kissed his lips tenderly. She held him in her arms, caressing him gently, trying to will comfort from her hands into his body. When she finally felt him relax, she asked, "Caradoc, what is it that makes a grove sacred?"

He tensed for a moment under her hands, but her touch seemed to soothe him, and he finally said, "A sacred grove is a place that has been touched by a god or goddess. Something special has happened there, or there are trees that have been tended lovingly by druids or priestesses. Often stones of power stand in the grove. Or perhaps it is as simple as the fact that it is a place where a god or goddess has spoken so clearly that the words were etched on the very soul of the land."

Alex spoke without thinking. "You mean like here."

She felt the jolt in his body her words caused, and he shifted so that his startled gaze met hers.

"Here?" he said.

Alex nodded. "Right here. It's where you asked me to stay with you, and it's where I finally knew, without any doubt, that with you is where I belong. I heard Andraste's voice telling me to listen to my heart, Caradoc. Right here," she repeated. "So doesn't that make this grove a sacred one?"

Tears pooled in the druid's eyes and he let them spill unashamedly down his cheeks. "Aye, love," he said in a broken voice. "It is a new sacred grove, named thusly by a wise young priestess."

"And you are a druid, right?"

"I am, indeed," he said.

"Then I am asking you to guide me through my initiation ritual so that I can accept the goddess and pledge myself to Andraste," Alex said in a rush.

Caradoc wiped his eyes. "Now?"

"Yes. I need to commit myself to Andraste, just like I committed myself to you today."

"In order to take part in an initiation ritual, you must be prepared to travel to the Otherworld."

Alex felt the color drain from her face. "You mean back where I was shattered?"

"Yes, love, but it will be different this time. You are whole. You are ready, and you have a guide."

Alex swallowed hard. "Well, then. Okay. I want to do this."

"Time passes differently there. Remember that it seemed we were in the presence of the goddess for just minutes, and almost an entire day had passed in the mortal world."

"Do you mean we might be gone a day or two, or are you talking months or years?"

"A day or two is normal, usually no more than that. Are you certain you wish to do this now, love?"

"I'm sure that most of our future is uncertain right now, so I'd like to do it, even if we're a couple days late catching up with Boudica. She can't engage Suetonius for at least a week, and we can't do anything without him and the missing medallion piece. If I perform this ritual right now then I'll be sure of the path I want to follow, no matter what happens."

"I'm not going to let anything happen to you," Caradoc declared.

Alex kissed him and thought, *it's not what might happen to me that I'm worried about....*

"Yes," Caradoc said. "I will guide you through your pledge to Andraste. It would be my greatest honor."

"All right," she said as he pulled her to her feet. "What do I do first?"

"First, you bathe, and bare your skin," he said with a grin.

"Again?"

TWENTY-THREE

With his arm around her, they walked to the stream. "This time your bath is symbolic of a type of death, as you wash one life from you and step naked into another." Caradoc squeezed her shoulder. "What you do now has more to do with spiritual love than erotic love."

"All right. That makes sense."

They were at the bank of the stream, and Caradoc turned to her. "You'll go in the water alone, love. Submerge yourself completely and do not pull yourself up. You must trust me to bring you out of the water, and your old life, into the new. Do you understand?"

Alex nodded. "I'm a little nervous."

Caradoc smiled. "We all were. All will be well, though. You know your goddess awaits you. Think of Andraste and the connection you share with the earth."

Caradoc didn't undress. He simply tied up his tunic and

stepped into the stream. "When you are ready, I will be here for you and we will begin."

Alex undressed slowly, thinking about how she was changing from an old life, where she didn't fit, to a new life. And that, no matter where it took her, this new path was the one she had to follow. She stood naked on the bank, not looking at Caradoc, but taking in the beauty of the darkening forest around her. It seemed right that she was doing this as the day ended. The symbolism for death and rebirth was complete.

She stepped into the stream and didn't flinch at the chill of the water, but she did look at Caradoc with widened eyes.

"Sorry, love. I can't make this easier for you. Part of birth is painful, and I must let this happen naturally for you."

She gave him a nervous smile and then dropped down into the water, cringing automatically at the cold. Alex drew in and released three deep, long breaths, then held a fourth and submerged herself in the stream, lying flat. She wasn't sure what to do with her hands, so let the water lift them until they floated just below the surface.

She wanted to give in to panic, but remembered Caradoc's advice and, holding her breath, thought about Andraste and how much her life had altered as she'd started to understand her connection with the goddess and the earth.

It wasn't just her life that had changed. She herself was different. The bitterness and chip-on-her-shoulder attitude she'd carried around with her since she was six years old was gone, as was the loneliness of not belonging. She truly was being born anew in this ancient world.

Caradoc's strong, warm hands grasped hers and pulled her out of the water and into his own cloak, which he wrapped around her. Lifting her from the stream, he dried her thoroughly, but silently. When he was finished, he said, "Now we must enter the Otherworld through its eastern gate—the gate of new beginnings. We will first confront the gatekeeper. He is an Otherworld guardian. He will challenge you. If your heart is pure, your intention true, you have no need to fear him, just answer him honestly. Do you want to continue?"

"Yes," Alex said firmly.

"Very well." Caradoc unwrapped his cloak from around her. "You must present yourself to the goddess naked, showing the purity of your intentions."

Alex nodded.

"I will be beside you the whole way. Remember, Andraste has already chosen you and blessed you. You have nothing to fear."

"I'll remember," Alex said, though her lips were so cold they felt numb.

"Then we shall go." Caradoc walked to the eastern edge of the meadow and stood with Alex between two huge oaks that had grown so close to one another their branches were intertwined.

"The oaks are the perfect frame for the gate to the Otherworld. Their magical properties are healing, strength and longevity. Concentrate on these two old ones who have stood entwined together for generations, and open the eastern gate to the Otherworld."

For a moment Alex stood there feeling lost and confused and completely inadequate, and then the air to her right shimmered and Caradoc's mother materialized.

Your soul knows what to do, child. Listen to it....

"Thank you," Alex said softly to the ghost. Caradoc's brows lifted, but he didn't speak. Alex stepped between the two huge trees, spread her arms and placed the flat of her hands on their trunks. "I'd like to go through the eastern gate to the Otherworld and find my goddess. Would you please help me open it?"

Her hands began to tingle immediately and the air in front of her, which had been until then a soft even breeze, intensified until it blew around her in a mini-tornado, lifting her hair.

The element associated with the east is air, Caradoc's mother explained. *Though you are not as tied to it as you are the earth, it has responded to your call. You may ask it to open the gate for you.*

"Air, I ask in Andraste's name that you open the eastern gate to the Otherworld for me."

A huge gust buffeted Alex, blinding her with its intensity, and when she opened her eyes she saw in front of her a marble stairway that led up to a white marble door that seemed to lead only to the sky.

"You did well. And now we face the guardian," Caradoc said, taking her hand. They climbed the stairs and he opened the door. But before they could step through, a dark form, hooded in a cowled robe and holding a long, wicked looking sword, moved to block their entrance.

Who comes to the gate?

The voice alone chilled Alex's blood, but she lifted her chin and said, "I do. I'm…" She paused. Who was she?

If you do not know your true self, you will not be admitted to Andraste's presence. Go away, mortal! For you are not ready to serve our goddess.

"Oh, bullshit! I know who I am, but it's a little more complicated for me than just being one person—like just being a guardian," Alex said disdainfully. It totally pissed her off that this guy sounded like the last condescending, patronizing, wet-behind-the-ears lieutenant she'd had to work for and take orders from simply because she was enlisted and he was an officer. Whatever.

The guardian drew himself up to his full height so that not only did he tower over Alex, but he was a good two feet taller than the Celtic warrior who stood at her side. *Then speak your name, impertinent mortal, before I tire of your presence.*

"My name is Alexandra Patton and I am known in this world as Blonwen. *Both* are my names."

Alex could almost swear she heard the guardian sigh.

And who speaks for you?

"It is I, Caradoc, sworn to the service of Condatis, God of the Waters."

I know you, Druid. Are you quite certain you wish to speak for this impertinent mortal woman?

Caradoc's lips twitched, but his voice was sober when he answered. "Yes, I am quite certain."

The cowled figure turned his attention back to Alex, and in one blindingly quick motion, pressed the blade of the sword he held against the skin over her naked heart.

You are about the enter a place of power, a place beyond imagining, where time has no meaning, where birth and death, dark and light, joy and pain, meet and make one. You are about to step between the worlds, beyond time, outside the realm of your human life. You who stand on the threshold of the Otherworld, have you the courage to make the journey? For know it is better to fall on my blade and perish than to make the attempt with fear or subterfuge in your heart!

Alex forced herself not to tremble, and answered with the words that lifted from her heart into her mind. "I enter the Otherworld with love and honesty and trust in my heart."

The guardian lifted the sword and, with a mighty stroke, brought it down in an arc, embedding the point of it into the marble at Alex's feet. Then he bowed to her and stepped aside.

Then enter the Otherworld, and the presence of your goddess.

Alex stepped into a meadow completely ringed by ancient trees. In the center was a many tiered fountain that bubbled musically.

"This seems familiar to me," she whispered to Caradoc. "But I don't know how it could."

He took her hand. "It is Andraste's meadow, where I came to retrieve the shattered parts of your soul. You have been here before—you just weren't whole. Have courage." He squeezed her hand and then let go. "I have to present you to each of the guardians of the four directions. We begin with the east, and Air. Have courage."

Caradoc led her straight ahead to the east edge of the meadow. "Hail, Guardian of Air, behold Alexandra Patton known as Blonwen, who will be made Priestess of Andraste!"

The trees quivered, then their branches began to dance in a riotous wind. A beautiful woman moved forward out of the forest shadows. Alex noticed her feet did not touch the ground. Her hair was blond and so bright it almost hurt Alex's eyes. She was wearing something wrapped around her body that had no real color or texture, but still somehow covered her. With a start of surprise, Alex realized she was literally wearing air. The woman lifted her hand, palm up, and a crystal bubble appeared on it.

Behold, life from change and death.

Inside the bubble a chrysalis materialized, then broke open to expose a magnificent Monarch butterfly. Its spread wings burst the bubble and it fluttered gracefully away.

Caradoc bowed to the elemental, and turned Alex to the right, leading her to the southernmost part of the meadow. "Hail, Guardian of Fire, behold Alexandra Patton known as Blonwen, who will be made Priestess of Andraste!"

The forest shadows burst into orange light and a woman stood there, her glowing body wrapped in a diaphanous piece of cloth that Alex thought was the exact shade of candlelight. Her hair was fiery red and her eyes a deep amber that reminded Alex suddenly of Caradoc and his mother. The guardian smiled.

Well met, son of Eilwen.

Caradoc, not so formal with Fire, nonetheless bowed to her, but also smiled warmly. The elemental then turned to Alex. From the air she plucked a flame-colored rose and handed it to her.

Behold the rose, but beware its thorns.

As if on cue, one cruel thorn pierced Alex's finger. Automatically, she dropped the rose, which disappeared, as did the Fire guardian. Caradoc turned her to the right again and led her to the westernmost part of the meadow circle.

"Hail, Guardian of Water, behold Alexandra Patton known as Blonwen, who will be made Priestess of Andraste!"

The air rippled and, in a joyous rush of sea-blue water, a lovely woman was carried to the edge of the trees. Her skin was the color of the Mediterranean, her hair the green of sea plants. Her almond shaped eyes were sapphire depths. She was wearing crystalline water that wrapped snuggly around her body and was perfectly transparent. Her smile when she saw Caradoc was radiant.

Caradoc! My father will be pleased that you summoned me here! She turned her smile on Alex, and the feelings of jealousy Alex had been harboring instantly evaporated. *Ah, Priestess! So it is you who has won the heart of our druid. I wish you both the blessings and the bounty of the sea.*

The water elemental opened her hand to expose a shell that spiraled round and round to a point, that then seemed to spiral out again. *Behold how life never truly ends.* Instead of handing the shell to Alex, she gave it to Caradoc, saying, *I give you this gift, Druid, as it will just disappear should she touch it.*

Caradoc bowed deeply to her and the water elemental washed away, leaving her laughter to echo on the departing waves.

"One more," Caradoc said as he turned Alex again to her right and the northernmost part of the meadow. "Hail, Guardian of Earth, behold Alexandra Patton known as Blonwen, who will be made Priestess of Andraste!"

This time the guardian literally lifted from the ground at the edge of the forest. The Earth elemental was no less beautiful than the other guardians. Her skin was smooth and brown, and her body was decorated with raw crystals, leaving her full breasts and her round, generous hips naked.

Priestess, you and I have already begun to know one another. Earth's smile was warm, and reminded Alex of how she wished her mother would have smiled at her after she'd learned Alex could see dead people. *Know that you are close to my bosom, Priestess. Call upon me, and I will always try to strengthen you.* The Earth elemental held up her hand, in which was a lacey, insect-eaten oak leaf. *Behold how life feeds on life.*

"Thank you," Alex said, and as Caradoc bowed to Earth, the elemental crumbled and was absorbed back into the ground. Alex sighed, sorry to see her go so soon. "Now what?" she asked Caradoc.

Now you approach your goddess and, if you accept my charge, swear your life to my service.

Alex turned around to see Andraste standing beside the fountain in the middle of the meadow. And at the sight of her, so mysterious and yet so familiar, everything within her rejoiced.

TWENTY-FOUR

Caradoc took her hand and led her to stand before the goddess.
Greetings, child.

Alex thought the goddess was the most exquisite thing she had ever seen, and had to clear her throat before she could even speak. Finally, she managed to murmur, "Andraste, I'm sorry that for so much of my life I've been confused, and I didn't even know you."

The goddess smiled tenderly. *Are you so sure you did not know me, child? I always knew you, though your journey to me has been a long one.* Before Alex could answer, Andraste continued, *Are you ready to swear into my service?*

"I am," Alex said with no hesitation.

Then I charge you with this triple oath—to honestly seek to walk my path, to hold to the truth, and to revere and protect nature as well as your sister priestesses and brother druids.

"That's all?" Alex blurted in relief, thinking that she had been prepared to literally slay dragons to be in the goddess's service.

Andraste lifted one perfect brow. *I believe that is quite enough for several lifetimes, child. Do you accept my oath?*

"Yes, I do."

Then the goddess did something that utterly shocked her. She knelt and kissed Alex's feet, saying *Blessed are your feet, that brought you to me.* Andraste, Goddess of War and Vengeance, then lifted her head and kissed Alex's knees. *Blessed are your knees, that kneel at my sacred altar.* The Goddess of the Celts, Mistress of Forests, kissed Alex's core. *Blessed is your sex, without which mortal man would not continue.* The Great Goddess stood and kissed each of Alex's breasts. *Blessed are your breasts, formed in strength and beauty.* Andraste then kissed Alex on the lips and said gently, *Blessed are your lips, which shall speak my sacred rituals and lead the people in my blessings.* Finally, the goddess took Alex's right hand, turned it over and kissed the middle of her palm. *And blessed is this hand, which shall proclaim to all who see it that you have been chosen as High Priestess in my service.*

Amazed and filled with the warmth and power of the goddess's blessing, Alex looked down at her right hand to see the same deep blue spiral that she'd noticed on Caradoc's mother's palm. It now decorated her palm, too, and proved to every ancient Celt that she was truly a High Priestess of Andraste. Then the goddess made a sweeping gesture that took in Alex's naked body, from her feet to the top of her head.

This priestess belongs to me! she shouted in a voice that rang throughout the meadow.

Alex dropped to her knees before her and bowed her head. "Thank you, my goddess. I'll try really hard not to disappoint you."

Rise, child, and take with you this token of my protection.

She stood up and the goddess handed her an amethyst crystal wrapped in a delicate silver chain. Alex heard a small sound of surprise from beside her, and she looked at Caradoc.

Ah, Druid, I see you recognize the homage piece you paid me the last time you visited my realm, Andraste said to him.

"I do, Goddess," he said.

As it still holds your heartbeat, I thought it an appropriate token to give to this particular priestess. Andraste waved her fingers and the necklace disappeared, to reappear around Alex's neck, the purple stone resting between her breasts. She closed her hand around it and could still feel the steady thump–thump of Caradoc's heart. And then, as she was still holding the crystal, it warmed and magically turned liquid, literally soaking into Alex's skin and her heart beneath.

Alex didn't realize she was crying until the goddess asked, *What troubles you, child?*

She looked into Andraste's bottomless eyes and saw power and passion, as well as understanding and love.

"I'm afraid I won't be able to stay here, and I know this is my home." Alex gazed at Caradoc, who was watching her with a strained expression. "And I want to be with him, but when I really think about it, instead of just listening to my heart, it seems impossible."

Come, child, gaze into my fountain. Perhaps you will find your answer there. Andraste led Alex over to the bubbling fountain, from which shining crystal water cascaded with a sound too beautiful for mortal description. The goddess passed her hand over the surface and told Alex, *Look and think of your heart's desire.…*

Alex took a deep breath, thought *Caradoc is my heart's desire,* and gazed into the water.

What she saw amazed her. Though the two of them looked different in each scene, she saw image after image of Caradoc and her. Sometimes they were children playing together; sometimes she caught glimpses of passionate teenagers clinging together as they discovered the first ecstasy of physical love. She saw them around the ages they were now, only in the vision she glimpsed she was heavily pregnant, with two young children playing by a fireplace. And she saw herself and Carador in their old age, stooped, but still sitting close beside one another, hands and hearts linked.

Then the water rippled and the images were gone. It was then Alex realized what she hadn't seen.

Andraste didn't say anything, seeming to wait for Alex's question.

"I saw Caradoc and me together in many different lifetimes, but none of them were who we are now."

That is because your decision hasn't been made yet. Fate has set events in motion, but you still have free will—you still have choices. Clearly, my sweet priestess, you have not truly made your choice.

"But I have made my choice!" Alex said, not looking at Caradoc. "I pledged myself to Caradoc. I love him!"

The goddess nodded. *You do love him.* She glanced at Caradoc and smiled warmly. *And he loves you, too.* Still gazing at the druid, the goddess's eyes widened almost imperceptivity. *I see that you have a decision to make, too, child.*

Caradoc appeared surprised. "I have made my choice. As you said, I love Blonwen and have this day handfasted with her."

But love is often not enough. The goddess looked kindly from Caradoc to Alex. *Duty and the world often intrude, and the two of you have more worlds to deal with than most. Still, remember that you do have a choice. Fate spins the thread, but you can often use it to stitch together a life garment of your own dreams and desires.*

Alex opened her mouth to ask the goddess to please explain. What exactly had Fate spun, and how could she make things work with Caradoc. But the goddess had begun to change. Surprised, Alex watched as the lovely woman she'd pledge to began to shift her appearance from mother, to maiden, and then, jarringly, to a very old woman.

You must return, child. Time has passed while you have been in my presence, and you have a task you must complete below. I have made a way for you there.... Andraste waved her arm toward the edge of the woods directly in front of them. The darkness within the forest wavered and a path suddenly appeared leading into the trees, illuminated as if a playful summer sun shone down on it. *Follow my path and you will emerge where you are needed.* The goddess shifted form to a maiden, who smiled mischievously at Alex. *I would not have my newest priestess be made a spectacle of, though. This, then, is another gift from me to you.* Andraste flicked her fingers at Alex. The air around her shimmered, and then Alex, who'd completely forgotten that the entire time she'd been naked in the presence of the goddess, felt the weight of clothes settle over her body. She looked down to see that she was wearing a moss-green tunic and chemise that was embroidered with rowan flowers.

"Oh! It's beautiful! Thank you, Andraste!"

You please me, child. Stay true to yourself, and you will continue to please me. Her gaze turned to Caradoc. *Son of my beloved Eilwen, I charge you to care for my priestess.*

Caradoc bowed his head. *It is a charge I am honored to accept.*

Go then, and blessed be....

The goddess disappeared in a shower of diamond sparks.

"Come, love, let us follow the goddess's path together."

"That's what I want more than anything—to follow the goddess's path with you." Alex took his hand and together they walked into the woods of the Otherworld, following the illuminated path of Andraste.

They stepped off the Otherworld path and into a misty morning, soft and pale in a predawn eastern glow. Feeling a little disoriented, Alex looked wonderingly down at herself. Yes, her tunic was the gorgeous green one she remembered Andraste giving her.

"It wasn't a dream, love," Caradoc said.

She met his eyes and opened her right hand, palm toward him. "It is really there?"

He glanced at her palm and smiled. "It is, indeed."

Alex turned her hand over and caught her breath at the wonder and beauty of the spiral circle that danced around and around it. "I am High Priestess of the goddess Andraste." She spoke slowly, savoring each word.

"You truly are," Caradoc said.

Before he could pull her into his arms, half-naked warriors, fierce and formidable with their ancient tattoos and their weapon laden bodies, seemed to materialize from the fog surrounding them.

The lead warrior, a woman with blazing red hair, a golden breastplate and a torque of power, strode up to them and clasped Caradoc's arm.

"You came! I worried for you, kinsman," Boudica said.

"We had the goddess's business to attend to," Caradoc said, returning his cousin's embrace.

Boudica turned to Alex. "Blonwen, well met. Just when I had begun to despair that you would not be here to bless us before our great battle, I was gifted with a dream from Andraste. In my dream I saw you in a meadow before a fountain, and the goddess was marking you as high priestess." The queen reached for Alex's right hand. When she saw the spiral circle her smile was fierce, and she lifted Alex's hand for all the warriors to see. "I told you Andraste would not forget us! Blonwen has returned after a fortnight, bearing the goddess's marking!"

As the crowd cheered, Alex mouthed the word *fortnight!* to Caradoc, who blinked in obvious shock.

"Blonwen, High Priestess of Andraste, the Roman legions await our charge, which I will lead as the sun rises behind us. Would you bless us now, as dawn—and our fate—are upon us."

"Now? The battle is now?" Caradoc said.

"It is, cousin," Boudica said. "We have trapped Suetonius and his legions in a narrow valley just through there, past where the people have drawn the wagons. There is forest on either side of him, and a rocky cliff behind him. The only way out is through us, and we shall not give way to him."

"What are the legions' numbers?"

Boudica smiled that fierce grin of hers that was at the same time frightening and wildly beautiful. "We outman, *and outwoman* him, almost three to one."

Alex felt as if she were in the middle of an avalanche. They'd been gone *two weeks.*

"And yet the governor allowed you to trap him here?" Caradoc was saying, as if he couldn't quite grasp all that his queen was telling him.

"Allowed!" Boudica sounded indignant. "We have cornered him like the mad dog he is, and now we will rid our land of this Roman pestilence once and for all."

Caradoc locked his gaze with Alex. "Do you understand what is happening here?"

Alex knew what he was really asking her—if this was the final battle history reported, one that Boudica did not win.

"Yes," Alex said solemnly. "I do understand."

"And will you bless us before we go into battle, High Priestess?" Boudica asked, eyes shining.

"It's the only thing I can do," Alex said.

TWENTY-FIVE

The blessing ceremony was a blur to Alex. Later she would remember the warmth of the rowan tree and the way it made the spiral circle on her palm tingle. Her voice had been magically amplified so that the simple blessing that came gently to her mind echoed through the clearing mist, reaching even the families that barred the exit to what would become known as the Valley of Death. Boudica embraced her when she finished the blessing and she could literally feel the power radiating from the queen.

As Boudica shouted for the warriors to come to the killing field, Caradoc appeared at Alex's side with a skin of strong red wine.

"Drink deeply. You have not grounded yourself after our return from the Otherworld," he said to her as the tide of excited warriors swept them after Boudica. Caradoc put his arm around Alex, steadying her while they moved forward. She drank deeply, leaning closely to him. "It is a trap," he whispered to her.

She nodded.

"The legions have lured her here. They mean the attack to be on their terms, not ours."

She nodded again. "Here they can finally use the legions' phalanx maneuvers against the warriors. The Romans are a killing machine."

They stepped out of the trees and Alex gaped at row after row of Celts, all battle ready and barbarically ferocious. Behind them, to the east, was the open end of the valley, except that today it wasn't open. Lined across the exit, several deep, were wagons and carts, livestock, old men and women—and children. A great cheer went up as Boudica climbed up into the golden battle chariot that awaited her.

"No…" Caradoc's voice was filled with horror, but the word was drowned by the shouts of the Celts. His fingers dug into Alex's arm. "The people block our retreat," he whispered frantically.

"Yes." Alex felt as if she would be sick. "Our army can't get out. They're slaughtered, along with many of their families."

"I have to tell her!" Caradoc cried. "She has to stop it!" He sprinted forward, trying to get to his cousin, but his way was blocked by a press of her most faithful warriors, so that all he and Alex could do was to watch helplessly as Boudica faced her army and raised her arm for silence.

"Ah, gods," Caradoc said in a broken voice filled with despair. "There truly is no stopping this."

Alex held him tightly, her gaze riveted by the Celtic queen. She was a glorious sight, and knowing what would become of her broke Alex's heart.

Boudica spoke in a voice filled with the power of the righteousness of her cause. "It is not as a woman descended from noble ancestry that I come before you today, but simply as one of the Iceni. I am avenging lost freedom, my scourged body and the outraged chastity of my daughters. Roman lust has gone so far that not our very persons, nor even age or virginity are left unpolluted. But the goddess is on the side of righteous vengeance. A legion that dared to fight has perished. The rest are hiding themselves behind shields, or are thinking anxiously of flight. They will not sustain their courage against even the din and the shout of so many thousands, much less our charge and our blows.

"My people, if you weigh well the strength of the armies, and the causes of this war, you will see that in this battle we must conquer or die. I shall never let a foreigner bear rule over me or over my countrymen, never let slavery reign on this island. I will either live free or die free, but I will be free!"

The Celts answered their queen with such a passionate cry that it lifted the small hairs all over Alex's body. She wanted to rush to the battlefield with Boudica and fight for freedom, too!

Then an ominous, rhythmic sound began at the opposite end of the valley where the rising sun was beginning to cast golden light on shields and helmets. Like a human battering ram, the legions moved forward together, shields locked, deadly spears held at the ready, as somewhere behind the front lines meticulously trained soldiers banged sword hilt on shield.

As if drawn by the hand of her goddess, Alex's head turned and her eyes left the terrible phalanx of soldiers. On the edge of the rocky hill, behind and above the army, sat a tall man on a stallion black as pitch against the blushing dawn sky. He wore a crimson cape over his silver breastplate and was flanked by officers who held tall eagle standards with spread wings. As Alex stared at the man, a ray of sunlight touched the amulet he wore around his neck on a gold chain, and it sparkled as if winking at her.

"It's Suetonius, and he's wearing the amulet," she told Caradoc, pointing across the field at the general. "How will we get to him?"

"It is better he is there than within the phalanx. We would never reach him otherwise. At least on the hill he is flanked only by a handful of soldiers." Caradoc stared at Suetonius. "You said he is not human, not as we are?"

"He's humanoid, but definitely not as we are."

"And his race is determined to exterminate ours in the future?"

"Yes."

"They must be arrogant creatures," Caradoc said.

Alex snorted. "The woman who told me about them said that they believe the universe is theirs by right to rule. Every other race should be their slaves."

"They sound like Romans."

"They're worse," Alex said.

Caradoc narrowed his eyes. "Which tells me we can use his arrogance against him. Could I get close enough to taunt him, I promise you he would engage me, and that means I could draw him away from his officers."

"I like your plan, especially as it's the only one we have." *And especially as you won't be the one drawing him away,* she added silently.

She and Caradoc slipped into an opening in the front line of warriors and finally had a clear view of Boudica. "By the way," Alex whispered to him, "the Roman Empire falls. They're not even a superpower in my time."

Caradoc's smile was grim. "Though it's far in the future, that pleases me to know."

Then their attention was pulled back to Boudica as the Celts shouted again, and Alex watched as Mirain and Una rode through the parted ranks in their own chariot to join their mother. Both girls had on battle armor, and both were brandishing swords.

"No!" Alex cried. "Boudica is going to die today. Most of these people are going to die. The girls can't ride into battle with her." Alex grabbed Caradoc's arm and started forward. This time there was no press of warriors to stop them, and they sprinted to the queen's chariot. She was calling last-minute instructions to Aedan and the rest of her most trusted warriors.

"Boudica, I must speak with you," Alex called.

"Aedan, ready the archers. Have the Trinobante charioteers follow the archers on my command. You and my personal guard will join them." The queen leaped gracefully from her chariot and strode to Alex and Caradoc. "Has the goddess sent a message to me?" Boudica asked eagerly, so certain of her victory to come that she made Alex's heart hurt.

She cannot turn back now. Even if I told her the army was doomed, Boudica couldn't get the families out of the way in time to get free of the legions. And with a sudden, terrible intensity, Alex hated that she knew the future, and wished, no matter what might happen to her, that she could believe Boudica and her Celts would win.

"I do have a message from Andraste," Alex said quickly, forcing herself to look the queen in the eye. She wasn't lying— not really. Andraste couldn't want the girls to die. "The goddess doesn't want your daughters in the battle." Alex glanced to where they stood in their chariot, slender, white-faced girls hardly more than children. "They have seen enough violence. Andraste asks..." Alex shook her head and corrected herself. "No, the goddess *commands* that Mirain and Una not witness any more fighting."

Boudica studied Alex with her sharp green eyes. "Would it satisfy the goddess if I sent my daughters to join the rest of the families?"

"No," Alex said firmly. "Mirain and Una need to be away from this valley."

Alex saw it then, the flicker that went through the queen's eyes. Boudica knew what Alex was telling her. At that moment she understood her people would, at the very least, not take the day against the Romans. Alex watched her process the knowledge and then make her decision.

"Caradoc, I ask your oath that you will take my daughters to safety, and I charge you with their care until I am reunited with them."

Alex saw the emotions pass over Caradoc's expressive face. She could see the regret that once again he would be leaving a battle to others to fight. She also saw grief as he gazed on his queen and cousin for what he was realizing would be the last time. And then she saw acceptance.

"You ask, my queen, and I give you my oath that I will protect your daughters until we meet again."

Boudica squeezed his shoulder. "Thank you. By doing this you do me the greatest service of any of my men." She stepped away from him and called, "Mirain! Una! Come to me!" The girls instantly jumped from the chariot and jogged to their mother. She put an arm around each one. "You are going to go with Caradoc and Blonwen. It is the goddess's wish that you leave this valley and witness no more violence."

"But Mother, I will fight! You promised that I—"

"Mirain!" Boudica cut off her oldest daughter's tirade. "You will do as your queen commands so that you may one day be a wise ruler. And a wise ruler is one who doesn't thirst for blood, but only raises a sword to protect herself and her people."

"But that is what I *am* doing," Mirain said through gritted teeth. "I am raising my sword to protect myself and my people."

Boudica's face softened. "I know, child. Today I will be your sword." She touched Mirain's face. "The battle will be easier for me if I know my world is safe, and the two of you *are* my world." She turned to Una, who was crying silently. "Ah, little one, now is not the time to weep."

"You're sending us away because you're going to die," Una sobbed.

"She's sending you away because Andraste spoke through me and commanded the two of you leave the battlefield," Alex said.

"That's a lie! There is no goddess, and if there is, Andraste doesn't care about us!" Una retorted.

The air beside Una shimmered and Caradoc's mother materialized. She smiled sadly at Una and told Alex, *This child belongs to Andraste. Take her hand, Priestess, and show her that her goddess does, indeed, exist and care for her.*

Following the ghost's words and her own instinct, Alex stepped forward and grasped Una's little hand in her own. The child jumped and cried out as heat flowed through Alex's hand into hers. Then she pulled away, rubbing her palm against her tunic as if it still stung.

"Blonwen, what is this about?" Boudica asked.

"Show your mother your palm," Alex told Una.

The child turned her hand over. Her eyes widened and she gasped as she saw the spiral circle that marked her as belonging to Andraste.

Boudica's laughter was joyous. She lifted her youngest child off the ground in a crushing embrace. "You belong to the goddess, little one!"

Una was still crying, but when her mother finally released her she walked over to Alex and met her gaze. "The goddess has chosen me, even after what she allowed to happen?"

Alex squatted down so she could look at the child eye to eye. "The goddess didn't *allow* anything except free will. We get to make our own choices, so bad people choose to do bad things. That also means you can choose not to let rape define you. Choose Andraste and life, Una."

"I do." Una smiled tremulously through her tears. "I choose Andraste."

"You have made me very proud, my little one." Boudica embraced both girls. "Both of you make me very proud." She kissed her daughters and then, smiling, turned to Caradoc. "Lift Una to your shoulders and show the people that the goddess is with us!"

The druid did as his queen commanded, putting the child on his shoulders and carrying her to face the mass of Celts. Una raised her hand, palm out to her people, and when they saw the spiral circle, they began to chant, "Andraste! Andraste!"

Boudica moved closer to Alex as Mirain followed Una and Caradoc. She whispered quickly, "Is the war doomed, or is it just me who will not live out the day?"

Alex met the queen's gaze again. She would not lie to her, but she had to leave her with some hope. "You will be with Andraste this time tomorrow," she said. Then added, "I promise you the Celts will be a free people."

Boudica drew a deep breath and then released it in a sigh. "That is all I have asked for, and now, with your warning, I know my daughters will survive me. Thank you, Blonwen, for coming to me and being the goddess's voice. I shall see you again someday in brighter times, in the meadows of our goddess." She clasped her forearm, while Alex fought back tears.

"It has been an honor to know you, my queen," she said.

"I charge you to aid Caradoc in caring for my daughters," Boudica declared. "Guide them to be true and strong. Teach them that we cannot allow our past mistakes to dictate our future." The woman's eyes were shadowed with regret. "It is a lesson I learned too late. Do not let it be so for my daughters."

Before Alex could answer her, the queen whirled around and strode to Caradoc and the two girls, waving and smiling at her people as they continued to cheer.

Behind them, Alex could hear the Roman phalanx moving into position.

TWENTY-SIX

The battle began as Boudica ordered the archers to let loose a rain of arrows that darkened the morning sky. Alex and Caradoc were hurrying the two girls back to where the families had barricaded the entrance, and exit, to the valley.

"Don't look. Just keep moving forward," Caradoc said.

Alex didn't know whether he was talking to her or to the girls, but she couldn't reply. Her heart ached too much to speak. She had to leave Caradoc. Immediately. She couldn't go with him to carry the girls to safety. She couldn't take the chance that Suetonius would still be there when she managed to return to the valley. Carswell had told her that the knowledge of Boudica's end was sketchy, but historians pretty much agreed she'd survived the battle, to poison herself afterward. What if history hadn't been able to record exactly what happened to Boudica that day because the Centurian had found her body, taken her torque of rule and the other medallion piece, and no one left alive recognized the corpse was Boudica's without her proof of leadership?

Alex had to lose Caradoc and the girls and make her way through the forest to Suetonius. She had to get that medallion piece.

And if she did manage to wrest it from Suetonius, what was she going to do about Boudica's piece?

I'll worry about that then. At least I have free access to the queen.

"Quickly, Blonwen." Caradoc was helping the girls mount two of the four horses that had been hastily packed for them. "We need to go before…"

The druid had been speaking softly, for Alex's hearing only, but he couldn't complete the sentence: *before it becomes obvious their mother and their people are going to be slaughtered.*

Caradoc led the way. The two girls rode sturdy horses, with Alex bringing up the rear. They turned to the north, circling around the battlefield through the woods until they burst from the trees onto the Watling Road. There Caradoc pulled up and trotted back to Alex, calling to the girls to wait where they were.

"Do you have any idea where we are?" Alex asked him.

"Luckily, yes. We are in Dobunni land. My mother's brother ruled the Dobunni when I was a boy. Before I left for Mona, I hunted these woods often. And traveled up and down the Watling Road to visit kinsmen." Caradoc looked around, obviously getting his bearings. "Through there—" he pointed "—we will find an old shepherd's hut as the land gets hillier. We can take the girls there, be sure they are safe, and then return here to find Suetonius and your medallion piece."

"It's a good plan, Caradoc," she said. Alex wasn't going to lie to him, and she didn't. His idea was good—just not good enough.

"We'll ride hard, and return here before midday."

She nodded. He trotted over to the girls and explained they

were going to be traveling hard and fast through the woods, and to stay close.

"And don't look back," Alex added. "I'll be right behind you. You girls just concentrate on following Caradoc and not letting a branch knock you off your horse."

"Blonwen, am I truly a priestess of Andraste?" Una asked, her face still marked by her recent tears.

Alex smiled at her. "You are, sweetheart. And someday soon I hope I'm able to be your guide to the Otherworld so that you can pledge yourself officially to the goddess."

"May I go, too? Even though Andraste didn't choose me?" Mirain asked shyly.

Alex didn't hesitate. She knew deep in her soul she was speaking her goddess's will. "Yes, you can, Mirain. Pledge yourself to the goddess, and she will accept you, as she did your sister."

"We must ride now," Caradoc said, not unkindly.

Alex met his eyes. "Okay, let's go. And don't you worry about looking back, either. I'll be here, but my heart will be with you."

Una giggled and Mirain watched with open curiosity as Caradoc kneed his horse over to Alex, leaned and kissed her. Then, without another word, he turned his horse off the road, leading them, one after another, away from the echoing cries the breeze carried from the battlefield.

Alex followed for only a few minutes. The forest was incredibly dense and Caradoc was moving swiftly. She hadn't needed to tell the girls not to look back for her. Everyone, including Caradoc himself, had enough to do just keeping pace and avoiding being knocked out of the saddle by branches and brush.

She reined her horse up beside a huge oak. Keeping a tight hold on the mare, which was sidestepping and trying to follow the others, Alex pressed her right hand, the one bearing Andraste's mark, against the oak.

"I need you. I am…" Alex paused, and decided to use the

name that she was becoming more and more comfortable with. "I am Blonwen, Priestess of Andraste, and I need your help." As she had before, Alex reached out with that illusive sixth sense she'd had since she was a child, and was rewarded with a surge of power and her palm tingling with warmth. She drew a deep breath, and asked for something she would have considered impossible just days before. "Close the space behind Caradoc and the daughters of Boudica. Make the woods appear thicker there than in front. Don't let them realize I'm not with them."

Almost at once Alex felt the energy that had been building under her palm zap out into the forest behind her lover and the queen's daughters, as if the tree had been struck by lightning. She bowed her head and pressed it against the rough old oak. "Thank you."

Not allowing herself time to grieve, she jerked the mare around and urged her back the way they'd just come.

The final battle between the Celts and the Romans made the aftermath of the carnage at Londinium look like a mean kid's game. Alex wove her horse through the dense forest, circling around the Celts and heading for the hilly ridge where she'd glimpsed Suetonius. She didn't have any idea how she'd find him. She couldn't afford to get too close to the battle to check out if he was still standing on the ridge; she might actually get pulled into the fight. So she moved blindly through the forest, trusting her sense of direction and following her ears.

The sounds of battle filled the air. She could hardly see any of the fighting, just a glimmer of sun glinting off armor, but she heard far too much. The war cries of the Celts were terrifying. She understood then why history described Celts in battle as demons possessed. The bold woad patterns, their wild hair and tall, half-naked bodies were frightening enough. Add their unearthly shrieks and they truly did seem like demonic creatures.

But in the midst of the war cries, Alex heard, more and more, the screams and terror-filled cries of warriors being killed.

As if thinking of death had conjured it, the air on the battle side of the forest rippled, and a ghost stepped into Alex's view. She blinked in surprise and felt her stomach knot. The dead warrior was Aedan, one of Boudica's inner group.

"Priestess?" he said, looking confused and disorientated.

"Yes, Aedan, it's me, Blonwen. You don't have anything to fear," she said.

Instantly, he seemed less agitated. "I am dead."

It wasn't a question, but Alex nodded. "Yes. Were you with Boudica when you were killed?"

He thought for a moment, and on his pale, translucent face she saw the jolt of surprise as he remembered the events that had led to his own death. "No." His voice was rough with emotion. "We'd become separated." His eyes widened and he began looking all around them. "Is she here? Has Boudica fallen?"

"No!" Alex assured him. "I haven't seen her. I don't think she's been killed."

Aedan sighed in relief and relaxed his frantic search, but then moved toward Alex, speaking earnestly. "The Roman phalanx is too much for us. We can not stand against the legions' combined might."

"I know," she said softly.

"They will defeat us!"

"I know," Alex repeated.

Aedan stopped walking. "The goddess has shown you our defeat?"

"The Romans will win this battle, and this war," she said, not answering him directly.

"I do not want to leave her. I have been by my queen's side since Prasutagus charged me with her protection from his deathbed." Aedan looked back in the direction of the battlefield. "I had hoped that someday, when this war was over and we were free of Rome, I could be more to Boudica than just her sworn warrior."

Ah, Alex thought, *that was why I got such a weird, overprotective vibe from him. Aedan loves Boudica!* That would make it difficult for him to move on to the Otherworld. He'd want to stay and keep serving her and hoping that one day—

And with a start, Alex realized the warrior could still be of service to Boudica, though only indirectly and generations removed.

"Aedan, I have to get to Suetonius."

That snapped the warrior's attention back to her. "The Roman general—why?"

"I have been commanded to retrieve Boudica's medallion piece—the one the tax collector took from her torque. Will you lead me to Suetonius?"

The ghost's face took on new animation. "If you return the medallion to Boudica, will it change the tide of the battle? Will it protect the queen?"

It would have been easy to lie to him, to allow him to hope just a little while longer, but she couldn't. She was Andraste's priestess, and she would not lie.

"No, Aedan. Nothing can save our queen today. Soon, she will join you in the Otherworld, but I can promise you that the medallion piece needs to be retrieved to save future generations."

"I will give you aid, Priestess," he said.

"Thank you, Aedan." She paused and, remembering how Caradoc had killed a chicken and given Catus's young assistant its blood, added, "I don't have anything to sacrifice to reward you with blood."

He shook off her words. "My reward is serving Boudica in some way, even after my death." Then the ghost's form wavered and he disappeared.

Filled with nervous frustration, Alex could do nothing except sit on her horse and wait.

"Caradoc! Wait! We must stop!"

Caradoc heard the echo of a girl's voice between the crashing of underbrush and the blowing of his horse, and he pulled the gelding up and turned to face the others, who were lagging terribly behind.

When had they fallen so far back? Caradoc peered through the forest behind them. *By the trident of Condatis, these woods are dense!*

Breathing hard, the girls' horses finally caught up with Caradoc. "Girls, I know this is difficult, but we must—" He broke off as he realized Blonwen was not behind them.

"Caradoc, Una has to tell you something," Mirain panted.

"Two things, actually," her sister said.

"They can wait." Caradoc kneed his horse around the girls. "Blonwen! Blonwen!" he cried.

Una's small hand reached out to grab his tunic as he passed by her, and he jerked his horse to a halt, turning a black look on her.

The child didn't so much as flinch. She simply said, "First, Blonwen isn't behind us anymore. Second, your mother is here."

TWENTY-SEVEN

"My mother is here?"

Caradoc was trying hard to look stern, and before the Romans did what they had done to her, she might have been scared by such a look. But now Una really wasn't scared of much. Actually, she'd decided she didn't ever want to be scared again in her life. So instead of being afraid, she just nodded and said, "Yes, your mother is here." She pointed to the right, where Caradoc's mother was sitting on a fallen log, smiling warmly at her.

"Una, we don't have time for games. How long has Blonwen been gone?"

Sweet child, say exactly this to my son—'The scar in the shape of a horse's hoof on your backside says your mother is here, and she knows where Blonwen has gone.'

Una smiled back at her. "I'll tell him." Then she looked from the ghost to Caradoc, and repeated her words.

Caradoc's eyes widened in surprise. "Have you always been a Soul Speaker?"

"No, she hasn't." Mirain spoke up. "Just since the goddess marked her today. Una, would you ask the spirit if I'll be able to talk with the dead once I've been accepted into the goddess's service, too?"

"Mirain, she can hear you. She's right here." Una pointed again.

"I know that. I wasn't sure if it was polite to speak directly to her. And don't be so high and mighty!"

"Where is Blonwen?" Caradoc broke in before the two really started bickering.

She has returned to the field of battle to confront Suetonius, Caradoc's mother stated. *Tell him, child.*

"I shall!" Una said brightly. "Caradoc, your mother asks me to say that Blonwen has returned to confront Suetonius." Then her bright look faded. "That's bad, though. She's all alone and—"

Not for long, the ghost interrupted. *That is why I have come to you. I will guide you to safety while Caradoc joins Blonwen.*

"Oh! That seems a good idea," Una said, smiling again.

"What?" Caradoc and Mirain said together.

"Well, your mother says she's here to lead us to safety so you can go back and help Blonwen."

"I really wish I could see her," Mirain muttered.

"Truly?" Caradoc didn't waste time attempting to peer through the veils of reality to see his mother. Instead he studied Una's face, trying to read the truth there.

Yes, truly, the spirit said before the child could answer. *Tell him I will lead you to the old shepherd's hut on the south side of the Dobunni hills.*

"She's going to lead us to a shepherd's hut on the south side of the Dobunni hills," Una reported faithfully. She threw her sister an apologetic look. "I am sorry you cannot see her,

Mirain. Her tunic is very pretty, even though I can see through it." Her attention skipped back to Caradoc. "Do you really have a hoof-shaped scar on your bum? Can I see it?"

Caradoc seemed to grind his jaw before answering. "No, you cannot."

"Una, you shouldn't ask things like that. It isn't proper. Mother would be displeased with you, and I can't imagine the goddess would be happy, either."

"Oh, I am sorry, Caradoc," Una said.

Time is wasting, child. Caradoc must help Blonwen. Tell him he has to be there so that she is forced to do what she must.

"That's sounds mysterious," Una said.

"What?" Caradoc and Mirain asked together.

Una sighed. "She wants you to go because you have to be there so that Blonwen is forced to do something."

"What is it I must force her to do?" Caradoc tried, unsuccessfully, to keep the frustration from his voice.

Una looked questioningly at the spirit.

Only Blonwen has that answer.

"She says Blonwen is the only one who knows."

Caradoc blew out a long, agitated sigh. "Mother, are you sure I may leave the girls? The queen charged me with their safety. I am oath sworn to protect them."

You are blood of my blood and I shall carry out your charge until you return.

"She says that she can take your charge because she's your mother," Una paraphrased, getting tired of repeating every single thing the ghost said.

"Then I accept your offer, Mother." Caradoc smiled wistfully in the direction Una kept looking. "If you care for them half as well as you cared for me, my oath will be fulfilled." He met one girl's gaze and then the other's. "Be brave. I promise to return."

"We're not afraid," declared Mirain.

"Bring Blonwen and Mother back with you," Una said.

"You have my word that I will do my best." Caradoc wheeled his horse around and started fighting his way through the forest.

Eilwen stood, and with a sweeping gesture that took in all of the forest, she cried out, *Spirits of the old ones, I do thank you for answering the young priestess's need, but you must now allow my son to pass. In Andraste's name, I command it!*

The forest shivered, as if a giant had blown his breath through the trees, and when all was still again the woods had returned to their normal appearance.

Eilwen smiled up at Una. *Now I will take you to one of my favorite places, but we will travel more slowly than the druid led.*

"Good, I was tired of going so fast."

"What did she say?" Mirain asked.

"That we can slow down now," Una told her sister.

"That's probably because Caradoc and Blonwen are going to be sure Suetonius and the Romans will be defeated, so we're in less danger now," Mirain said.

"And Mother will come for us soon," Una added, clucking to her horse to follow Eilwen.

Eilwen remained silent and kept her face turned from the children so that they wouldn't see her tears of grief.

The general is just through there. On the other side of these rowan trees is a ridge that abuts to them. Suetonius and his personal guard are there, overlooking the battle.

Alex wiped her dripping face with the sleeve of her tunic. Aedan had led her up the increasingly steep and rocky hill for the better part of an hour in a hike that would have kicked a marine's ass. Thankfully, hiking was on her daily list of to-dos at the tallgrass prairie, so even though she was sweating, her breath was steady and she was invigorated instead of exhausted by the exercise.

"So if I step out from those trees, he will see me?" she asked the spirit.

He could, though his attention is trained on the battle.

Well, she could take care of that. She gulped, not wanting to dwell on the fact that she was soon going to get naked in front of a bunch of Romans, and try to grab a guy's necklace, and then disappear before *he* grabbed too much of *her.*

Priestess? Did you hear me?

"Oh, no. Sorry."

I said you cannot battle Suetonius alone. It is madness.

She smiled ruefully. "Well, I have been called crazy before."

I do not jest, Priestess.

She sighed. "You don't need to worry about me. See this?" She held up her arm so he could see the ESC cuff. "It's magic."

Truly?

"You have my word on it. So don't worry." Alex paused, and then spoke the words she sensed he needed to hear before he would move on. "Your service is done now. There is nothing more you can do here. Andraste's meadow waits for you. Your Boudica will join you there soon, on that you have my word."

Impulsively, Alex walked to the first tree in the rowan grove that flanked the battle ridge. "Aedan, what was your father's name?"

The spirit startled in surprise. "He was called Tearlach, Priestess."

Alex raised her spiral tattooed palm and pressed it against the rowan's bark. "Hello, magical tree," she said softly. "I need to call a spirit from the Otherworld to me." The warmth that danced around the spiral circle in her palm was answer enough. She smiled. "I am Blonwen, Soul Speaker of Andraste, and I summon from the Otherworld the spirit of Tearlach, father of Aedan."

The now familiar veil between worlds parted, and a man stepped through the opening. He was tall and blond, as was his dead son, and he looked around in confusion until his gaze found Aedan.

"Son? It is you?"

"It is, Father," the warrior answer in a choked voice.

"Was it an honorable death? Did you serve the queen?"

"I vow that I did," Aedan said.

The older spirit nodded. "Then I am proud of you, my son." He looked at Alex. "Soul Speaker, I answered your call. Is there a task you would have me perform?"

"There is, even though I don't have any payment for you. I ask that you guide Aedan to the Otherworld. He has served his queen and her people well."

"Soul Speaker, there is no payment required for such a task." Tearlach held his arm out to his son. "Come with me, Aedan, to where there is no pain or regret or sadness, and the meadows of Andraste are eternally green."

Aedan went to his father and embraced him.

Alex ignored the tears that were leaking down her cheeks and said, "May Andraste's love greet you, Aedan, and may you finally get your heart's desire when your queen joins you in the goddess's meadows."

Just before they stepped through the veil together, he looked back and bowed his head respectfully. "Thank you, Priestess…." And the two spirits disappeared.

Wiping her cheeks, Alex thanked the rowan, and then began focusing herself. "Now, Alexandra Blonwen Patton," she said aloud. "It's time to get this job done."

Resolutely, Alex stripped. She laid her clothes neatly over a rock, close to the edge of the woods. She didn't actually expect to be able to get back to them before she pressed the ESC crystal, but it made her feel better to think it might happen.

Hell, anything was better than thinking about popping back to Flagstaff and the middle of the lab naked.

"So I won't think about it," she said.

Soon she was naked except for her ESC cuff, just as she had been when she and Caradoc traveled to the Otherworld and she pledged herself to Andraste.

Caradoc...

Alex bit her lip and blinked hard. Crying was stupid. It didn't help for shit, plus Aedan had already made her bawl once, and if she wasn't careful she'd look red-eyed and snotty-nosed—which was not the look needed to lure Suetonius away from his men.

"The sooner I do this, the sooner I'll be able to come back, find Boudica, get the other piece of the medallion and then decide what to do about Caradoc. My husband." The word *husband* had such a magical sound to it. "I'll make it work—somehow."

Alex returned to the rowan. This time she pressed her naked body against the rough bark—not in a sexual way, but as if she was being embraced by a loving mother. "Please help me to know the right thing to say, and then give me strength to do what needs to be done."

Alex walked through the rowan grove to the edge of the trees. Just as Aedan had described, there was a ridge that abutted to the grassy place beside them. Alex stayed in the rowans' shadows, assessing the situation.

Suetonius was easy to recognize. He was the tallest and most muscular of the men and his cape of scarlet was as unmistakable as his silver breastplate. He was just a little below her, easily within climbing distance. Half turned away from her, he had his eyes fixed on the battle below.

Following his gaze, Alex looked down at the battlefield. Death and destruction spread below them. The Celts were hurling themselves at the legions' phalanx. The tall, woad-painted warriors were fighting bravely, rushing the shield wall of the Romans as they shrieked their battle cries. But it was obvious to Alex that there was no way the Celts could win. Yes, there were substantially more of them, but they were too vulnerable. The style of warfare the Romans had forced them into was going to be their destruction.

It wasn't going to be fast, though. There were simply too many Celts. The wall of Romans was moving forward, but more slowly than Alex had thought. She knew that eventually they would, as a single force, rush the fleeing Celts, trapping them between their swords and the families that unknowingly blocked their escape. But now it almost appeared to be a brutal stalemate, where pawns were being killed and immediately replaced by other players.

As if he was reading her thoughts, Suetonius's deep voice carried to her on the wind. "The barbarians should have been dispersed by now! On what are our soldiers waiting? The appearance of Jupiter himself? As if a god would bother with this rabble!"

"My lord! The field is thick with barbarians. They outnumber us many times over."

Suetonius glanced at the officer who stood to his right. Then, almost more swiftly than Alex's eye could follow, the general backhanded the man across the face.

"If we need more men to exterminate the rabble, then you shall join them."

The blow had knocked the officer to his knees, but he stood quickly, saluted and rushed away.

Supposedly to join the fighting, Alex thought. *Wow—this Suetonius is a total asshole! But now he's an asshole surrounded by three instead of four men.*

She was readying herself to step out of the shadows and call to him when Suetonius strode to the very edge of the craggy precipice and shouted down at the legions below. Alex had to stifle a shocked gasp at his magically amplified voice, but it seemed to come as a surprise only to her and the Celts, who were faltering in the battle and stepping back in wonder.

Conversely, the Romans who weren't in the front line of battle just paused and looked attentively up at their general, as if him speaking with an invisible megaphone was the norm.

Centaurians are a ferocious race with vast powers.... The thought surfaced in the memories planted in Alex's mind.

"No kidding," she muttered to herself. And then Suetonius began to speak.

"Romans! Ignore the racket made by these savages. There are more women than men in their ranks. They are not soldiers—they're not even properly equipped. Stick together. Throw your javelins, then push forward. Knock the rabble down with your shields and finish them off with your swords. Think of the booty and women that await just down this valley. Win quickly and I will forfeit my share, and instead divide it amongst you. You will be rich men!"

The legions' answer was more of a snarl than a battle cry, and they went back into battle with redoubled ferocity.

"That should end the day. I grow bored with this sodden country and its unnatural female ruler," Suetonius said in a more normal voice, stepping back to join his remaining officers.

His words were the final goad Alex needed. She walked out of the shadows, naked except for her cuff. She could feel her hair around her bare shoulders, a wild red-gold mane, crackling with energy after her request of the rowan.

"What a big, brave man you are!" she called down to him. "Taunting the Celts from the safety of your hill."

Suetonius and his officers spun around. One man held a spear at ready, the other two notched and drew wicked-looking arrows. Suetonius was armed only with a short sword, and he did not draw it.

"What is this? One of the dryads I've heard so much about?" the general said with a flippant smile.

"I'm not a dryad. I'm a priestess who has come to offer you a challenge," Alex said. She forced her hands onto her hips so that they wouldn't automatically cover her body, and lifted her chin, ignoring the ogling stares of the men.

"I will gladly accept your challenge, after I have defeated your people." He glanced at the officer with the spear. "Marcellus, take the chit to my tent. You may fondle her, but do not *spear* her. I do not thrust after any man."

The officers chuckled at Suetonius's pun, but before Marcellus began to climb up to her, Alex said, "Oh, please, it's not that kind of challenge, and your *spear* is obviously too little to reach me here. My challenge is something I'm guessing you want even more than rape. I just heard you say you wanted this battle to be over quickly. Beat me and you'll have your wish."

Suetonius's hand stayed Marcellus. "How could a battle possibly be won or lost on the fate of one woman?"

"How could a battle possibly be led by one woman?" she quipped in return.

"Explain yourself!" he commanded.

Alex noticed that while his men's eyes roamed up and down her body, Suetonius kept his gaze locked with hers. Her stomach flipped nervously. Part of her plan was that her nakedness would throw him off—distract him.

"I'm Boudica's high priestess to Andraste. I am her omen— the living sign that our goddess is with her and that her cause is just. If you capture me and hang me from this ridge, so that the queen and our people can see that you've killed me, they will lose heart. The battle will be yours."

"The battle will be ours with or without killing you, woman."

Alex raised her brows and tossed back her hair. "Are you really so sure of that? I distinctly remember you running away from Londinium like a scared little girl when Boudica showed up there and burned it to the ground."

"Bitch!" he snarled at her. "I have never run from a woman!"

Alex frowned in mock confusion. "So it wasn't you who grabbed Boudica's medallion from Catus, jumped on the first fast horse you could find, and raced down the Watling Road, leaving a whole bunch of Romans to burn in the temple of Jupiter? Don't I have the right general? I thought you were Suetonius. All right, well, my mistake. I'll go find the real man." Alex turned and started to walk nonchalantly back into the rowan grove.

"Stay here! I'll get the daughter of a whore myself, and I won't wait until my tent to show her the spear of a Roman!" she heard Suetonius say.

TWENTY-EIGHT

Heart pounding, Alex rushed to the largest rowan of the grove and put her back against it, facing the direction Suetonius should appear. "Help me," she whispered to the tree. "I just need to grab the medallion and then I can get away from him. Please help me." Everywhere her skin touched the tree's bark, she felt warmth rush into her, along with a wonderful sense of calm.

The calm ended when Suetonius burst into the grove.

He wasn't human. How could the Romans not see that? He was massive, not just in height, though he would tower over even the tallest Celt, but his muscles were huge. And his hair and facial features were off—there was something too bestial about his hair and too brutal about his equine nose and his wide, dark eyes.

She knew she hadn't made a sound, but his eyes instantly found her. He smiled, and she thought that one small twitch of his lips might be the most frightening thing she'd ever seen in her life.

"Ah, there you are, hiding under the tree. Are you certain you are a priestess and not a dryad?"

Alex couldn't speak, which made his smile widen. Instead of continuing his rush toward her, he slowed, stalking her.

Her body felt frozen, her mind numb. She wanted to run, but couldn't make her legs work. All she could do was cling to the tree's warmth and stare in horror as her death approached, Boudica's medallion glittering from the gold chain around the general's neck.

Courage, Priestess! At the edge of her vision Alex could see the ghost of Boudica's husband, the old king of the Iceni. He lifted his fist in a salute to her. *You are not alone.*

Be brave, Priestess! All will be well. Another spirit materialized beside the first. Alex recognized her as the woman who had been the first warrior to die at Londinium.

Take heart! Courage! called the old man who had appeared to her not long after she'd arrived.

We are with you! cried one of the other warriors she'd helped cross to the Otherworld.

"I'm not alone," she told them, and stood a little straighter.

Suetonius's serpent smile didn't falter. "Have men hiding in the wood, do you? You'll find I'm very difficult to kill."

"I talk to dead people," Alex told the approaching general. "That's who's here with us. The woods are filled with ghosts."

For just an instant Alex saw the haughty confidence falter. Was that fear that flickered through his dark eyes? It was gone too quickly for Alex to tell for sure.

"Very soon, woman, *you* will be a dead person." He spoke in almost a lover's tone, as if the idea excited him.

All I need to do is get the medallion! Then I'm out of here. Alex drew a deep breath. Her breasts lifted and his gaze lingered on her nipples. Pushing back her fear and disgust, she said, "I think you'll discover I'm hard to kill, too." She met his gaze, when it finally lifted to her eyes.

"You're a female. Soft. Weak. Submissive. You will not be hard to kill, but I do think I will take my time with you."

"I'm a high priestess. That means I'm not a normal woman." And for perhaps the first time in her life she was sincerely grateful she wasn't "normal."

"I vanquished an island filled with priestesses and druids. Why should I fear you?"

The whole time they'd been talking he'd been stalking closer and closer to her. Finally he was so near that if she reached out she could touch him—or grab the medallion that dangled around his neck.

"You should fear me," she said in a sexy purr she knew would take him aback, "because I'm not from this time, so have more tricks up my sleeve!" Alex snatched the medallion in her fist and jerked, snapping the gold chain. She whirled away from him, putting the tree between them, and reached for the crystal button in her ESC cuff—

Suetonius moved with inhuman speed. He grabbed her hand just as her fingertip touched the crystal, and pulled her around the tree to him.

"A female from the future? One of the bitches who think they can exist on our level?" He wrenched her arm around and down, so that she was forced to her knees before him. "I knew I'd find one of you here."

She kept the medallion clenched in her fist and glared up at him. "We have never been on your level. We've never been that low."

He backhanded her so hard her vision exploded in stars and the copper taste of blood filled her mouth.

"Stupid female! You cannot possibly stand against us, just as the barbarian queen cannot stand against Rome." He hit Alex again, and this time blood gushed from her broken nose, but she kept hold of the precious medallion.

He laughed at her.

"The piece is what you came after, huh? Oh, I shall make sure you have it. I'll burn it with your body after I finish with you!"

He picked her up and slammed her facedown against one of the nearby boulders, so hard that her breath was forced out of her. Teetering between consciousness and oblivion, Alex tried to draw breath past a terrible pain in her side. She felt Suetonius fondling her butt roughly, digging his fingers between her cheeks and running them down to her woman's core, where he shoved them inside her.

"So small…" he growled. "It will be good to stretch you out."

Alex struggled to draw enough breath so that her vision would stop going gray, but the piercing pain in her side made it impossible for her to do so. Her mind was shrieking, *press the ESC cuff,* but her body wouldn't obey. She couldn't feel her hands. All she could feel was Suetonius moving behind her as he pulled himself free of his uniform and rubbed the wet bulb of his shaft against her nakedness.

"I think I've decided I like females from the future of this planet. You are very—"

The arrow caught Suetonius high in the left side of his chest, with such force that he staggered back several paces from Alex. She rolled from the boulder, clutching her side as Caradoc ran up to her.

"Blonwen!" He bent over her.

"No!" she gasped, trying to blink the blurriness from her vision. "You're not supposed to—" The shadow over his shoulder had her crying, "Behind you!"

Caradoc whirled around, holding his short sword up at the ready. Suetonius's incredible speed allowed him to dodge the blade and connect his fist to Caradoc's chin, knocking the druid off his feet.

But the quickness with which Caradoc rebounded surprised even Suetonius, who bared his teeth and drew his own sword from its scabbard at his waist. He reached up and pulled the arrow from his own chest with hardly a grimace. "You will be my exercise before I go back to servicing the female," he said.

"You touch her again only if I am dead," Caradoc answered.

"That was my intention, boy."

"Remember he's not human!" Alex called.

Suetonius lunged at Caradoc, slicing a long, bloody line across his chest. "Yes, do remember I am not a mere human."

Caradoc circled with the Centaurian, keeping just outside his sword reach. While he moved, he raised his free hand palm up, facing the sky, and with a grim smile said, "I am not a *mere* human either, creature. I am a druid, beloved of Condatis, God of the Waters, and through him I, too, wield power. Let it rain!" he roared.

The sky instantly began to roil. Clouds blew into being, bruised and angry, in the otherwise clear blue of the day. With a crash of thunder, they opened, and rain began to fall in wet ropes.

Suetonius laughed. "Do you think water will harm me?" He lunged at Caradoc again, slicing through the meat of his left biceps, but the druid danced back before the blade could do lethal harm.

"I did not call the waters to harm," Caradoc said, feinting and stabbing. A bright stain of scarlet bloomed on Suetonius's right shoulder.

Alex suddenly understood what Caradoc meant. He seemed to draw energy from the pelting rain. He said he hadn't called the water to harm Suetonius, but it definitely was a hindrance to him. The ground was already becoming soggy and slick, and rain ran in rivulets from his dark hair, causing him to brush it off his face to clear his vision.

It had the opposite affect on Caradoc. His steps were sure on the wet ground and the rain didn't obscure his vision—it glided gently down his body. Alex thought again how selkie-like he looked.

She was actually beginning to hope, when Suetonius laughed again.

"This has been amusing, but it has gone on long enough."

The general attacked with blinding speed. Caradoc was a skilled warrior with a druid's powers, but he was no match for the Centurian. Soon he was bleeding freely from a dozen wounds. With a terrible hacking motion, Suetonius cut through Caradoc's right thigh, causing the warrior to stumble back and drop to his knees. Still he held his sword up, parrying Suetonius's increasingly lethal lunges. The Centaurian drove him mercilessly back, cutting and hacking and bleeding him until Caradoc was pressed against the same boulder Alex had been thrown over. She was still crouched at the side of it, watching in horror as her lover fought to his death right there, within her reach.

Within my reach…

Alex knew what she had to do. Ignoring the searing pain in her side, she scramble on all fours to the nearest rowan tree. Using it to brace herself, she stood. Then, with the bark pressed against her back, she said, "I need a burst of power, like the one I used to hurl the spirits back, only bigger." Alex felt the heat building through her body, and prayed silently that it would be enough. She threw out her arms, pointing at Suetonius just as the Centaurian lifted his sword over Caradoc and said, "It is time for you to join your water god."

The burst of hot power from the tree sizzled through the rain and caught Suetonius by surprise, throwing him back.

Using the adrenaline rush from being the tree's conduit, Alex ran to Caradoc and dropped down beside him. He was weaving unsteadily on his knees in the rain, obviously close to passing out. She wrenched off the ESC cuff and put it in his hand, along with the medallion.

He gave her a confused, blurry look and said, "You must use your magic to return to the future—"

"If you didn't die here they can fix you. Tell Carswell I'll get the other piece. When you're well, she'll send you back for it. I'll be at that hut you said wasn't far from here. I love you, Caradoc!"

Before he could speak, she pressed the ESC crystal, and was blown back by the force of power that opened a rift in time and pulled Caradoc into the future.

The rain stopped the instant the druid disappeared.

"You bitch! What have you done?" Suetonius jerked her to her feet. Alex cried out as he lifted her, shaking her as if she were no more than a doll. "Where did you send him?" His face was close to hers and she could smell the sourness of his breath.

"Go to hell," she said through gritted teeth.

Still holding her off the ground, he slammed her against a tree. "What year?" he yelled.

"You can kill me, but I won't tell you."

Anger flared in his eyes, and just as quickly was replaced by scorn. "I don't need you to find him. All I need do is wait for his return. A hut, you said? Near here? The other piece of the medallion will be retrieved from Boudica's corpse, and someone will be waiting for your druid in the hut, but it will not be you." He rammed his hardening shaft against her. "First I'll finish what you and I started, then I'll see to Boudica and your lover."

"No! I'm not going to let you do that."

Suetonius sneered. "I am about to rape and then kill you, female. There is nothing you can do to stop any of this."

"You are absolutely right about that." And while Suetonius fumbled between his legs and held her cruelly against the tree, Alex blocked the vile Centaurian from her mind and focused on the magical rowan at her back. She closed her eyes and found her calm center. And then, with eyes still closed, she said. "I am a Soul Speaker, and I wish to send out a call."

"What are you saying, female?" Somewhere at the edge of her mind, Suetonius was speaking as he rutted against her. Alex took no notice of him at all.

When she opened her eyes she looked over the Centaurian's shoulder at the veil of reality as it parted to reveal the mists of the Otherworld.

With a voice magnified by the earth power of the rowan, Alex shouted, "In Andraste's name I call forth all the souls that this Centaurian, Suetonius, has murdered. Let everyone who has been wronged by him come forth and, for the prize of blood, you may take your vengeance on him!"

Suetonius was shaking her again. "What are you doing now, you—"

His voice broke off as the air around them began to boil with mist, and from the mist tendrils curled out, just as they had done in Alex's dream so long ago. This time the tendrils were feeling for the Centaurian.

He dropped her and stumbled back, looking wildly around him, batting at the mist as if it were a swarm of insects. "Be gone! Leave me!"

The mist grew thicker, taking on separate forms. Alex saw what must be hundreds of souls materializing around them. Suetonius's eyes widened in horror.

Unnoticed by the Centaurian, Alex stumbled to where Caradoc's sword lay. Not caring about finesse or swordplay, she hefted the blade in both hands, threw herself at Suetonius and stabbed it into his side.

The Centaurian gave a great cry and knocked Alex away. As the sword pulled from his body, a rush of blood followed it.

"Your blood payment is there!" Alex said, pointing at Suetonius. "He is the sacrifice."

She watched as the specters converged upon him, attaching to his form like ghostly leeches. When he began to scream Alex stopped watching. As she turned away, she murmured, "Celts, you are avenged...."

TWENTY-NINE

Alex had to find Boudica. She didn't think about Caradoc; she simply had to believe he was alive. Carswell would save him. All Alex had to concentrate on was staying conscious and finding the queen.

Her clothes were where she'd left them, neatly and optimistically folded. Alex told herself the pain of her cracked ribs was good—it kept her conscious. There was something wrong with her vision. It seemed she was looking down a graying tunnel. Had she hit her head? She didn't really remember. Alex lifted her hand, feeling around, and winced when her fingers found the lump above her left ear. Concussion? She'd worry about it later.

Alex found her horse next. She'd left him when Aedan's spirit had led her into woods too dense and rocky for the mare to travel. Now she was grateful for the animal's steady temperament as she swayed drunkenly in the saddle, doing more of trying-not-to-pass-out than actual riding.

Still, she kept the mare's head pointed in the general direction she knew would bring them out of the forest, near where the Celts had drawn their wagons across the exit to the valley.

When Alex finally came to the edge of the trees, the day was waning and the battle was finished—as was Boudica's war. Alex pulled the mare up, and from the lengthening shadows of the forest, stared across a sea of carnage. What she saw was so horrible her mind couldn't completely comprehend it. There were dismembered bodies…gutted bodies…still-alive and writhing bodies. Women, men, old and young, in a valley turned black with blood and the cawing birds that were already feeding. Roman soldiers waded among them, plundering the dead and dying. Amid all of the horror, Alex saw souls wandering, dazed and disoriented.

"There are just too many of them." She spoke aloud to herself, trying to take comfort in the familiarity of her voice.

Guide them home….

The words drifted through Alex's mind at the same moment she realized what she had to do. Wearily, she kneed the horse toward a huge oak that towered over all the other trees in the area. She pressed her palm to its bark.

"I need your help." The warmth danced around the spiral in her palm. "Please open the veil to the Otherworld. I'm a Soul Speaker and Priestess of Andraste. I need to guide these spirits home to the goddess."

Power from the ancient oak flowed into her, warm and sure. The air in front of her, through which she could see the battlefield, rippled, and then the veil between worlds parted.

"Spirits of Boudica's Celts! Come to me!" Alex's voice sounded weird. Though it was magnified by the power of the oak, it wasn't so much the loudness that had changed. Rather, her voice had a completely different timbre, echoing through the Valley of Death like a lamentation from the Underworld that had escaped to haunt the living.

She saw the Romans pause in their looting and, as the souls of the dead began to follow her voice, they shivered and made signs against the evil eye. Alex was grimly pleased to note that several of them left off their grisly looting and hurried away. None of them even glanced her way.

As the ghosts got closer, Alex pulled more of the warmth from the tree and straightened on the mare's back, smiling at the ghastly, milling group. "It's me, Blonwen, Andraste's priestess." She saw recognition on several of their semitransparent faces. "You've done well. Andraste is proud of you. The goddess is waiting just through there..." She motioned to the parted, shimmering veil. "Join her and leave behind the pain and sorrow you have known here."

There was no hesitation among the spirits. They moved forward—not rushing, just walking to their next life as if strolling down a forest path. Some of them nodded at her as they departed. Some even called farewell. All of them moved on—except the tall, regal woman with the blazing red hair.

The dead queen's spirit had come to stand beside the Otherworld entrance. She watched silently as the dead who had been her subjects and friends passed on.

"Boudica!" Alex cried.

The queen's gaze shifted to her. "I failed, Priestess."

"You gave your people hope, and those who died here died free," Alex said.

"Tell me, Priestess, would that be enough for you had this—" she gestured at the bloody field "—been your life's work?"

"That's not what you'll be remembered for. I know, because I came to you from the future, and there you're remembered as a strong queen who led her people in a righteous revolt against Rome."

"The future? Truly? Are my daughters safe there?"

Alex wasn't sure what had happened to the queen's daughters. She assumed Caradoc had sent them on to safety when he'd discovered she was missing, but history was foggy about them; she really had no idea if they survived their mother long. "I am from the future, but it's a distant future, one where you and your daughters are written about in history. I can tell you, though, that Caradoc and I got them safely away from here, and I have not seen their spirits pass to the Otherworld."

The queen closed her eyes and seemed to crumble in on herself. "Yet if they live, they will be slaves of Rome." She looked up at Alex. "In your time, are the Celts free?"

Alex smiled. "Yes, very."

"That is something, then."

"But to be sure we stay free, I need your help."

She held out her transparent hands. "I am little help like this."

"Just tell me where your body is. I need to take the medallion piece in your torque to the future. It has magical powers there."

"The torque will be burned with my body on a warrior's pyre."

"Where? You have to tell me!"

The dead queen pointed to the west. "Ride through the forest there and you will come to a sandstone ridge. Beyond it is a wood we call Andraste's Wald. They build my pyre there."

"I have to go. I have to get that medallion before they burn it." Alex turned her horse. "Goodbye, Boudica. I have been honored to know you."

"I should come with you, Priestess."

"No." Alex's reaction was so gut deep that she knew she was speaking the goddess's will. "Move on to the Otherworld. Your time here is finished. You fought so hard for freedom. Don't stay now and make yourself a slave to the past."

Boudica bowed her head slightly in acknowledgment. "You should remain here, Blonwen. This time suits you, and I have a feeling your time here is *not* finished. Fare thee well, Priestess of Andraste." The queen's spirit moved through the veil, the last of the dead to leave the valley, and the curtain between worlds shimmered once more and then was gone.

Alex dug her heels into the mare and headed west.

The warm power of the oak had been buffering the pain in Alex's body as well as lending her strength, and as soon as she broke contact with it, agony slammed back into her full force. Her vision blurred and she pressed her arm against her side, trying unsuccessfully to lessen the pain of her cracked ribs.

"Help me, Andraste!" She thought she shouted the words, but the sound that emerged was hardly a whisper.

The air in front of her shimmered and a beckoning spirit appeared. *This way, Soul Speaker.*

Alex turned the horse's head, knowing only that she must follow the spirit.

Through here, Priestess. Another ghost materialized ahead.

To me, Soul Speaker. Ride to me, said another, farther off.

Barely conscious, Alex clung to the back of the horse and followed the path laid by the voices of the dead to the sandstone ridge and Boudica's funeral pyre.

Caradoc's first impression of the future was that it shone like the light of a trapped sun. Half-dead, suffused with pain, he slammed into what he now knew was called a *laboratory,* clutching the medallion and still screaming "No!" at Blonwen. There was a great and terrible cacophony of sounds, as jarring as the light, and women who wore strange dress rushed to him, speaking a language he could not understand.

Caradoc bellowed and struck out at them, not caring that they were women, too deep in shock to remember this was Blonwen's time…Blonwen's people….

Then a voice cut through the chaos, and in his own language said, "Be at peace, warrior. We are friends of Blonwen."

Caradoc looked wildly around the alien room until he found the small women with the intelligent green eyes. "Carswell?" he rasped.

"Aye," she said.

With a hand that shook as if he were an old man, he held the medallion out to her. "Take this and send me back to her. She is in danger."

The woman nodded and walked to his side. She took the medallion, glanced at it and then looked expectantly up at him.

"Blonwen means to retrieve the other part of it, but she cannot do it without my aid. Send me back! She may be dead already."

Carswell's touch was gentle when she rested her hand on his arm. "Warrior, if we do not heal you, I'm very much afraid you will soon be dead yourself. Now, tell me your name."

"We don't have time for this. Send me back!"

"I will, but not until you can be of some use to her. You know you are in the future, don't you?"

"I do."

"Then believe me when I tell you we do have time."

Caradoc hesitated.

"Did Blonwen trust me?" Carswell asked him.

"She did."

"Then you must trust me, too."

"My name is Caradoc, son of Eilwen, kinsman to Boudica, Queen of the Iceni."

"Thank you for your trust, Caradoc."

A woman rushed up to Carswell with a sharp tool, which, to Caradoc's surprise, she pierced him with. Too late, he jerked back, arm burning.

"Everything is going to be okay. You're safe now…."

And the room went black.

★ ★ ★

"Priestess?"

"I—I'll follow in a second. I have to rest right now. Head spinning…" Alex was slumped over in the saddle, her face pressed to the mare's mane. The horse had come to a halt. She knew she should sit up and continue to follow the ghosts, but she hurt so badly, and if the mare took one more step she was going to throw up all over the animal's neck, which wouldn't be good for either of them. If she could just rest for a little while…

"Priestess, let me help you."

"You have. You are. Just—" Alex shrieked as the ghost actually touched her. She opened her eyes to see the confused face of one of Boudica's inner circle of warriors, who was very obviously solid and alive. "Neill?" she asked, trying to remember his name while she pressed her arm to her ribs and took short, panting breaths.

"Aye, Priestess Blonwen. Let me help you down now."

She nodded and then focused on the not passing out as the big Celt eased her from the horse. She stood there, half leaning against the mare, half kept on her feet by the warrior, and mostly unconscious.

"Bring water for the priestess!" Neill shouted.

She felt the skin held to her mouth and automatically drank thirstily, even though the water was brackish and filled with the taste of her blood. When she was done drinking she leaned against the mare and trembled, trying to focus her mind on the here and now. But thoughts of Caradoc kept swirling through her memory. That first kiss when she'd gotten so angry at him…their handfast…their lovemaking. *Please let him be safe and alive.*

"We knew you would come, Priestess. We knew you would be here to guide our queen into the Otherworld."

"Otherworld…" Alex repeated faintly, thinking that she very much hoped Caradoc was in her *other world,* alive and being cared for.

Then she smelled smoke, and reason beat through the haze of pain and exhaustion. She lifted her head and blinked to clear her vision. Her horse had come to a halt before a low sandstone ridge that had a shallow stream running between it and the edge of what appeared to be an endless green forest, covering rolling hills. Between the stream and the trees was a huge pile of wood—obviously fallen logs and timber scavenged from the forest. On top lay the body of Boudica, Queen of the Iceni, the torque of power still around her neck.

There were half a dozen or so bloodied and beaten survivors of her inner circle, men and women warriors, clustered around the pyre. Two of the warriors held torches made from branches. They were all looking expectantly at her.

"No!" she cried, lurching away from the horse and Neill, and limping toward the pyre. "You can't burn the torque. I need...I have to have it."

"Priestess!" Neill caught up with her easily and took her arm, trying to help her walk. "The queen did not pass on the torque before she drank poison. She disbanded us and bade us flee to Andraste's Wald, where we are each to seek our freedom until better times. The torque must burn with her."

"No," Alex repeated stubbornly. "She would want me to have it."

"Priestess?" Neill sounded as shocked as the other warriors looked. "You are not in the line of royal succession."

"I don't mean for myself." She waded into the stream, almost pulling Neill with her. "I don't want to be queen. I want it for Anasazi."

"Anasazi?" Neill said. "Priestess, Boudica knew no Anasazi."

Alex shook her head, sending waves of dizziness through her. "I didn't mean to say that. I meant to say Andraste."

"Priestess, you have been wounded and harshly used. You are not in your right mind. The torque must burn with the queen, as she did not pass it on, and none of her heirs are living." He spoke gently but firmly to her. "This, too, is the tradition of the goddess."

"But her daughters got away. They're alive."

"At the end, Boudica believed them to be dead, as no one could escape the Roman's wrath. We must follow our queen's will."

"No! You don't understand. I have to have it!" Alex wrenched away from him. Unable to stand on her own, she fell to her hands and knees in the water. Ignoring the rocks that cut her skin, she kept moving through the stream toward Boudica's body.

"Light the queen's pyre. The Romans cannot be far behind us. We will not let them desecrate Boudica's body." Neill glanced sadly down at Alex. "Grief has driven the priestess mad. We will bring her with us and care for her, as the queen would wish us to."

The warriors touched their blazing branches to the pyre and Alex began to sob. She'd failed. She looked wildly around. Maybe if she could get to the woods she could pull some power from one of the trees—enough to clear her mind and make her body work, just for a little longer....

"Please help me…Andraste…." She bowed her head, praying with all her will. Then, remembering how Caradoc had drawn magic from water, she added, "Condatis, please…help."

"Warriors of Boudica—will you pass the torque of the Iceni to me?"

Alex lifted her head to see Caradoc, strong and whole and well, step from the deep shadows of Andraste's Wald.

"We will!" the warriors shouted as one.

Caradoc sprinted to the burning pyre and, reaching through the flames, pulled the torque from the dead queen's neck. Without ceremony, he stretched it open so that it fitted around his own. Then, while the Iceni bowed to their new king, he rushed to the stream and drew Alex into his arms.

Telling the warriors to get ready to ride, Caradoc carried her into the forest. He went several yards into the woods before he stopped and gently laid her on the moss at the base of an ancient oak. She blinked away dizziness as she gazed up at him and tried to smile, wishing she was still in his arms—wishing she was strong enough to pull him to her.

"You're not dead," she managed to say.

"No, I am not, but you almost are." He reached as if to touch her battered face, and then pulled back. "Ah, gods! Look what that creature did to you."

"He's dead," Alex said.

"Good." Caradoc pulled the torque from around his neck and punched his thumb through the circlet that held the second medallion piece, popping it out. He took her hand, opened it, placed the medallion on her palm and then curled her fingers around it.

"You got it," she said, trying to think clearly enough to understand why Caradoc seemed so strange—so distant.

"All I did was pull it from the fire. You got the torque, Alex. You defeated Suetonius. You led me here." He took the ESC cuff from his forearm and fitted it around her wrist. "And now you are going home."

"I'll give it to Carswell. Then I'll come back. Where will you be?"

"No. There's no coming back."

Her brow wrinkled in confusion. He sounded so cold. "Yes there is. Carswell can send me back here, just like she did you."

"No!" He spoke sharply, then drew a deep breath, and when he continued talking his voice was emotionless, as if he was explaining directions to someone who had gotten lost. "This isn't your world, Alex. You don't belong here. Look at you. You're almost dead. I'll be running and hiding—probably for years. You won't keep up. You won't survive."

"But Carswell will fix me. When I come back I'll be healthy again."

"There is no coming back for you, Alex," he repeated.

"Why do you keep calling me that?"

"Because it is your true name. Forgive me. I did not mean to hurt you. I should not have allowed what happened between us to go so far. I do not want you to return to me. You would be in my way. I couldn't survive if I had to take care of you, too. And after coming so close to death, I find that I want to survive. Alexandra Patton, I break our handfast. Fare you well."

Before Alex could stop him, Caradoc pressed the ESC crystal.

After she disappeared he bowed his head and wept.

THIRTY

Alex leaned back against the rough bark of the scraggly hack-berry tree and tried to see the beauty of the Oklahoma sun setting into the tallgrass prairie. The tree even pressed a tentative warmth into her skin, which made her smile and pat the bark absently, as if the little tree was a slightly annoying but well-loved pet.

"I'll learn to be happy here," she said, more to herself than the tree.

I think you should go back to the druid.

Alex sighed and didn't even bother to look at the ghost. "Hello, Andred."

Well met, Alex. Alex could hear the smile in her voice. *Now, as I was saying, I think you should go back to the druid.*

"I thought we decided to agree to disagree on that subject."

You decided. I disappeared and gave you a month to calm down and come to your right mind again. Now I am here to return to my point, which is you returning to the druid.

"I'm not going to talk about it."

You need to talk about it, said the ghost.

Alex looked at her then. She didn't want to admit it, but she had missed Andred. "I thought you'd gone for good."

The spirit smiled. *No. I'll be coming by here as long as you're around.*

"No, Andred, that's not right." Alex had never considered that *she* was what was tying this strange young ghost to the world. "You need to move on. The Otherworld really is very nice. You don't have anything to fear."

I know that, Blonwen.

"I asked you never to call me that."

It is your true name.

"It's not! It's a made-up name for a made-up woman who would be dead for more than a thousand years if I had stayed. It can't be my true name."

Go back to him. Your soul won't rest until you do.

"Oh, bullshit! I don't buy all that soul mate stuff—not since mine told me he didn't want me anymore. I'd be in his way there. He said so."

For a smart woman you're behaving rather stupidly about this.

Alex rounded on the ghost. "He doesn't want me! And I'm not going to go back there just to be rejected by him again. I'm not stupid, Andred. I'm weak! I couldn't take him sending me away again."

Alex, the ghost began.

"He gets married!" she blurted, blinking back tears. "You think I didn't want to believe he sent me back just because he was afraid for me? As soon as I was fully conscious, I asked Carswell who he was. Obviously, she'd found out that he'd survived the battle. If he hadn't she wouldn't have been able to heal him. She gave me the file on him." Alex began to recite, almost by rote: "Caradoc, son of Eilwen, kinsman of Boudica, druid and warrior, survived the slaughter of the Celts to become king of the Iceni, but his life was not typical of a Celt. Historical evidence shows he lived in Rome for seven years in free custody. His trial was recorded in history, and is interesting in the fact that he was allowed to marry the widow of a Roman nobleman. Though he refused to sign a treaty with Rome, he did agree not to take up arms against them, and was eventually able to return to his people. It was through Caradoc that the royal blood of Briton survived." Alex wiped her sleeve across her eyes, pissed that it could still make her cry. "What am I supposed to do—go back and be his mistress? *He got rid of me and married a Roman woman.*" She enunciated the words carefully, even though it broke her heart to say them.

Did you ask about this Roman woman?

"No. Why would I want to know about the woman he married?"

Stop allowing your hurt to blind you and think with your mind and not your broken heart.

"He had children with her!"

The ghost sighed. *Had you done any research, you would have found out that two of those children, girls, were too old to have been the Roman widow's daughters.*

"Okay. Well. Then he did save Una and Malian." Something bound tight within Alex began to release. "Good. I'm glad. I liked the girls. A lot."

The widow must have liked the girls a lot, too. History reports she raised them as her own. Unusual, that, for a woman to raise the daughters of a queen her people conquered.

"Maybe she didn't know that part. Maybe Caradoc didn't tell her, to protect the girls."

Andred scoffed. *Do you really believe Boudica's daughters would pretend to be any other woman's children? The widow had to know their true identities.*

Alex stared at the ghost. "You couldn't mean you think that

I…" Her words faded as her pulse suddenly kicked up. Alex started to pace. "No. I am definitely not the widow of a Roman nobleman. Impossible."

Andred met her gaze. *Time travel is impossible. Is it not?*

"You really believe it could be *me* he marries?" Alex thought her heart was going to beat out of her chest.

Caradoc marries an obscure widow who suddenly appears in Rome, liberally sprinkling coins about, so much so that she bribes the government to allow her to marry a royal prisoner. Sounds like quite an unusual woman for her time. It seems almost as if she was dropped there from somewhere—or some when—else. She paused and added, *Ask yourself this. Do you believe everything Caradoc said to you, and everything your goddess showed you, was a lie?*

"No," Alex said softly. "No, I don't."

Then why have you not returned to him?

"I—I have to call Carswell."

The ghost nodded. *That is an excellent starting place.*

"Who are you?" Alex asked breathlessly.

Andred smiled and lifted her right hand, holding it palm out. Even semitransparent, the spiral circle, twin to the one that would decorate Alex's palm for the rest of her life, was clearly visible. *Do you not recognize me by now? I am just another face of your goddess, child. And I have been watching over you for many years. You are well healed. Don't you think it's time we both went home?*

Sobbing with happiness, Alex dropped to her knees at the goddess's feet.

They could shackle him, imprison him and torture him, but Caradoc would not bend to the Romans' will. He would not sign a treaty with them, not after they'd butchered his people, burned his lands and slaughtered his queen. But he would pretend cooperation, up to a point. He would not strike out at them and kill them in their sleep, as he wished he could. If he did they would murder Una and Mirain. The fact that they held the girls hostage insured he wouldn't sacrifice himself, after running through as many of them as he could take with him to the Otherworld. It insured the Romans could say they had the king of the Iceni in free custody, and parade him around so that his people believed he complied with them and would not revolt again.

Caradoc's lip lifted in a sneer. But there was only so much they could force him to do. This new trick of theirs—selling him to a widow—went too far. His freedom was gone; his pride was not.

"Here, now, Caradoc, look lively. This is your new home." The Roman officer had halted their march. Caradoc stood, expressionless, as the soldiers made coarse jokes about him as if he couldn't hear them.

He almost didn't. He'd heard it often enough in the past week to ignore them. It seemed a great deal of speculation was going on about whether he would be the widow's rutting Celtic boar, or her prize bull stud.

Knowing the Roman debauchery he'd already witnessed, Caradoc had no doubt the woman had both in mind.

The great carved doors of the villa finally opened, and Caradoc was led within the opulent foyer. Though his shackles echoed garishly off the sea-blue walls, he could hear another sound even over the clanking iron. Water. The druid's eyes widened as he entered the villa. There were fountains everywhere. He could even see through to the open-air courtyard, where a waterfall cascaded into a pond.

"Never seen so much water in one villa," one of the soldiers said.

"Widow added it. A stoneworker told me she said she wanted to be surrounded by water."

Caradoc's stomach tightened. Could Condatis be at work?

He'd felt his god had forsaken him since he'd left his homeland and begun living among his enemies. Though, were he honest with himself, he would admit that he hadn't reached out to his god. Not since he'd sent *her* away.

Caradoc turned his face to the marble wall in the foyer of the opulent villa so that the guards who always shadowed him could not see the emotion he still could not hide when he let himself think of Blonwen.

Carswell had healed him and then sent him back, after what seemed far too long, to the hut where Blonwen had said she would meet him. He'd found only the girls there, newly arrived, as only hours had passed, rather than the months his recovery had truly taken.

Instead of panicking, Caradoc had turned to his god, calling on Condatis to lead him to his love, and the god had, indeed, shown the druid where to find Blonwen. She had been immersed in water, calling on Condatis's aid herself.

It had been a simple thing to press the ESC cuff, return to Carswell, explain Blonwen's new location, and then—finally— go to her.

What he'd seen when he'd pulled her from the stream had been the final nudge Caradoc had needed. After seeing the world in which *Alex* lived, and knowing the world to which he would take her—a world filled with violence and slavery and death—he knew he couldn't allow her to return to him.

Goddess, how he missed her! Sending her away—hurting her—had been like cutting out a piece of his soul. And since then he'd been numb inside. He had no heart left to call on his god. Were it not for the pledge he'd made to Boudica to care for her girls, he would have no heart left to live.

Yet the water of this villa soothed his soul.

"The lady will see him now," a large dark man called, from outside a door that opened to a room nearer the pool. Another dark man, so similar to the other they might be twins, stood at the opposite side of the door. Both were heavily armed. They were obviously slaves, personal bodyguards Roman nobles bought to protect themselves.

Caradoc steeled himself. He was a prisoner, but he would not be used by this woman. He'd lost his heart, his love, his soul—but he still had his memories. In his mind, he and Blonwen were still handfasted. When Caradoc had broken the vow, he'd been careful to break it only with her future name. *Blonwen* would always be his wife, and he would not allow anything or anyone to sully that bond.

"Let's go meet your new mistress!" A soldier prodded Caradoc with a spear.

But when they got to the doorway, one of the dark guards stepped forward, blocking the soldiers' way. "Only the Celt enters. The rest of you are to leave."

The soldier laughed and shrugged. "If the barbarian here rips her throat open with his hands, we won't be held accountable."

"The lady has already so noted your responsibility is finished," said the guard.

Still laughing, the soldiers ambled out. When they were gone, the guard bent and, with a key he produced from a bag around his waist, unlocked Caradoc's shackles.

Caradoc stepped out of the iron for the first time in his months of captivity.

Still expressionless, the guard said, "Our lady bids you enter." His twin opened the door.

Released from the heavy shackles, Caradoc felt as if he flew into the room.

It was dark within, the space lit only by soft morning sunlight filtered through sheer linen curtains that billowed in the breeze from floor-to-ceiling windows. He could see a female figure, her back turned to him, silhouetted against the light. The room was big; its central feature was a huge bed. Caradoc drew a deep breath. The lack of shackles and the breeze that carried the scent of water into the room might have lightened his soul, but it would not change his resolve.

"Lady, I thank you for the kindness you have shown in removing my shackles, but I would that we begin this…" here he paused, searching for the right word "…this transaction with honesty. My body is not my own to give. I have given my oath in a handfast, made permanent," he added. "I will serve you as a slave, but I will not break my oath."

She turned around then. He could see that she was weeping silently. Her face was washed in tears, but she was smiling.

Her face!

"Then you didn't really want to send me away?"

The sound of the sea rushed in his ears as he shook his head, not believing his eyes. "When I sent you away I lost myself."

"Well, you're found now," she said.

They moved at the same moment, coming together with a great cry of joy. Caradoc kissed her and ran his hands over her face, saying her name over and over, trying to convince himself it wasn't a dream.

"Ah, love! How I have ached for you!" He held her close and then at arm's length, looking her up and down. "You are healed? Carswell worked her future magic on you?"

The woman wiped her eyes and smiled at him. "Now that I'm with you, yes, I'm really healed."

"Will you stay? Here? With me?" Caradoc held his breath and waited for her answer.

Blonwen lifted her wrists, which were both completely free of an ESC cuff. "I am here, with you, forever."

As Caradoc took her into his arms and their lips met, the sound of a goddess's joyous laughter mingled with the rain that began to fall softly outside, making beautiful music.

★ ★ ★ ★ ★

Ready to sink your teeth into more?

Look for brand-new Silhouette® Nocturne™ titles every month wherever books are sold.

Sensual and dramatic tales of paranormal romance await you....

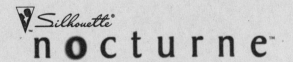

Silhouette®
nocturne™

www.silhouettenocturne.com
www.paranormalromanceblog.com

SNSERIES2TR

Do you crave
dark and sensual
paranormal tales?

Get your fix with
Silhouette® Nocturne™!

Here are other romance stories you may enjoy!

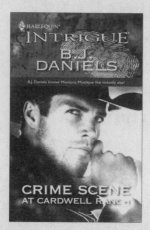

Harlequin Intrigue®
Breathtaking romantic suspense.
Crime stories that will keep you
on the edge of your seat.

Silhouette® Romantic Suspense
Heart-racing sensuality and
the promise of a sweeping
romance set against the
backdrop of suspense.

Harlequin® Blaze™
Fun, flirtatious and steamy
books that tell it like it is,
inside and outside the
bedroom.

Dark, sexy and not quite human. Introducing a collection of new paranormal short stories by top Silhouette® Nocturne™ authors.

Look for
AWAKENING THE BEAST—

with tales woven by some of the most spellbinding authors, including Lisa Renee Jones, Olivia Gates and Linda O. Johnston. Let them take you on a thrilling ride, where you'll catch a glimpse of sensuous, sexy men who share their wildest desires in ways you thought existed only in dreams....

Available October wherever books are sold.

Ready to sink your teeth into more?
www.NocturneBites.com
www.paranormalromanceblog.com